the
Lost
Years

ROWEN LEE

HIDE BEHIND PRESS

Published by Hide Behind Press, Portland, Oregon

Edited and designed by Girl Friday Productions
www.girlfridayproductions.com

Cover design: Kathleen Lynch
Interior design: Paul Barrett
Project management: Sara Spees Addicott
Editorial management: Bethany Davis

ISBN (paperback): 979-8-9861640-0-7
ISBN (e-book): 979-8-9861640-1-4

Library of Congress Control Number: 2022914870

First edition

Prologue
→ BONDED ←

I was lost and desperate. Desperate for a way out, a way in, a way through—I don't know what, but I wanted someone to grab my hand and tell me, "This is your path, this is what's best." And I wanted to close my eyes and follow. So I did. I thought it would be easier that way.

"You got a cigarette?" a man asked me as I waited at the crosswalk on my way to class. It was pouring down rain, and the heavy clouds mirrored his aura. His face was hardly visible under his black jacket hood, but I could see his hands trembling, his reddened knuckles, the dirt under his fingernails.

A younger and less jaded me would have been scared of him and timidly walked away. But when he looked up, his eyes looked blank, empty, and indifferent. Like nothing fucking mattered, except that cigarette. I had seen eyes like his before. I wondered what used to make him spark, what used to make him feel alive before he ended up on that street corner, asking me for a cigarette.

I gazed into his lost eyes with my own. "I'm sorry, I don't smoke."

He nodded and put his head down, and I continued through the downpour to my morning lecture thirteen blocks away. No true Oregonian uses an umbrella.

My lecture hall was full of two hundred eager-looking students with recorders next to them in case they missed a point in their note-taking. I sat down and pulled out my spiral notebook, which was filled with doodles, journal entries, and poems I'd come up with while pretending to give a shit the way they all did.

"You're late, Maleeka," my cousin Waleed whispered to me as he moved his recorder and notes over to make room for me. He took up most of the space at our shared table. He was a big guy, kind of like an oversize teddy bear you'd see on a Christmas display at Macy's, with a round face and solid black eyes. He had moved to the States from Syria when he was five years old. I taught him how to pronounce American words without an accent and how to write his lowercase *r*'s so they wouldn't look like *v*'s.

"You think I care?" I told him, avoiding eye contact.

Waleed was used to me being in a funk at school. He knew how much I hated college.

"You okay?"

"I don't belong here."

"Don't worry; I can help you, Leek," he whispered out of the side of his mouth, keeping his eyes concentrated on the podium. He had often promised me he'd let me run his doctor's office one day and would pay me well so I could drop out if I wanted to.

"I don't want help." I shook my head and started writing, writing nothing about the periodic table or covalent bonds. The path I was bonded to took me to the urban university Maskin State as a civil engineering major contemplating an arranged marriage to my much older first cousin.

Dear Journal,   Nov. 15th, 2004
    I don't even know who I am anymore.

• • •

Secrets have fucked with my mind for so long
I'm holding on tight cause I finally belong
In all their acceptance and all their love
I'm finally the girl that they need

Keep me here guarded and cover my dreams
Wrap me up in your praise so I don't have
                              to think
Controlled by your guidance
Arranged by your mind
Convinced I can please you
Encouraged by pride   (is that enough?)

Dear Dad, (god knows I'll never give him this)
    Crazy to think I used to have such big dreams!
Dreams of writing, even singing. Dreaming
of ways to be an inspiration. Dreams of
living my truth. But here I am stuck in a
room full of aspiring brain surgeons,
chemists an engineers b/c you think it's best.
I've even agreed to an arranged marriage
to Amin, even though I feel sick about it.
    You think I should be flattered he agreed
to marry me and I should be relieved
knowing he would take care of me and
respect me b/c we are family . . .

That's not love Dad. I know what real love is . . . but you would never know.

I know you want what's best for me, but I can't imagine this would be it. Still, do I have any other choice?

The life and love I once wanted for myself lives in another universe. A place where I can live my truth and fullfill my dreams. A place with no fear, violence, guilt, expectations or judgment. A place where I become the person I want to be with everyone's love and support. I place I know won't ever exist.

You want me to be the strong one, the one who keeps us all together. I am hanging on to that to give me purpose, knowing that will make you proud and give you peace. But it's not fair and it's not always working.

I know I'll never be able to follow my heart. I'll never be a singer, I'll never be a writer but I don't think I can be an engineer either.

And I don't know if I can marry your nephew.

My mom always told me nice boys don't want a girl with a reputation. But I wasn't after a nice boy. My freshman year of high school, my friends and I ran into Marc Osbourne with his friends getting drunk in a park after hours. He stared at me through the crowd while I made small talk with the other guys. So I did what any interested girl would do. I laughed hard at mediocre jokes I would otherwise not find as funny, and I smiled at him while taking swigs off the shared bottle of vodka. He made his way over to me, grabbed my face, and kissed me. My plan had worked.

Monday morning, the headlines hit the halls: Maleeka Munir fooled around with Marc Osbourne in a field . . .

The stares shot like laser beams. All eyes were on me. People whispered to one another with a head nod, like *that's who* and *no way*. Before I could escape their gazes, I saw my brother's high-top Converse sneakers marching toward me. Turns out people were staring at him too.

Rasheed, my brother, was a junior, two years older than I was, and though we went to the same school every day, he never talked to me. He wouldn't even drive me to school in the morning. If I did cross him in the halls, he never even made eye contact. Sometimes my girlfriends would holler out, "Hey, Rasheed!" knowing it would piss him off. I always stayed quiet.

"Is it true?" he asked me while his friends rallied around him.

I could feel the warmth take over my complexion. My ears were on fire. I wanted to seep into the ground and disappear, but I had no way out.

"Rasheed, it's not what everyone's saying."

He shook his head, clearly impatient with my bullshit. "Just tell me if it's true!"

I couldn't deny everything the way I often did with my parents. Rasheed was too smart for that. All I could do was nod.

"God damn it, Maleeka," he said as he stormed past me, followed by his entourage.

"Rasheed, wait!"

"What's wrong, Rasheed?" A guy laughed by the lockers down the hall. "Not pleased with your sister's taste in dick?"

Rasheed grabbed the collar of his jacket and threw him against the lockers.

"Oh my God!" I covered my face so I wouldn't have to watch as the hall monitor separated the two of them.

"Get the hell out of here, Rasheed!" He pushed Rasheed off the guy.

"Me?! He just told me—"

"I said get the hell out!" he yelled with his finger in Rasheed's face.

Rasheed stormed off. I was worried he was going to go confront Marc.

Rasheed was the only boy in our family. He was named after my dad's father, though he looked nothing like him. He took after my mom's side. Tall with green eyes and light-brown, wavy hair that my mom loved—she said he looked like JFK Jr. Being the only son and named after our grandfather was a big deal, and he knew it. He had big shoes to fill, and he did it well. Mom always said he was an easy kid to raise. Every choice he made was molded by what Dad thought was best. And he knew our parents thought the world of him. I thought he was arrogant, and he judged me for not being perfect like he and my older sister were.

The bus stopped at the corner of my street, and all the kids who lived in the neighborhood stood to file out.

"Good luck, Maleeka," a guy said as we got off the bus.

The boy was my age. I'd known him most of my life. He lived in a cul-de-sac nearby, and he used to play with my brother in the street, but only my brother. My dad caught me taking him to our backyard one day to show him our treehouse, and he freaked out. The boy never came close to our house again.

"Thank God your dad is out of town," my mother, Brenda, told me when I walked in the house. She sat in the fancy front room we were never allowed in growing up. It was staged for perfection with white sofas, lace pillows, and beautiful souvenirs from all over the world displayed like they were in a museum. It was Mom's space; she sat there every morning with a cup of coffee and every evening with a glass of wine, reading her Bible in a gorgeous, high wing-backed ivory chair right next to our grand piano.

As I entered the room, she looked at my shoes, signaling me to take them off. I put them by the front door and sat on the edge of the sofa. "You're not going to tell him, are you?"

Rasheed didn't let her answer. He barged into the room. "What do you need, attention? Is that why you did it?" he yelled, fuming with anger and disappointment as if I were his daughter.

"No! It's not like that, Sheed."

"You know the only reason he went for you was to get at me, right? Do you understand that?"

Marc Osbourne was the lead singer of Absence, a high school punk-rock band that was a known rival of my brother's band, With Remorse. A fight between them broke out after a show the summer before, so the bands never played at the same venue together again. It was embarrassing enough for his little sister to be talked about in the halls for rolling around with a guy in a field, but it was the ultimate humiliation for him to have it be with Marc Osbourne.

I didn't want to believe it. I thought Marc and I had a connection. I mean, before he kissed me goodbye, he told me my eyes were "fucking gorgeous." I didn't want that moment to have anything to do with Rasheed.

"Do you know what people are saying about you? They're calling you a . . . God, this is so embarrassing." Rasheed stopped himself before calling me a slut or a whore. I knew he couldn't bear using those words in relation to his little sister.

"I'm sorry, but please don't tell Dad. He'll kill me, I mean he will seriously beat my ass. He'll lock me up! I don't even want to think about what will happen."

My mom nodded and took a sip of her wine. Given the circumstances, her happy hour had started early that day. "He'll put it on me because I let you go out Saturday night with your friends." She finished off what was left in her glass, shaking her head. I knew she too thought through the worst possible scenarios if Dad found out.

"I promise, Mom, I will never talk to him again." I looked over at Rasheed. "I'll stay away from him, just please don't tell Dad."

Rasheed took a deep breath and nodded. I knew it wasn't for my sake, but to save Mom and even Dad. He said it would kill Dad to know what I did.

My mom sent me to my room for the rest of the evening while she and Rasheed ate dinner. I didn't mind. My room was the only place in my house where I could be whatever I wanted without worrying about what they thought of me. I was relieved not to be around their judgment and disappointment. They took all the fun out of that night for me. I was celebrating a day before, and now I was forced to apologize for a night I had wanted more than anything else.

Dear Journal, April 2nd, 2001

I know I told them
I'm sorry, but I'm not!
I wish I knew who told everyone.

· ·

I feel their eyes, as I walk by
Feel your thoughts, all over my skin
I'm the talk of the halls
The girl in the story
the one that was caught with him

The glare in your stares pass on judgments
The way you're "concerned" is a joke
You're really just after the gossip
not caring that I could get hurt

You turned my night so slutty
When really I could have done more
You've stollen my fun, made it dingy
making me a sound like a whore

I heard my mom on the phone through my bedroom door, telling whoever she was talking to how I crossed the line. She said I was out of control and not like my siblings. She was right, I wasn't like them. My brother and sister were both studious. They strived to excel in school. I wasn't into school aside from the social life. I fought to live a life like my friends. It created a constant battle in our home, especially with my dad. He insisted I shouldn't get too close to my American friends because "we aren't like them" even though his wife too was American.

"Your sister's on the phone for you," my mom said as she walked into my room without knocking. She threw the phone on my bed and walked out.

My sister, Raneem, was four years older than I was, a freshman at Harvard, studying political science. I knew she had never kissed a boy. She never spoke up or broke the rules.

"God, Maleeka, how did you get yourself in this mess?"

I wanted to tell my sister how much I liked him and how beautiful his eyes were. To tell her the way he looked at me, and how he bit his lip and said, "God damn," when I took my shirt off. I wanted to tell her he called me gorgeous, and nobody had ever called me gorgeous before. But I couldn't do that. Instead I said, "I know, I fucked up."

Raneem was supposed to be my example growing up. And I get why. She was perfect: tall and angelic, with a fair complexion and light hair she inherited from our mom and distinguished eyes with dark eyebrows passed on by our dad. As beautiful as she was, she had a dark side. Mom called her moody, but it felt deeper than that. It would come out of nowhere; she would disengage and isolate herself. But nobody outside our home could tell. She worked every room she entered. Everyone adored her; their faces lit up when she was around, and all the attention would be on her, even though I'd be standing right behind her.

"You really did," she told me.

I knew my place in my family. When I was young, my brother and sister would call me "the accident." On bad days, the joke that I wasn't planned for made me feel like I wasn't wanted, but on other days, it made me feel less watched to my own advantage. Like I was there, but not planned to satisfy their desires or fulfill their dreams. It wasn't on me to be the perfect daughter or son; they already had one of each of those. The lack of pressure gave me freedom my siblings didn't have, and the lack of attention gave me an urge to rebel.

"I'm not like you, Raneem. You and Rasheed are so perfect."

"Trust me, Maleeka, I'm not perfect."

"They think you are."

"Are they going to tell Dad?"

"They promised they wouldn't."

"Good. God, he would go crazy. I think he'd rather his daughter be a heroin addict than a whore."

I laughed at my sister's assumption of what my dad would prefer, but part of me knew it might be true. We had a bunch of rules enforced by our dad, who was the head of the house. He had moved to America from Syria when he was nineteen years old, and even though he married my mom, he was against the American way of most everything. The schooling, the sports, the friends, and the overall lifestyle that I wanted. He wanted us to focus on school and family, that's it. Everything else was a distraction from that to him. And the biggest ban in our home was boys.

I'll never forget the first time I laid eyes on Marc Osbourne. A few months before our hookup in the field, there was a punk-rock show in the community skatepark of our town. I begged my mom to let me go with my best friends. It was never easy leaving the house when Dad was there. The easiest way to do so was to leave when he wasn't home and have my mom deal with his questions. Dad made the rules, and Mom went along with them; she didn't want to "make waves" is what she'd tell me when I'd ask her to speak up so I could live like a normal teenage girl.

"Mom?" I said as I walked down the curved staircase leading to the kitchen of our home. She looked stressed out as she fumbled through her purse and grabbed her keys. I could always tell when Mom and Dad were fighting. Her face would be red, her stare would be off, and their framed picture from an Olan Mills photo session would be face-down on the shelf above the dining room table. Just as they all were that day.

"The girls called. They asked if I could hang out."

She lifted up her head and let out a big breath.

"Please, Mom, I really want to go," I told her before she could say no. "I'm always missing out on all the fun."

She pulled her hair back and shook her head. "Just go, Maleeka."

I ran out of the house, relieved. I was out free and couldn't wait to spend the afternoon with my best friends.

"Leek!" my best friend, Lauren, said as she opened her front door.

"Hey, Ren!" I gave her a hug.

Lauren Weigh was what most girls wanted to be: tall and thin, with long blond hair and a wardrobe you'd see in a *Seventeen* magazine. She taught me what it meant to be a real friend. Not only a hanging-out-at-recess-and-passing-notes-in-class friend. She was my first after-hours friend who encouraged me to push the boundaries. Dad hated it, but I loved spending time with her and her family. She didn't have a sister, so I took on that role.

"I am excited you're coming," she said as we walked down the street together.

"I know. Me too." I couldn't wipe the smile off my face.

"Is your dad home?"

"No, my mom told me to go. I think she was sick of listening to me whine."

"That's funny, my mom was pushing me out the door to come." Lauren laughed.

Lauren's mom, Shelly, was a retired cheerleader and encouraging of our social lives. She was full of questions and curious about the latest "juice" (that's what she called it) of what was going on. My mom never gave a shit the way Shelly did. She never seemed interested in who dated who or who won homecoming or who I had a crush on. She was above it, called it "drama," and insisted life went on after high school.

We walked a couple of blocks to meet our friend Samantha, who sprinted toward us. Her mom stormed into the house and slammed the door.

"Is everything okay?" Lauren asked her as Samantha walked past us without looking back.

"She's crazy!" Samantha shook her head.

"What happened?" Lauren asked as we ran to catch up with her.

"She's in a mood again. She probably got in a fight with her boyfriend, and she's taking it out on me. I don't want to deal with her shit."

"I'm sorry, Sammy," I told her. "Forget about her, we're going to have fun today."

"I know. I'm glad I'm with you girls." She buried her head into my shoulder with a smile.

Samantha Beck was a magnet. She attracted crowds with her big personality, and I loved being in the center of those crowds, standing next to her. She had long brown hair she would straighten stiff in perfect panels around her face. Her tan was always on point, and her charm matched with her figure had all the guys after her. She was the only one of us who came from a home split by divorce. Like many divorces, it was messy, which made her gravitate to her friends.

I sang out the lyrics to MxPx's "Punk Rock Show" to get Samantha to smile, and Lauren joined me.

"Come on, darling." I took them both by their hands. "Let's go see a punk rock band."

It was hard to find good girlfriends. Most girls at school took themselves too seriously, but the girls I soaked up my time with knew how to let loose, especially when we were together. Each one of us had our individual personalities, but when we were together, we fed off each other, and our zest, laughter, and love kept us connected.

We walked to the next neighborhood, where our friend Emiko lived. Emiko Doi was a quiet, mysterious girl. I didn't notice her until I was forced to sit next to her in elementary school because I talked too much in class. Her parents were immigrants from Japan with five girls, and Emiko was the oldest. She cared for her parents, who were held back by the language barrier, and her siblings were much younger than she was. She resembled a little Tinker Bell, but with edge. As we got closer to her house, I could spot her dyed platinum-blond pixie hair against the trees as she waited for us.

"No way!" she said to me as we approached her.

"Hey, Em."

"I can't believe you got out."

I laughed. "You guys make it sound like I'm a prisoner on bail."

"The way you got out is more like an escape." Lauren laughed. "The warden doesn't even know you're gone yet."

"I think of you more like a Disney princess," Emiko said.

"I am *not* a princess!" I laughed. Raneem was the princess, not me.

"A badass princess, fighting for life outside of the one your father wants for you." She smiled at me.

"Oh God, so I'm Ariel."

"No way, you're Jasmine," Samantha said, and started to sing the chorus of "Arabian Nights."

We all laughed as we approached the skatepark to find it packed with kids, some skating on the grounds and others throwing themselves into a mosh pit of sweat.

Punk-rock music was for the rebels. It brought assembly to the misfits. More than the music, I think they connected to the attitude. It wasn't cool to be punk rock; if you were punk rock, you didn't want to be considered cool. We girls stood out with our bright attire and bare legs. We looked like we'd walked out of a Gap commercial. I wore pink linen shorts with a white V-neck tank top and the newest line of Dr. Martens sandals. I popped against the crowd in black. We got a few looks from the older girls, who were veterans of the crowd, and the guys that wore a big X on their back. They embellished their crosses with safety pins and studs to make it clear to everyone in the halls and on the street what they were.

"Yeah, Marc-o!" I heard someone scream in the audience, and looked over on stage to see him standing there. He was on a pedestal, wearing baggy cargo pants that fell over his black skater shoes and a white T-shirt. I love guys in white T-shirts. It's effortless, and you can see their bodies through the fabric. His hair was jet black and wavy; it looked soft without any gel in it. And his eyes were the same color as the clear blue sky behind him.

I was in a teenage movie, slow-motion-type shit, and the perfect song came on and calmed the crowd for the soundtrack of the scene. They were covering AFI's "Morningstar." The slow intro was sweet and mysterious as I assumed him to be. I loved hearing his voice clearly asking if he was the star beneath the stairs, or the ghost upon the stage, or anything. And at two minutes and thirty seconds, he screamed into the microphone after the drummer laid in hard.

Chills. If you've never heard the song, play it. You'll see what I mean.

His eyes were closed as he wrapped both hands around the mic, crushing the life out of it. He had his shoulders back, and I could see the veins popping out of his forearms. The passion pulsed from his insides out. Plenty of people can sing. They sing in their cars, in church choir, even in a whiskey bar with a mic. But not all singers can perform. It takes a captivating soul to reach out to people, to engage with them and hype them up with more than their voice. And Marc did that.

I wasn't the only one in awe; they had a pretty big following. One of my best guy friends, Jake, was their biggest groupie. We saw him standing by the stage with a bottle of water in his hand. Jake glanced over at us and shot his head right back to the stage.

"Let's go say hi to Jake," Lauren said.

"I'll stay back here with Sam," Emiko said, volunteering Samantha to stick back with her.

Emiko and Jake were voted the cutest couple of our eighth-grade class. We were all close to Jake and spent time with him goofing off at the mall or going on long walks in the neighborhoods. But once we were in high school, he branched out with a more rebellious crowd, making their relationship rocky.

"Hi, Jake," Lauren said.

"What's up, guys?" he said, with his eyes still stuck on the stage. He was busy playing water boy.

"They're pretty good," Lauren yelled over the music.

"How would you know?" He laughed as the song ended, bringing the volume down, while the crowd cheered.

Marc nodded to the crowd and headed our way.

I adjusted the straps of my tank top and took my hair out from behind my ears. Did he notice me? Was he coming to say hi? God, I was an idiot. He was thirsty. Jake handed him the water bottle as I stood still, staring at his chiseled jawline and long eyelashes resting on his lower eyelid while he gulped his water. He put the cap on, handed it back to Jake, and caught me staring. He gave a little grin with a head nod to who I'm sure he assumed was another groupie. I was the ultimate groupie. No, I wasn't throwing my bra onstage or asking him to sign my tits. Instead, I was plotting out our love story, picturing him as my boyfriend. Imagining myself holding his hand while walking into a show, smiling at him while standing on the side of the stage where all his best friends stood, and kissing him after his set, showing everyone he was mine. I was in my head, in my own fairy tale, and nobody there, not even my dad, could take that away.

Dear Journal, March 3rd, 2001

I've seen blue eyes before
But never in that shade
Guys have caught my
    attention
But never this way

It felt like a movie set
a stage like he was on
I couldn't take my eyes
    off him
While he sang his punk rock song

His aura seems rough, but his smile so sweet
His head nod welcoming the only girl in pink

I don't think I've
    ever been more attracted to
someone in my life. He isn't the most
gorgeous guy in the world, but something
about him got to me. I didn't want to leave.
I wanted to spend the rest of the day close
to his stage. But Lauren wanted to leave
to go see Zach

Zach Darling was a senior who put eyes on Lauren our first week of high school. And she was equally attracted to him. He had blond highlights at the tips of his brown spiked hair, and his pearly smile popped against his light-brown complexion. He was popular, and known by all. One thing people knew him for was that he dated the hottest girls, and I wondered if Lauren was flattered to be his newest pick knowing that. But senior guys going for freshmen were mocked by the guys our age. They called them pedophiles and warned us they were going for "fresh meat." All our guy friends hated that Lauren was tied up with Zach. He took up all her time, and ours too. Everything we did was centered around him.

It took a couple of weeks for Mom to get over the hookup she found out about. I missed out on a few hangouts and sleepovers until she finally let me have the girls over.

"Why isn't Em here?" Lauren asked, lying on my bed, doing her nails.

"She said she has plans," I told her.

"With who?"

"I didn't ask."

"Is Zach picking us up tonight?" Samantha asked Lauren. It was a regular occurrence to sneak out and meet Zach and his friends at the park and smoke cloves for a couple of hours. We girls loved them; they tasted like cinnamon and made crackling sounds while we smoked them.

"I told him I'd call once Leek's parents go to bed."

My parents went to bed at the same time every night, ten o'clock, and they never checked on us after hours. Not like Lauren's mom. We would stuff the bed with pillows, and I made sure to always keep my music on so they would think we were still in there in case they were to wake up. We kept our shoes off as we tiptoed down the staircase covered in thick, red Mediterranean carpet, and I would press on the door as I unlocked the top latch, because it made less noise that way. We had mastered the process.

Walking down the street was another level of the game. We couldn't stall. We had to move quickly and dodge the cars driving by in case it was a relative. Most of my dad's family lived in our neighborhood, and the streetlights were spotlights. I kept my head hidden until we made it to the corner where Zach and his friends waited.

"What's up, Maleeka?" Kai, Zach's sidekick, said.

I gave Kai a hug. I'd befriended him when Lauren and Zach got together. He had light-brown hair, hazel eyes, and a cute, crooked smile. I'd had a crush on him until I realized I was friend-zoned when he started telling me his biggest secrets. One of which was that he had a fat crush on Sam.

He let go of me as Samantha walked up to us. "Hi, Samantha," he said, giving her a kiss with his cute smirk.

I often called Samantha a siren. She was a pro at getting guys to fall in love with her. Most of our guy friends did. She gave them attention and flattered them while allowing them in enough to see some vulnerability. She knew how to make them feel needed and adored.

"You guys want to drive up to Mission Point?" Zach asked the group.

"Yeah, let's do it," Lauren said. "You girls have to see this place."

Kai whispered in Samantha's ear, and she nodded, following him to the back seat of Zach's car.

"You ride with Jason, Leek," Lauren yelled out.

I looked over and saw Jason leaning against his old-ass station wagon with a beer in his hand. I didn't know Jason well, but he was with us the night of the epic hookup, feeding me vodka while Marc stared at me.

"Are you serious?" I said back to Lauren.

"Come on, Leek. We're all going to the same place. We'll see you there," Samantha insisted.

"Hop in, Maleeka," he said as he threw his beer can in the ditch and got in the driver's seat.

I got in his car, annoyed with the fact that I was stuck riding with Jason, the guy nobody else wanted to ride with. He played Bad Religion loud, but he still managed to ask what seemed like a million questions.

"You hang out with these guys a lot?"

"Yeah, I guess."

"They're cool."

"Yeah, I guess." I looked out the window.

"Whatever happened with Marc-o? You guys ever hook up again? You seemed pretty into each other." He laughed.

"We were drunk, Jason." I glared over at him.

"So you never got together with him then? It was just a hookup?"

"I haven't seen him since."

The Friday before Marc and I hooked up, he was kicked out of school. He smelled like weed, so his teacher sent him to the principal's office. When they searched his backpack, they found more on him. He was expelled for having drugs on campus. I was disappointed to find out he wasn't there Monday morning after the fact, but considering everything, it was better he was no longer in those halls.

"Marc's wild, but he's a good guy. It's too bad his band broke up," he told me at the red light as he lit a cigarette with the car lighter underneath the stereo.

"They broke up?"

"Yeah, it sucks. Everyone was pretty bummed about it."

I wanted to ask why, but I didn't want Jason to think I cared. I didn't want to give any more ammo involving Marc to anyone. Especially Jason. The girls said maybe it was him who told the world about our hookup.

I sat quietly in the passenger seat the rest of the way there and thought about that night with Marc. Up until then, I often referred to myself as "the agent." Like I was a middle-aged man booking gigs for the main girls. My best friends were the most beautiful and popular girls in our class, and if a guy wanted a shot at them, they knew to come through me. And I would act as the spare tire or the extra in their scene, never the leading lady. But it had been different with

Marc. With him, I wasn't a tagalong or the best friend of the main girl. I owned that night. Even though I promised to stay away from him, I couldn't stop thinking about him. I wasn't over it yet.

As we pulled up, I jumped out of the station wagon to join the girls.

"Wow, this place is beautiful!" I said.

"It's pretty, huh?" Jason said as he grabbed a pack of cigarettes out of his jacket.

"Do you have any cloves?" Lauren asked Zach as she hopped on the open cab of Kai's truck.

"You hooked?" He laughed as he pulled out a pack and handed us each one.

I took my clove and walked off to sit on the metal guardrail at the edge of the cliff. Staring off at the view, I couldn't help but wonder what the hell I was doing there. I knew there was no way I would be there if it weren't for my friends.

"Is Maleeka okay?" I heard Jason ask the girls.

"She's fine," I could hear Samantha say.

"You good, Leek?" Lauren called out to me.

I turned back and smiled at them. "I'm fine."

"You sure? You don't look okay." She jumped off the cab, about to walk up to me. Zach grabbed her hand before she could.

"Leave her, she's fine," he said to her. I don't know if he meant for me to hear it, but I did.

"I swear, I'm fine. I want to look at the view."

"You're just bummed your guy isn't here tonight." Samantha laughed. The girls all knew about my secret crush, turned into hookup, turned into "I think I really like him." But the guys all assumed it was just a drunken-night hookup.

"Who's her guy?" Zach asked them.

I shook my head, looking back at the view. "Nobody," I called out. "I don't have a guy."

I thought they'd get the hint and change the subject, but I could hear them whispering. Zach laughed while inhaling his clove and pushed it out with a few coughs, still able to yell out, "Are you fucking kidding me?" He coughed more. "Are you hung up on that stoner?"

"You act like you've never smoked," I told him without looking back at him or the crowd. I'd rather look at the pretty lights.

"Okay, I smoke, but he's a fucking pothead. You must be desperate." The guys all laughed, even Jason, who seemed to be friends with Marc, even a fan of his band.

"Zach!" I heard Lauren call out and her hand smack into his gut.

"He's right, Lauren. Marc is bad news," Kai said.

"I'm telling her how it is. Ask anyone. Those guys are all stoners."

I turned around to stare Zach down. "I don't need you to tell me how it is. He's not my boyfriend. It's none of my business."

He put his arm over Lauren's shoulder. "He's not your boyfriend, but you let him feel you up? That's the only reason he thinks your eyes are gorgeous," he said, with his hands in the air, making quotes like it wasn't true. "If you believe him, you are definitely desperate."

"Zach, seriously, stop." Lauren clenched her teeth at him.

I hated that Lauren had told Zach what Marc said to me. Everyone knew we fooled around, but only the girls knew he'd said my eyes were gorgeous. I turned back around to stare out to the bright lights of our town beneath us. I wondered where he was down there, what he was doing. I wished I could be with him, not here.

"Don't listen to Zach," Jason said behind me. I could see his shadow on the ground. "I told you, Marc's a good guy."

I nodded my head.

"Zach can be a dick," he continued.

"Why'd you laugh?" I looked up at him.

He shrugged his shoulders. "Sometimes you laugh 'cause everyone else is."

"Yeah, I guess."

"Maleeka, I know they told you I told everyone about you and Marc, but it wasn't me."

I nodded my head again. I didn't need Jason to elaborate or convince me who it was. The only person who knew about our hookup who would be capable of humiliating me was Zach, the one humiliating me that night.

I scraped my clove onto the rail. "Jason, can you take me home?" I didn't need to be there. I didn't need to risk getting in more trouble with guys like Zach Darling.

"You got it."

"Home? Maleeka, we just got here," Samantha said.

"Stay. You guys don't have to go with me," I said, even though I didn't want my friends staying there. I thought they could all do better than these guys. Sure, they weren't punk-rock stoners, but they *were* dicks.

"Maleeka—"

"I swear, Ren, I'm not mad." I knew she was going to ask me if I was. "Stay."

Samantha looked at Kai and back at me. She whispered in his ear before calling out, "Wait, Maleeka, I'm coming with you."

"You don't have to."

"I don't want you to be alone."

"I'm fine, Sam," I told her.

"No, Sam's right," Lauren said.

"You're leaving?" Zach's eyes bulged out.

"Yeah. You stay, though," Lauren said.

"Let her leave and stay with me. I'm your boyfriend."

"I can't do that, Zach."

Zach and I never made it easy for Lauren. It was a mutual tolerance. We were both fighting for her time. When they started dating, I'll admit I got a little butt hurt. I hated having to share Lauren. And he didn't give her up easily.

"That's messed up, Lauren. I see what your priorities are."

"Zach, please. I'll call you later." She gave him a quick kiss and walked toward us, leaving him behind.

I looked over her shoulder to see him with his hands clenched at his waist as he shook his head. I couldn't tell if he was pissed at Lauren or at me.

A WHOREHOUSE

The car ride home was quiet other than Jason's music blasting. I sat in the front while the girls sat in the back. I'm sure they were having nonverbal conversations about what happened, with wide eyes and clenched jaws. I could picture Lauren's remorseful eyes and Samantha gesturing with her hands that it was no big deal and I'd get over it soon enough. I kept my eyes out the window while Jason drove, nodding his head to the beat of the music and playing drums on the steering wheel.

He dropped us off at the corner, and we got back into the house and into bed without waking anyone up. Until the house phone went off.

"Fuck!" I jumped off the bed to grab it.

We had a phone in almost every room of our house, including Mom and Dad's. Dad woke up. "Hello," I heard him say as I too picked up the phone.

"Is Maleeka there?" It was Zach.

Dad didn't even answer him. Boys weren't allowed to call the house. He hung up the phone without saying a word to him, assuming this guy would get the point.

"Lauren, it's Zach. Call him before he calls back!" I threw the phone at her, but it hit the floor.

"Shit," she said as she fumbled to pick it up. "I forgot to call him when we got home."

Every guy friend I had was scared of Dad. They knew the rules about our home, and better yet, they respected them. They didn't call the house unless I gave them a specific time to do so, and it was never at midnight. Zach wasn't my friend, though. He didn't give a shit about Dad or about me. The phone rang again. This time it was in Lauren's hand, so she answered at the same time Dad did.

"Who is this?" Dad yelled through the receiver. I couldn't tell if I heard him through the phone or through the hall.

"Look, I don't want to talk to Maleeka. Is Lauren there?" I heard Zach say with an attitude.

"God damn it! This is not a whorehouse!" He hung up, raging toward my room.

The bass in Dad's voice made the whole house shake. Raneem always told Dad he yelled too much. He would joke that he wasn't yelling, he was talking. "That's how Arab men talk," he'd say. So when he did yell, it was intense. He lost his mind. The girls rushed to hide in my walk-in closet as his footsteps got closer.

He barged in, screaming in Arabic so only I would understand him. How I was out of line and how my friends were trouble. I yelled back at him, begging him to calm down and stop screaming. The only way he could hear me was if I screamed back. It only set him off even more.

"Karim, stop!" Samantha called out as he grabbed my antique wooden computer chair he'd helped me stain when I was twelve years old. I knew what was coming and turned away to block my face as he threw the chair. It smashed into my back before rolling to the floor, like the jaws of the girls in the closet.

"Okay, Dad! I'm sorry!" I screamed at him, scared something else would get thrown.

He paused for a second and looked at the girls huddled together in the closet. He shook his head at me. "You're out of control," he told me in English, and walked out of the room.

I released a breath and let my shoulders fall. "Fuck." I didn't know what to say to the audience staring at me with eyes wide open. I put the spotlight on someone else. "Lauren, Zach can't call here like that!"

"I know, Leek. I'm sorry." She tried to put her arm around me, but I didn't want anyone touching me. I dodged her reach and picked up the chair as the girls turned their attention to the floor.

I grabbed the phone to give to Lauren. "Call him back. Hurry."

Lauren sat at my desk on the chair Dad had chucked at me to call Zach. I could hear his tone through the phone, unable to make out the words, but I could tell they weren't pleasant. He was mad she left and didn't call him like she said she would, and every time she said sorry, I'd cringe. I was angry at her for being sorry and not telling him he'd crossed the line. I was angry at her for calling him back, even though I told her to. Samantha got in my bed next to me, crying. Why would she be crying? She wasn't the one who was smacked with a chair. But it couldn't have been easy to watch that.

"What did he have to say that couldn't wait until morning?" Samantha asked Lauren when she finally got off the phone.

Lauren didn't answer Samantha. Instead, she looked at me. "I'm so sorry, Leek."

"It's fine. Keep the phone off the hook," I told her.

Samantha looked at me with tears in her eyes. "Maleeka, does your Dad—"

"Can we drop it." I didn't let her finish.

I didn't want to go into detail about my dad; I knew they wouldn't understand. It was nothing they'd ever seen before. I, on the other hand, was immune to my dad's hot temper and mean throw. It was part of his scare tactic and the way he expressed his anger. It was normal in our family; the men in my Syrian family all had tempers. But him doing it in front of my friends felt different, more terrible somehow. I saw it through their eyes. Him showing them our world embarrassed me more than being called a slut for messing around with Marc.

I closed my eyes and pretended to fall asleep while Samantha and Lauren snuggled up to me. I could hear Samantha still sniffling and Lauren say, "That was so fucked up." I wanted it all to end. I wanted the night to be over so they could leave and I could go on as if it never happened.

After the girls left that morning, I found my mom in the front room, having a cup of coffee. She was reading the Bible and didn't look up at me. It was standard at my house for the day after a fight to be still. No conversation about what happened, no discussion, no sorrys. Stillness that would go on until we were "over it." But I had to say something.

"Is Dad home?" I asked her.

"He went to his mom's house," she said with her head down.

"It's not fair, Mom, the call wasn't even for me."

"You know your dad, Maleeka." She kept reading.

"He didn't care when that chick called for Rasheed last week."

"It's different, you're a girl."

I couldn't tell if Mom was mocking my dad's double standard or if she agreed with it. She wouldn't even look at me. She didn't feel for me.

"He threw a chair at me!"

She finally looked up at me. "You know your dad, Maleeka," she said again.

When my parents would fight, their combats were explosive. That's what initially encouraged me to start writing in a journal; it was my only release to retell the story, as if I was documenting it. I was a young journalist telling the grimy details of two worlds colliding. Mom would drink to try and mask her frustrations until her words became daggers, stabbing until Dad would explode. He never touched my mom, but anything else in his way was affected. Objects would be thrown, and things would break. There was always a mess to clean up the next day, whether a glass smashed on the floor, a television thrown off the entertainment center, or ketchup splattered all over the wall.

I didn't know where to turn. I couldn't go to my friends, who were traumatized by it. And I couldn't go to my mom, who wasn't fazed by it. So I spent the day in my room, alone, listening to my favorite artist and writing in my journal.

When I told my older cousin Megan that Eminem was my favorite artist, she looked at me like I was crazy. She thought he was sick and crude, and to quote her, she said, "I figured a cute, happy girl like you would be listening to LeAnn Rimes." She had no idea.

I connected to him even though I was nothing like him. I didn't live in no trailer park. I had a beautiful three-story house with a great big front door and crystal chandeliers that could be seen from the outside through the windows. My dad never left us; he spent a ton of time with us and money on us. And my mom wasn't unstable like Marshall Mathers's—well, maybe a little. But putting our differences aside, I could relate to him through his angst. The way he enunciated words and emphasized syllables with passion and emotion while spitting brilliance in his bars had me mesmerized. And I loved singing along with anger and emotion because I felt angry too.

I couldn't control the vibe of the entire house, but I had total control over my room. I loved my room. It was a representation of everything I was. It had deep maroon walls to depict my moodiness, with pictures, song lyrics, and posters plastered on top to cover the darkness with inspiration. And on my ceiling I had six big letters for me to read every night before I'd fall asleep: *DREAMS*.

Dear Journal,   April 15th, 2001

My dreams are what give me hope
and keep me going. Dreaming to make
some sort of a difference by being
inspirational to fucked up teenagers
like me.
I know on the outside it seems like I
have it all, a ton of friends, a big
family and nice things ...
But I'm lost.
I can't wait to get out of here.
They don't care about me. I know
they're all mad at me about last
night, but I'm mad too!

THEY ARE CRAZY

Monday at school, the girls all left me notes in my locker that told me how much they loved me and how much they hated my dad. I appreciated their gesture, but I kept my distance. One of them told someone who told someone else, and by the end of the day, kids at school were calling my dad a child abuser. I stayed close to Emiko. I felt less embarrassed around her. Even though she knew the entire story, she hadn't seen his eyes, or mine. She only imagined the worst rather than having witnessed it.

"People are talking," I told her as we walked out of last period.

"Who cares, Leek? Everyone knows your dad is strict."

"There's a big difference between people assuming my dad hits me and them knowing it happened."

"Let them talk. They don't matter." Emiko smiled, looking over my shoulder. I turned around to see Jake smiling too. I guess they'd made up.

"I knew it," I said, looking back at her.

"What?"

"You were with him this weekend, weren't you?"

She nodded as he approached us.

"Hey, Leek," he told me after he kissed Emiko. "You coming with us?" he asked me.

"Come, Maleeka," Emiko said. "We're going to hang out at Jake's. You shouldn't be alone."

I looked across the parking lot to see Lauren and Samantha walk toward Zach and Kai. I didn't want to go home and be alone, and I would rather be the third wheel with Emiko and Jake than be around Zach.

"Yeah, I'll come."

Jake sat on his sofa, with a guitar, covering "Santeria" by Sublime while Emiko played house in the kitchen, making him a peanut-butter-and-jelly sandwich. She put it on the coffee table in front of him and sat next to him as he leaned in to give her a kiss to tell her thank you. I loved what they had together; they reminded me of a sweet married couple from the fifties, a June and Ward Cleaver, aside from the pack of cigarettes in Jake's flannel pocket and Emiko's hoop earrings that were bigger than her entire ear.

"I wish I knew how to play the guitar," I told them.

"Learn," Jake said, handing me the guitar as he leaned off the couch to grab his sandwich.

"Yeah, I should," I said, plucking the strings. "'I could be a mother fucking riot,'" I said, quoting Bradley Nowell.

"You look good." He laughed as a ding came out of the computer on the desk I sat at. I should have respected his privacy and not turned to look at it, but it was right in my face; it was hard not to see who it was.

It said, *What are you up to?* and the sender's screen name was Marco83. Marco as in Marc, 83 as in his birth year, it had to be him.

"You got a message," I told him.

"Who is it?" He came up behind me to read the chat box on his screen. He reached over me to respond.

I ran the guitar pick along the strings with no idea how to play a chord and let him finish his conversation. And as he backed away from the computer, I had to ask.

I took my hand off the neck of the guitar and rubbed my own. "Has he ever asked about me?"

Jake slouched on the sofa and put his feet on the coffee table while he looked at me, confused.

"I mean, 'cause of that night and everything."

He nodded his head and grabbed Emiko's hand. "Oh, yeah, no. He's never brought you up to me."

That hurt my ego.

"Maleeka, Marc's not the type to ask about a girl. He parties with girls, gets fucked up with girls. He doesn't ask about girls. I'm sure he hasn't thought about you since. He was fucked up and wanted to get some."

"Jake!" Emiko slapped his hand.

"What? I'm being honest. I don't want her to get her hopes up for nothing."

Jake and I were close, and because of that there were times he was a little too honest with me. In eighth grade I asked if he thought I was fat, and he told me I could lose weight if I wanted to. "It wouldn't hurt," he'd said.

"Yeah, for sure," I told him. "I was just wondering."

"You think about him?"

I didn't want to say yes, but I couldn't say no either, so I didn't say anything. I put my head down and picked at my nails.

"Maleeka, Marc's my boy, but he isn't going to go for you."

"What's wrong with me?" I looked at him with a defensive stare.

"Nothing. You don't get it. You guys are different."

"What, the punk-rock thing?" I rolled my eyes.

"Opposites can attract," Emiko chimed in. Emiko and Jake were considered different when it came to music. She was obsessed with JLo and only listened to Sublime when she was with Jake.

Jake shook his head. "It's not only the music, Maleeka. Shit, you're planning spirit week for our school, and he got kicked out for having weed on him!"

I tried to say something, but he didn't stop.

"You guys don't hang out with the same people, or have any of the same interests. You're not like him. He hooked up with you. That's it. Trust me, he's not going to go for you. You guys are diff—"

"All right, Jake, just drop it."

"You're pissed."

"I'm fine."

It was true; I looked nothing like the crowd Marc hung around. My hair was full of blond highlights, and I wore name-brand clothing.

And I didn't have anything to do with the punk-rock scene. Maybe if I was stoned and listening to Strung Out all day with a nose ring, Jake would think we'd be compatible.

AN ARTIST

I wasn't about to have another person tell me to stay away from him. I didn't need that from Zach, Rasheed, or even Jake. He thought our hookup was random, and we had never met before. But Marc and I had made a connection before the hookup. Before he was "fucked up and getting some."

After I saw Marc at his show and before we fooled around, I was stuck in detention. The girls were at the JV soccer game without me while I sat in a stuffy audiovisual classroom with twenty students I didn't know, because I was tardy for Global Studies too many times. I pulled out my journal to write and doodle a bit.

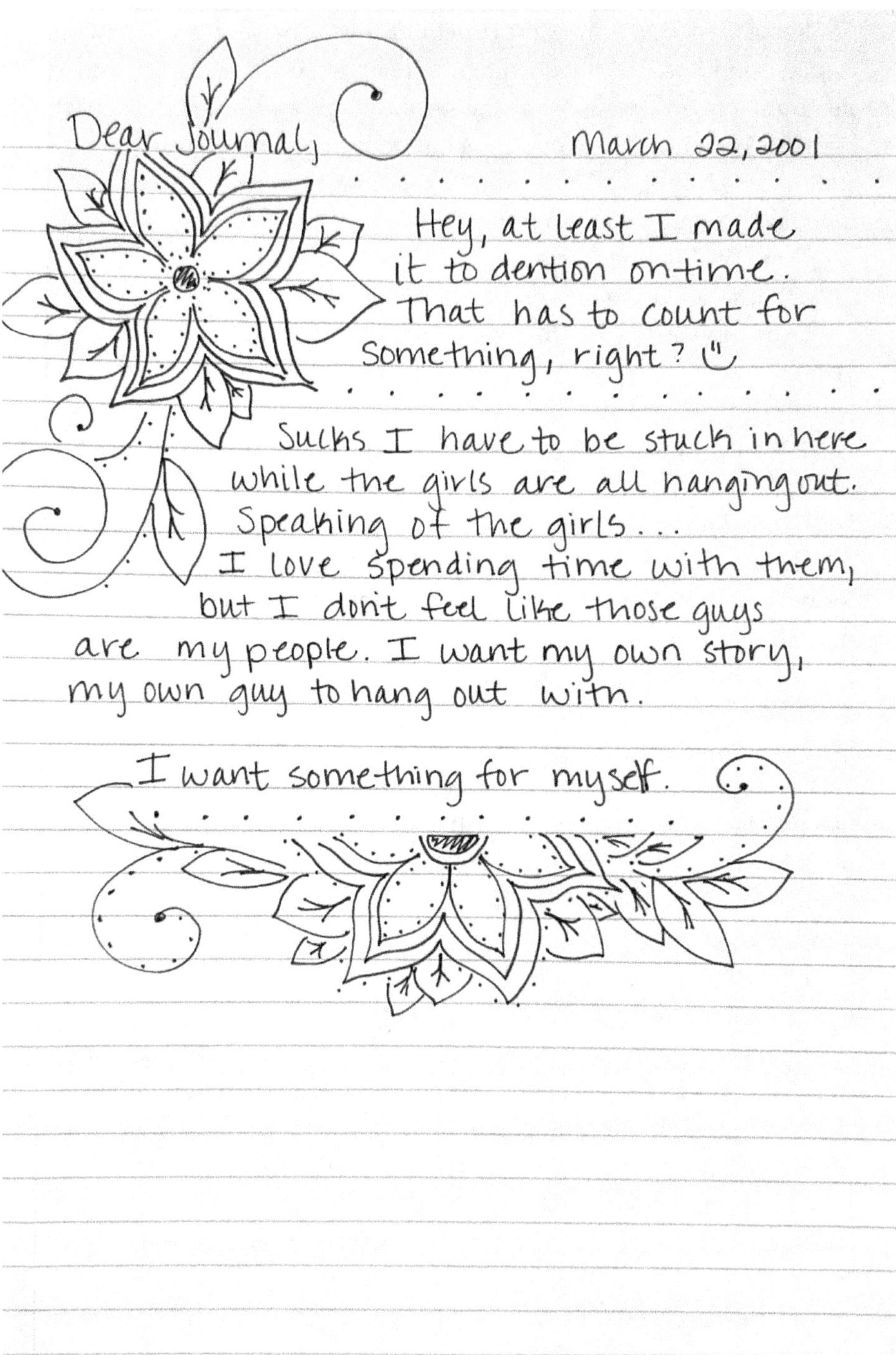

Dear Journal,   March 22, 2001

Hey, at least I made
it to dention on time.
That has to count for
something, right? ☺

Sucks I have to be stuck in here
while the girls are all hanging out.
Speaking of the girls...
I love spending time with them,
but I don't feel like those guys
are my people. I want my own story,
my own guy to hang out with.

I want something for myself.

Someone walked in and sat behind me. What nerve to show up to detention late. He slouched low in his seat so his feet were underneath my chair. I could smell the trouble on him; I knew what marijuana smelled like. I kept doodling and moved my feet forward so they weren't touching his. The teacher called out names for roll call, and halfway through she got to mine.

"Mah-Mal—" she stuttered.

"That's me," I said before she got too far into it.

"How do you say it?" She looked up at me over her wide-rimmed glasses.

"Maleeka."

"What a beautiful name," she told me before getting to my last name. "Munir. Oh, you're Rasheed's sister, right?"

"Yeah, I am." I smiled.

"I can't believe I have a Munir in detention," she said with big eyes. Rasheed would never be in detention. She moved on from me and made it to the guy behind me.

"Marc Osbourne," she called.

"Here."

My stomach dropped. What were the chances? Immediately, I was glad to be there. I didn't care about the soccer game anymore. Not like this was a social hour, but still, Marc Osbourne was right behind me. I didn't know what to do, where to put my hands, or how to sit. I grabbed my pen and flipped to a clean piece of paper to doodle, hoping it would ease the nerves.

I heard his desk creak, and the space between us tightened up.

"That looks dope," he whispered behind me.

I choked; I didn't know what to say. All I could do was laugh nervously and try to keep my calm. He was cool enough for both of us.

"I'm Marc," he said from behind my back.

"Maleeka," I said quietly with my head turned to the right.

The detention administrator was also the school's AV tech expert, and within a few minutes, she got a call that the intercom wasn't working on the field.

"I'll be back," she said. "I trust you'll all be quiet and still here when I get back."

"What are you in here for?" he asked me after she left the room and the other kids started talking.

I didn't know if I should turn around. Maybe I would appear too eager. But it would be rude if I didn't, so I did.

"Too many tardies." I wrapped my hair behind my ear. "You?"

"Same." He smiled at me.

No way! I thought to myself in excitement of our coincidental meetup. Being late put us both in the right place at the right time. I thought it was fate. We made eye contact for a second, and I remembered the last time I stared at his blue eyes.

"You're in a band, right?" I asked him.

"I am." He smiled. "How'd you know?"

"I've seen you guys before. I was at the Punk in the Park show."

"Oh yeah, what'd you think?"

"You're good."

"I wouldn't pin you to be at a show like that."

I looked at my pink acrylic nails and high-end-department-store outfit and nodded my head. "I was there."

"You like to draw?" he said, raising his eyebrows at my notebook.

"I wouldn't call it drawing. It's more like doodling."

"Can I see that for a second?"

I looked at my journal, apprehensive to hand it to him. All he'd have to do was flip back a few pages to find out how big of a crush I had on him. He stayed on the page, luckily.

"Do you mind?" he asked, reaching for my pen.

"Sure." I gave it to him and watched him as he added contributions to my doodling. He brought depth and dimension to my name in block letters. And he added detail and shade to my pretty flowers, giving them more depth and edge.

"You're an artist." I smiled at him.

"You could say that. So are you, apparently."

"My flowers? Please, they're silly."

"Nah, come on, take the compliment. They're cool." He smiled and ripped the page right out of my journal. "Can I keep this?"

I nodded. "Sure, I guess they are pretty coo'."

"Coo'?" He looked at me funny while folding up the piece of paper and putting it in his book as his new bookmark.

"Yeah, coo' is silly for 'cool.'" What a stupid thing to say. I wished I could take it back until I noticed him tilt his head with a big smile.

"You're cute, Maleeka."

"Should I add on an extra twenty minutes?" our director came in asking us all. "To make up for all the chatter."

Everyone shut up.

"Not another word," she said.

I turned back around to face the whiteboard. I got back to my journal while Marc read his book. I hated that she had come back so soon. I had to go another thirty minutes with him right behind me without hearing his voice or admiring his demeanor. Finally, her apple-shaped buzzer rang on the shelf behind her, and everyone shuffled their belongings to get out of there as fast as they could. Marc was the first one out of his seat. I turned back to grab my bag off the chair.

"Pink shorts," he said, putting his backpack over his shoulder.

"What?"

"I saw you at the show." He smiled. "You were wearing pink shorts."

He remembered me. He remembered the color of my shorts. Was he staring at me that day as hard as I was staring at him?

I smiled back at him. "Yeah, that was me."

"See you around, Maleeka."

After Jake told me Marc would never go for me, I went home on a mission. I sat at the computer in my family's shared office and added the screen name Marco83 to my buddy list. He was still online. I twirled my hair around my finger. Jake was wrong; I knew it deep down. And after getting a chair thrown at me and nobody giving a shit, I cared less about my promise to stay away from him. Part of me wanted to stick it to my family, and another part of me wanted to stick it to Jake for thinking Marc wouldn't go for me. But most of all, I wanted to do something for myself.

I typed out, *Is this Marc Osbourne?* in the chat box and pushed send.

It was 7:32, and I waited. My back was toward the hallway, with a full view of the computer if you got close enough. Every time I heard footsteps, I would minimize the chat box and pull up my game of solitaire. I kept my eyes on the screen, waiting, and by 7:38, he responded.

Marco83: Let me guess, Maleeka Munir?

Leek55: How'd you know?

Marco83: Your screen name is Leek55 . . . MaLEEKa

Leek55: you're smart :)

Marco83: How've you been? I didn't think I'd ever hear from you again.

Leek55: why would you think that?

Marco83: Circumstances, I guess.

Leek55: well . . . here I am :)
Marco83: I'm glad. How's school going?
Leek55: ughhh school . . . you're lucky you got out
Marco83: Ha, maybe. Though it was not by choice.
Leek55: still you're lucky
Marco83: I'm not that lucky, it makes it impossible to see you.

That made my stomach drop. I brushed my bangs back and shook the nerves out of my fingertips before typing . . .

Leek55: the wall isn't the same without you . . .

Everyone called that wall the "pothead wall." It was the wall where the hottest skaters, also known as the biggest stoners, hung out. Marc used to run that wall before he was expelled. After the punk-rock show, I would walk by it every day, out of my way, to check him out and show off whatever I was wearing. I thought my long route was inconspicuous and only I knew what I was doing. Until one day I walked by in baggy orange cargo pants with a tight white tank top that showed skin underneath my belly button. I heard a girl standing next to him say, "That girl in the orange pants is obviously in love with you."

Marco83: You still walk by every morning?
Leek55: I don't go out of my way anymore
Marco83: We should have talked more when we had the chance.
Leek55: we have the chance now :)
Marco83: You're right. :)

I wondered if he was smiling as big as I was. The colon and parenthesis didn't do justice to how big my smile was.

Marco83: Tell me about you Maleeka.

He didn't know much of anything about me, other than my morning routes, my doodling in detention, and what I looked like topless.

Leek55: what do you want to know?
Marco83: Starters, where are you from?
Leek55: you mean where am I FROM from?
Marco83: Ha! Is that what people ask you?
Leek55: all the time
Marco83: Tell me, where are you FROM from?
Leek55: my dad is from Syria
Marco83: So you're Syrian.

I had a hard time telling people I was Syrian; I was only half. There were stereotypes to being Arab, most of which I didn't identify with. But I wasn't like my American family either. I didn't really know what to say I was.

Leek55: no . . . my dad is

Marco83: Then so are you, you should be proud of who you are. Do you speak Arabic?

I was impressed he knew the language for a Syrian was Arabic. Most would ask me if I spoke Syrian. And when I'd mention my family was from the Middle East, they'd ask me if that was in Africa.

Leek55: some

Marco83: Fuck yeah, how did I get so lucky to hook up with such a beautiful Syrian girl?

Leek55: she was a little tipsy :)

Marco83: Damn, you think I could get her to hang out with me sober?

Leek55: I think she'd like that . . .

Dear Journal,   April 24th 2001

Marco83: Fuck yeah, how did I get so lucky to hook up with such a beautiful Syrian girl?
Leek55: she was a little tipsy :)
Marco83: Damn, you think I could get her to hang out with me sober?
Leek55: I think she'd like that…

I have been talking to Marc online all week! I know I promised to stay away from him, but I don't care!
He is everything I thought he would be. And he's so interested in everything I am. ♡ ♡ ♡ ♡ ♡ ♡ ♡ ♡ ♡
Rasheed is wrong- he's a good guy. And Jake is wrong- he wants to see me again. ☺

He said I am a beautiful Syrian girl. I don't think anyone has ever told me I am beautiful. I know I'm not the prettiest girl in the world, I know I'm not skinny, but when I talk to him I feel better than I ever have.

a Pretty BIG Deal

"I hate this dress," Samantha told me as I zipped the back of her formal dress in Lauren's double vanity bathroom. She and Lauren were the only two freshmen girls going to the senior prom. "I look fat."

"You're crazy, Sam. How can you tell someone like me you're fat?" I told her, tucking in the strings used to hang up the dress.

I was more developed than my best friends. They all wore a 0 or 00, depending on the brand. The size on my T-shirt tag and the stretch in my jeans was considerably bigger than my best friends', making me feel like an Amazon. My thick thighs and DD cup never let me appreciate my tiny waist. I wore a 10, and it was hard to be a 10. Sexy was supermodel sexy, Kate Moss sexy. Flat chests and hip bones pushing your jeans out from your flesh, and all three of my best friends had that. I thought my girlfriends were the most beautiful girls in school, and I think most people at school would have agreed. As much as I adored them, it was hard to stand next to them at times.

"Because I am!" She threw her matching shawl on the hamper.

"Calling yourself fat is basically calling me a fucking whale!" I raised my voice enough for Lauren and Emiko to notice.

"You're not a whale!" Samantha told me.

"Then how are you fat?" I shook my head. The other girls kept their mouths shut and their heads down, letting us go at it.

She adjusted her strapless dress under her arms. "I just hate this pudge that sticks out."

"Oh yeah, well, what about my pudge? It's obviously bigger than yours."

"So I'm not allowed to say I'm fat even though that's how I feel?"

"No! You're not! I would give anything to have your body. I am stuck in this lard while you're complaining about your skin, not even your fat, inside your armpit!"

"You guys, stop, you're both beautiful," Lauren finally interjected. We could have gone on forever.

"Yeah, guys, don't be so insecure," Emiko said.

I was insecure, and it hurt to hear Samantha complain about a body I would die to have. It got quiet for a long twenty seconds. Someone had to change the subject.

"Maleeka, did you tell the girls about your date tonight?" Emiko said.

"Date?!" Samantha shot her head up at me and grabbed my arm. "No way, you're going out with Marc?"

"He asked me online if I'd want to hang out." I smiled.

"Maleeka! Why didn't you say anything?" Lauren smiled at me like she was making up for every offensive remark her boyfriend said about Marc.

"Lauren, don't tell Zach."

"I promise." She put her hands up as if she were showing me her fingers weren't crossed.

"Please, all of you. Don't tell anyone."

"We won't. God, we can't have any more chairs thrown at you," Samantha said, trying to be funny. We all laughed, even though we all thought that night was fucked up.

"Girls!" Shelly called out to us. "The boys are here!"

Shelly had gone over the top with a lavish spread of food and drinks. All the parents were there, snapping pictures of their striking kids dressed in formal wear by the beautiful staircase outside leading to the front door. Shelly had decked it with greenery and fresh roses from the market. My parents would never do that. When I went to the Sadie Hawkins dance a few months before, I got ready at Lauren's, and Dad didn't even see me in my dress. He sure as hell wouldn't ever have taken pictures of me with my date.

"Doesn't she look beautiful?" Shelly said to me as Lauren got close to Zach on the staircase. Shelly told Lauren she was beautiful all day; it was so easy for her to do so. I envied the way she spoke to her; my mom never told me I was beautiful. I told her once I wished I looked like Lauren, and she told me to lay off the chocolate.

Lauren wore a white silk dress that clung to her hip bones. And Zach wore an all-black suit with a white tie. They looked like a wedding-cake topper. "So beautiful," I agreed with her.

"You are such a good friend to have come, thank you."

"Of course, Shelly, I wouldn't miss it for anything. This is a big deal to go to prom as a freshman."

"It is a pretty big deal." Shelly nodded her head, staring at Lauren and Zach and back at me. "Zach's a sweetheart, don't you think so? Did you see the flowers he brought me?"

Ugh, the flowers, yes, I saw them. Zach brought Lauren a corsage, and he also brought Shelly a bouquet of flowers, and she thought that was the sweetest thing in the world. Shelly didn't stop talking about them. She showed each person the flowers as they walked into the house, me being one of them, twice.

I pressed my lips together while nodding along with Shelly. "He's lucky to have her. She's the best out there."

Shelly put her arm around me as Lauren's dad, Glen, approached us. "You're such a good friend, Maleeka," she said.

"She's the best." Glen smiled at me. "You should be going with them, Maleeka." Glen always made me feel like I deserved everything Lauren and the others had. He asked me often if there was any guy out there worth my time and insisted when it did happen, the guy would have to be "so damn special" to stand by me.

"If I were still in high school, I'd take you, Maleeka," Lauren's brother said, appearing out of the open garage door.

I laughed, shaking my head.

"I'm serious, Maleeka, you could rock a strapless dress better than the rest of them."

"Thanks, Quinn." I smiled as he put his arm around me.

Quinn was Lauren's older brother who graduated from high school the year before. Well, I shouldn't say that—he would have graduated from high school the year before if he hadn't dropped out. He was a bad-boy heartthrob with an olive complexion, green eyes, and a chiseled jawline. I thought he was hot and charming, almost like a real-life Rhett Butler.

"Don't you want a picture with your big brother?" Quinn called out to Lauren before she jumped in Zach's car to head out. "You look gorgeous, Ren," he told her as he walked up to them. "Come on, Zach, I'll let you be in it too." He pulled Zach in, and they all said cheese.

I wanted everything Lauren had. A mother who was interested in my life. A laid-back father who allowed me to be normal. A brother who talked to me and called me gorgeous. And even a boyfriend to take me to the prom, not a boyfriend like Zach, but still a boyfriend. Instead I went home to wait for my parents to fall asleep so I could sneak out to see Marc.

Cupcakes & ACID

I had never been on a date before, if that's what this night was supposed to be. I had hung out with boys, but never alone with a boy I liked, and certainly never alone with a guy I promised I would stay away from. What do you wear for a night like that? I stood in my closet, looking for an outfit to wear. It was a fancy closet, with drawers and shelves for anything you'd need to store: scarves, belts, purses, and shoes. Dad was reluctant to let go of his expectations, but he let go of his wallet often. He gave us whatever we wanted without hesitation. I think he wanted to provide us with everything so we would always need him.

I wanted something edgy and hot to make a guy like Marc attracted to me. I passed on bright colors and picked a black low V-neck. Black was sexy; it was dark and mysterious, and it made everyone look thinner. I put on my Abercrombie jeans and reached for the studded belt Lauren got me after she knew I had a crush on a punk-rock boy. I covered my cheekbones with bronzer and put clear lip gloss on after spending an hour straightening my hair perfectly.

At ten thirty I grabbed my shoes and took one more look in the mirror. I couldn't walk out of the house looking like that. I grabbed a baseball hat and a zip-up sweatshirt and tiptoed down the stairs, holding my breath until I shut the front door.

We made plans to meet midpoint between our houses on the home-team bleachers of the football field. The vacant bleachers gave me the option to sit wherever I'd like. I made my way to the top; there was less light hitting up there. I took off my baseball cap, applied a new layer of lip gloss, and sat on the cold metal bleachers, pretending to be casual, but my leg bouncing called me out. I moved to perch on the edge of the bench to keep my legs looking slender, but I realized I looked overly eager. So I leaned back, crossed my legs at the knees, and put my sweatshirt over my thighs.

"Maleeka Munir," he called out at the bottom entrance of the stands.

"Hi." I smiled, stalling for a minute while I stared at him. He walked up the steel steps toward me, looking self-assured, his shoulders back and his head up. I didn't know what to do—stand and greet him or have him sit? My hands were shaking, so I kept them interlocked in one another.

"Come here." He put his hand out, forcing me to let go of myself. "You look beautiful," he said before giving me a hug like we had done this before. He wasn't nervous at all, not like I was. Hugging him sober on a planned date was harder for me than making out with him on a night unplanned for while tipsy. "Sorry I'm late," he said as I backed away from his grasp.

"You're not late, I just got here." I was lying so he wouldn't feel bad making me wait twenty minutes that felt like forever.

"I had to make a pit stop." He reached into his pocket.

"Cupcakes?" I smiled.

"You said they were your favorite."

Late one night in the middle of our online chatting, I told him my favorite treat when I was young were Hostess cupcakes. I loved the fake chocolate taste of the icing and the soft cake filled with cream. It had been a while since I last had one.

"Thank you, Marc."

"Wait." He reached in his other pocket and pulled out a small square-shaped cardboard carton.

I laughed. "Milk too."

"That's how you like them, right?"

I nodded my head. "Yeah, you're right."

"Let's sit." He raised his eyebrows to the bench I had been waiting on.

I couldn't wipe the smile off my face if I tried. I had the biggest crush on him, and here I was, hanging out with him alone. I was there for myself, and he was there for me and only me.

He sat down to open the carton of milk while I watched him struggle. Those things were never easy to open. You had to fold back at the right angle to get a clean opening when you pulled it out.

"They need to make these a twist-off cap." He smiled.

He looked innocent as he fussed with the carton of milk. I grabbed the cupcakes and opened them up so he didn't have to do all the work.

"You want one?" I asked before taking one myself. Every well-mannered Arab girl knows you're supposed to offer before you eat.

"You'd share?"

"Of course, God knows I shouldn't be eating one, let alone two of these."

He looked at me funny. Not like what I said was funny, but like what I said was completely ridiculous.

"Take one." I extended them closer to him.

We sat and talked about our day. I told him about the prom I helped plan in student council and how beautiful the girls looked. And he shared with me his wild excursions with his friends and the weed he bought being the best strain he'd ever had.

"I didn't know there were different types of weed," I told him. I wasn't well educated on cannabis.

"Have you ever smoked weed before?" he asked me.

"Once, with Quinn." Marc knew Quinn. He knew all of Lauren's family. They had gone to the same private grade school together, and Shelly befriended his mom in the parent-teacher organization.

"Oh yeah, how was it?"

"I didn't feel anything. Maybe I didn't do it right. The bong was a little intimidating." I laughed and finally took my first bite of the cupcake. I didn't want it, considering how late it was and how many calories were in it, but I had to accept the gift with grace. It would be rude otherwise.

"Not everyone gets high their first time." He took a big bite of his cupcake, so big that it was almost gone. "So, tell me, Maleeka, what's the worst thing you've ever done?" he asked me with a full mouth.

I covered my mouth in case there was leftover chocolate in my grill. "Pretty much everything I've done with you."

He laughed. "Shit, am I corrupting you, Maleeka?"

"I guess so." I laughed. "What about you?" I grabbed the carton. "Have you done anything besides weed?" I took a drink of milk to wash down the cake in my mouth.

"I did acid last weekend."

"Acid!?" I said, choking on the milk in my throat. "Why would you do that?"

"Just to try it." He ate the last of his cupcake and brushed his hands off in between his legs, like it was no biggie.

"Wow." I looked at my feet.

"It's just acid, Maleeka. It was something fun to do with the guys one night. It's not like I'm going to be doing heroin." He laughed.

I kept my head down, staring at the grooves on the bleacher step underneath me, unsure of what to say. I didn't think it was cool to try acid. I thought it was over the top and reckless. Maybe Jake was right when he said Marc and I were different.

He leaned close to make eye contact with me. "You look spooked."

"Sorry." I snapped out of my stare and looked up at him. "I don't know what to say."

"Say whatever's on your mind."

I couldn't say what was on my mind. I didn't want to offend him. I couldn't tell him I wasn't comfortable with him doing acid or that I thought it was too much. I couldn't question his boundaries or insist he have any. He was who he was, and I thought if I wanted anything to do with him, I'd have to accept that. I remembered my mom giving her sister advice in regard to her husband and failed marriage: you could never change a man.

"Acid sounds so scary."

He leaned back, shaking his head with a smile on his face. "It's not so bad, and honestly it was a one-time thing, just to try it."

"I would never try acid."

"Well, what would you try?"

"I don't know, I'd probably just keep it organic. Maybe I'll try mushrooms someday."

"Mushrooms are fun. If you ever decide to do them, you have to do 'em with me." He smiled.

"Deal," I said, stoked he was planning out our future, even if it was a night tripping out on mushrooms together.

"You feel like smoking with me?" He pulled a bag out of his back pocket. His pockets were filled with goodies.

I grabbed the ends of my hair and twisted them around my index finger, trying to wrap my mind around the idea of getting stoned with him alone.

"No pressure, we don't have to." He put the bag back into his pocket. I grabbed his hand.

"Yeah, let's do it." I had to impress him. I wanted to show him I wasn't different from him or his friends the way Jake said I was.

He showed me how to use his pipe, and like a gentleman, he gave me the first hit while lighting it for me. The strong wind pushed me to get close to him, keeping the flame going. He looked at me as he roasted the green weed, and as I released the carb and blew out my hit, I coughed, and couldn't stop.

"You okay?" He handed me what was left in our shared carton of milk.

"Yeah, I'm fine," I said in between coughs. "Sorry, this is so embarrassing."

"It's okay to cough," he said. "That means you're going to get really high."

I kept coughing while he took a hit easily.

"You sure you're okay?" he asked as he brushed my hair off my forehead with the lighter in his hand.

I looked at him with my arm over my mouth, nodding. It was a small gesture, but so sweet, like he was taking care of me.

We went back and forth taking turns a couple of times until he got a phone call. I was grateful for the break. While he talked on the phone, I pulled my lip gloss out from my tight jeans to reapply.

"You wanna get out of here?" he asked me as he put his phone into his khaki cargo pants.

"Sure," I said, not knowing where we would go or how we would get there.

"My buddy Carson is on his way to pick us up. He wants me to smoke him out."

"Carson Meyer?"

"Yeah, you know him?"

I knew exactly who Carson Meyer was. He was the drummer in their band, and I saw him around at school on the pothead wall. He was a punk-rock boy with shaggy black hair and a pale complexion. He was the one who Rasheed threw up against a locker after finding out about me and Marc.

"I've seen him around."

His friend pulled up in his big truck with a cute girl in his front seat who was in a cherry-red beaded formal gown. They had come from the prom. She was sweet when Marc opened the door. She turned and said hello while Marc let me in first.

"Maleeka Munir? What are you doing hanging out with trouble tonight?" Carson laughed.

"He's not that bad." I smiled at Marc.

"Does your brother know you're kicking it with Marc tonight? Careful, Marc." He made his voice go an octave deeper and puffed out his chest. "He'll kill you, you motherfucker." Carson laughed. I wondered before if Rasheed confronted Marc after finding out we fooled around, and it was obvious by Carson's impersonation he did and said something about killing Marc.

Marc chuckled a little and looked over at me. I couldn't laugh along with them. What if Rasheed found out I was high with Marc in Carson Meyer's truck? Immediately I wished I weren't there.

"Listen, Carson, don't mention to anyone Maleeka's with us tonight. All right?"

I looked at Marc, relieved he asked so I wouldn't have to.

"Yeah, man, whatever. Your secret is my secret, Marc," Carson said as he looked at Marc through the rearview mirror, still driving.

"Cool," he said as he patted on the back of the driver's seat and leaned in his to smile at me. I mouthed, "Thank you," to him without speaking, grateful he took care of Carson because I sure as hell didn't know how to.

We headed to the back roads behind our town that lined the Misty River. It was a luxury we had to be close to beauty, and it made for good spots to get stoned with your friends. Carson pulled off to the side of the road, giving us a front-row seat to the moon reflecting on the river while we hot boxed his truck. And I got high. So high. I thought it was embarrassing to cough uncontrollably in front of Marc, but coughing in front of the strangers was even worse. I couldn't walk away or excuse myself. I had to bury my head into my arm as I hunched over into my lap to try to muzzle the sound.

Marc looked over at me. "You o—"

I nodded fast to get him to drop it and not draw any more attention to me. But it was too late. Carson turned around.

"You sure?" Carson handed Marc a bottle of water to give me.

"Yeah." I grabbed the water bottle to take a sip, trying to wash it down. My throat burned.

"Here." I handed the bottle back to Marc. "Sorry, I'm okay."

"Don't be sorry." He smiled at me.

I wanted all the attention off me as the effect of the weed hit. I tried to keep up with the back-and-forth energy between the guys, while Carson's date ate chips in the front seat with her feet on the dashboard and her dress hiked up to her knees. I envied her ease. She was chilling, enjoying those chips. I could tell by how she licked her fingers after each bite. I couldn't relax.

The guys didn't shut up. They were giving each other shit about which band was better, Strung Out or NOFX. I wondered if I should mention I knew the song "Don't Call Me White" by NOFX. Jake used to play it for me because I wasn't white. Or would saying that make me sound stupid? That thought put Jake back in my head. Maybe he was right. I wasn't cool enough to kick it with these guys. I was a paranoid amateur. I didn't know how to engage with them while high.

"You listen to punk rock, Maleeka?" Carson asked me, interrupting my thoughts.

I nodded back as I took a big swallow of as much spit I could find in my dry mouth. "I listen to all kinds of music."

"Who's your favorite punk-rock band?"

"Um, Blink 182 is good," I said. Raneem loved Blink 182.

Carson laughed. I knew what he was thinking; it was written all over his face. He thought I was a joke, like Blink 182 and their nude music video. I had to redeem myself. These guys didn't think Blink 182 was considered punk rock.

"I also like Pennywise," I interjected to save face. "I like their song

'Perfect People.'" I had heard "Perfect People" once in Rasheed's truck, and I designated the chorus as my secret family anthem.

"Pennywise is cool," Marc said as he smiled at me.

The paranoia was in overdrive. I wanted out. It was my first time getting high, and all I wanted was to be in my bed at home, alone.

"You guys wanna go to Zach Darling's?" Carson asked us. "He has a bunch of people over." I didn't think Marc and Carson hung out with Zach, but a party is a party no matter whose house it's at.

Marc looked at me.

"You don't want to go, Maleeka? I'm sure your girls will be there," Carson said.

"I can't, it's so late." I couldn't walk into a party with Marc Osbourne and Carson Meyer.

Carson drove us back to town and headed toward my neighborhood as if it were no big deal to do so. I asked him to stop at the corner. His truck couldn't be outside my house. I grabbed the latch of the door to jump out. "Thanks for the ride, Carson," I said. "Nice meeting you both."

"Anytime," Carson told me.

"Nice meeting you too, Maleeka," the girl said, looking back, munching on her second bag of Fritos.

"Good night, Maleeka," Marc said as he scooted closer to me before I jumped out. I didn't know if he wanted a hug or an acknowledgment. I said bye to everyone except him. I wasn't thinking straight. All I could think about was my long journey back home and into the house.

"Oh, sorry." I laughed. "Good night, Marc." I smiled, looking back before I jumped out of the truck. I put my sweatshirt and baseball cap back on and walked home.

Dear Journal,   May 12, 2001

FIRST date

he wants you to get high.

I came home high. So high.
But honestly, he got me high before
that hit.

Reasons tonight went well...
1. He told me I looked beautiful
2. He brought me cupcakes
3. The way he brushed my hair off my
   forehead
4. He lit the bowl for me
5. He opened the door for me
6. He told Carson not to tell on me
7. He asked if I was okay
8. And before I left he made sure to
   say goodnight when I forgot to say
   anything to him

Reasons it didn't go well...
1. He tried acid

It wasn't summer yet, but school was almost out, and spring was at its end. The weather was mild, not warm enough for a swimsuit by a pool, but enough sun for cotton shorts and a tank top with our straps tucked in as we all lay out in Lauren's backyard to try and get a tan.

"What's new, Leek? It feels like we haven't hung out with you in months," Lauren told me, pulling up her lawn chair next to mine.

When you spend every day after school and every weekend together, a couple of weeks apart can feel like months.

"Yeah, we miss you, Leek," Samantha said.

"I know, I'm sorry, guys. I'm done being the spare tire." I tried to make it a joke, I had a smile on my face while I said it, but they didn't let it be funny.

"You're not the spare tire, Leek! Quit saying that shit," Samantha said with her arm over her face to block the sun.

"There is no reason for me to hang out with your boyfriends every night."

"We aren't reason enough?" Lauren said, trying to guilt-trip me.

"Guys, let Maleeka do her thing, even if it is staying home to talk to Marc on the internet," Emiko told them.

"How often do you guys talk?" Lauren asked me.

"Yeah, Leek, tell us everything." Samantha sat up at the edge of her seat.

I was glad to hear their interest and their support. I kept so many secrets in my life, but never from my best friends. I told them every-thing, and even let them read our online chats I printed to put in my journal.

"He is so into you," Samantha said after reading our latest conversation out loud to the others.

I couldn't stop smiling.

"'I can't wait to see you again, *babe*'?" Samantha said, dropping the journal on her lap. "He called you babe!"

I put my face in my hands, still smiling. "Ugh, I know, I love it when he calls me babe."

"I give you two weeks until he asks you out," Lauren said.

"I don't know about that."

"Come on, Maleeka, this guy likes you. Don't let your insecurities ruin it for you," Samantha said.

"It's not that. He told me the other day he isn't looking to date right now."

"You talked about dating?" Emiko asked.

"Not exclusively, just in general. He said he didn't want to sound like a stereotypical guy, but the reason he isn't dating anyone is because he's not ready for the commitment that comes with a girlfriend."

"I bet you can get him to change his mind." She smiled at me.

"I don't know, I can't date him anyway. We're just friends."

"Well, what's your friend doing tonight?" Lauren asked. "Let's call him. Give me his number." She picked up the phone.

"I don't have his number."

"What? How do you *not* have his number?"

"It's not like we can talk on the phone. Could you imagine if Rasheed found out or picked up while we were talking?"

"God," Samantha said, "your family is always getting in the way of any fun."

Lauren got up off her chair and went inside while we girls continued in on radical scenarios of what would happen if the family knew I talked to him online. She came back outside with a little brown leatherette notebook.

"Let's call him," Lauren said, reminding me Shelly used to be friends with Marc's mom. She flipped to the Os to get his number and dialed.

"Lauren, wait!" I leaned out of my chair.

She put her hand out to stop me from grabbing the phone.

"Hello?" Marc said on the speakerphone.

"Hi, Marc?"

"Yeah."

"It's Lauren Weigh, you busy?"

"What's up, Lauren. No, what's going on?" I could tell he was shocked Lauren was calling him.

"I'm sitting here with Maleeka. Do you want to talk to her?"

"Dude!" I whispered.

Marc laughed a little at her bold call that had me on the other side of the deck, biting my nails.

"Yeah, let me say what's up," he said.

Lauren smiled big and handed the white cordless phone over to me.

"Here," she said, "he's all yours."

I grabbed the phone with rockets exploding in my gut. I was nervous. I never heard his voice on the phone. It sounded deeper and raspier than in person.

"Hi," I said, still biting my nails, and made my way back over to my chair to sit down and chat with him. I reached my finger over to take it off speakerphone, and immediately all three girls opened their eyes wide and shook their heads. They wanted to hear it all.

"What's up, Maleeka?"

"Just hanging out with the girls. Sorry, are we bothering you?"

"Not at all, I'm glad Lauren called." He laughed.

"Ask him if he wants to hang out," Lauren whispered so he wouldn't hear her.

"Are you doing anything tonight?" I asked him. "Do you want to get together?"

"Yeah, definitely. I was going to go kick it with Jake, but I want to see you."

I looked at the girls, who were cheering me on silently.

"Tell him to come over," Lauren whispered again.

"And have him bring Jake," Emiko also whispered with a smirk on her face.

The guys came over before Shelly called it a night in her room with a movie. She opened the front door for them, and I could hear her call out, "Marc Osbourne! How are you, sweetie?"

Like all our "juice," Shelly knew about Marc. She took us out to breakfast one morning and all she had to do was ask if I was interested in anyone. Shelly made it easy to tell her everything. And she knew Marc through his mother's eyes, so she encouraged it and told me she thought he was misunderstood by others.

Marc gave her a big hug.

"How's your mom doing?"

"She's doing well, I'll make sure to tell her I saw you."

"Please do, and give her my love. God, we had good times together."

"Okay, Mom," Lauren said, interrupting their conversation. "Come downstairs, guys."

Shelly walked over to put her arm around me. "I'm going to watch TV. If you guys need anything, let me know."

"Good night, Mom." Lauren pulled me away from her. Lauren was often annoyed by her mom getting involved with our lives.

"Good night, Shelly. It was great seeing you," Marc said with a smile. I loved how he was mature and polite with Shelly.

Lauren's room was big; it took up most of the space on the lower floor of their split-level home. It had enough space for her queen-size bed on one side and a seating area on the other. It looked staged for a television show. The walls were white, but everything else in her room was pink. Her bedspread, her beanbag chair, the twinkle lights she had pinned on the wall. Even her computer was pink. Samantha was on the bed. Emiko sat on the love seat with Jake, I sat on the computer chair, and Marc got comfortable on the pink fuzzy beanbag chair.

"It's obvious you're not even listening to my story," Lauren said, standing in the middle of the room, when she noticed Marc staring at me.

"Come on, Lauren, I'm listening!" He laughed. "Start over, when was the first time you got stoned?"

"Forget it!" She laughed, throwing her pillow onto his lap while he kept laughing. He looked cute holding on to her sequin pillow.

"Come on, Lauren, tell him. We were in her backyard," I said.

"Quinn got her high. Isn't that cute? Her big brother got her high for the first time." I smiled at him.

"That's very cute, Lauren." Marc smirked.

"Yeah, okay." Lauren rolled her eyes with a smile on her face. She walked over to the desk I sat at. "He can't take his eyes off of you," she whispered to me.

I straightened my back to sit upright, realizing the way I leaned over showed a ton of cleavage. My boobs were what I thought were the only attribute about me that set me apart from the others; they were much bigger than the girls'. It was the only compliment I ever heard from guys—"Your boobs are huge." But I wanted Marc to see more to me than my boobs.

"Do you have any weed?" Samantha sat up on the bed and asked Marc. After Quinn smoked her out, she realized how much she liked it, and she wasn't shy to ask for it.

"Yeah, I have a bag," Marc said.

"You guys wanna go for a walk?" Lauren said.

"Yeah, let's do it," Jake said. "I'm not about to have Shelly catch me smoking on her property."

Emiko and Samantha led the group down the street in the direction of the park. The same place where Marc and I hooked up before. I followed, assuming the whole group was going.

"You're not coming." Lauren turned back to stop me.

"What do you mean?"

"He's waiting for you." She smiled at me and looked at Marc, who hung out by his car after handing Jake a little weed. She ran to catch up with the others, and Samantha called out, "Have fun, Maleeka!"

"I'm glad you stayed. I don't think I could kick it much longer without doing this." He grabbed my face to kiss me.

We made it into the back seat of his messy car. It smelled like cigarette smoke, and there were papers, wrappers, and soda bottles everywhere. He threw them all on the floor and got close to me. I was nervous, it was easier to throw myself on him while I was tipsy, but I was sober. He grabbed me again with force, and his kiss made me feel like a ten. Not a size ten, but a ten on the charts. The most beautiful I could possibly be on my imaginary chart. I hadn't been up there since the last time I kissed him in the dirt. His assertive demeanor and even his voice had me turned on, which made me feel sexy again, less un-sure and insecure, and more myself. I put his hand up my shirt until I gave him the go-ahead to take it farther down to my pants. I wanted the pleasure—the legs shaking, the sweat, the urge to keep it all in.

"Oh my God, Marc," I whispered in his ear while he sucked on my neck with his fingers inside me. "Marc," I gasped, but he kept at it. I couldn't go much longer. I called out again, "Wait!"

"Are you okay?" He backed off and looked at me with his bright-blue eyes.

I leaned my head back into the crease of the back seat while nod-ding with my hands wiping the hair off my face. "I'm sorry, I can't . . ." I took in a deep breath. "I can't breathe."

"I must be doing something right." He laughed, leaning on his side.

"You're funny." I smiled at him, admiring his eyes.

He caught me staring and looked right back at me. "And you're gorgeous."

"Yeah, right. You're crazy." I shook my head, looking the other way.

"You aren't good at taking compliments, are you?"

He called me out. I mean, he was right, it was obvious, but I didn't think he'd call me out.

"Maleeka." He grabbed my face. "Believe me, you're fucking gorgeous."

I was fueled by his fixation, making me feel beautiful, and I wanted to thank him. I pushed him against the rear door in the back seat with loads of passion, taking charge. All he had to do was sit back and enjoy. Emiko had given me pointers on how to get the job done.

"You want to smoke?" he asked while zipping up his pants after I was done getting him off.

"Yeah, sure," I told him, with my hair all over the place. He climbed to the front seat to grab a joint and turned on the car to play music.

"What is that?" I jumped out of my seat once the music blared in the speaker with a robotic voice in the intro.

"Black Sabbath," he told me. I looked at him like he quoted some dark, biblical terminology, confused. "'Iron Man'?" he told me to elaborate.

"I have no idea what that is." I laughed with my hand over one ear. "Do you have something more laid back?"

"I know what to play," he told me as he crawled back over to change the CD in his Walkman with an adapter attached to the tape player. "You like the Beatles?"

"Yeah, I like oldies." I put my top on and leaned against the car door with my feet up on the seat.

He sang the opening line to "Strawberry Fields Forever" while leaning back in his seat, and smiled at me as he took a couple of hits. The smoke filled up the car and danced with the beat, circling before settling into the air. He nodded his head and continued to sing along to the words I had never heard before. Fooling around with him and getting high after, both things I would get hung about.

"Look at those windows!" Samantha called out loud enough for us to hear her.

I got out to greet them with bloodshot eyes and messy hair.

"Did you get the dick?" Samantha asked me as I got out of the car.

"You're so foul, Sam," I told her while Marc got out of the car and lit up a cigarette.

"Seriously, Leek, what were you guys doing in there?" Emiko asked. "Those windows are all fogged up!"

I laughed. "We were hanging out."

"So you got the dick!" Samantha laughed, looking at Lauren, who was shaking her head, laughing.

"You guys are annoying." I walked off before I looked back at Marc, who smiled at me and my girls. "Good night, Marc."

"Good night, babe," he called out to me. My stomach dropped with that word—*babe*.

GREATEST COMPLIMENT EVER

Dear Journal,   June 3, 2001

→ 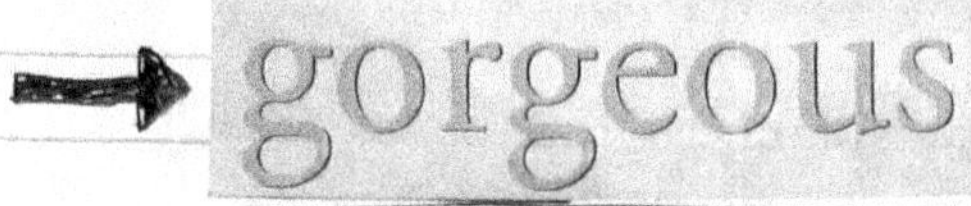

←

→ 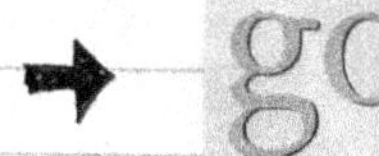

WHAT A WORD!

...GORGEOUS...
Bigger than beautiful.
More than hot or sexy.

It's hard to believe someone when they tell you you're gorgeous when you don't believe it yourself. But it's not just him telling me so, it's also the way he kisses me, stares at me and grabs me that makes me believe everything he's saying.

Raneem was the first girl in our Syrian family who went away to school. Not a couple of hours away, but on the other side of the country. The girls in my family could have easily gone away on scholarships like she had, but they weren't allowed. It was looked down on for a girl to leave her parents' house before marriage. But Raneem and I joked my dad was a closet feminist. He told me when I was eight years old I could be whatever I wanted, even president of the United States. His brother laughed and said, "Women shouldn't have that much power." Dad was proud of Raneem. I remember watching him tell his parents, who didn't know how much of an honor it was for her to be there. He stood firm in their living room with his chest puffed out, explaining to them what kind of college Harvard was. I could tell he loved telling people where she was when they'd ask. Good thing he had Raneem. He sure as hell never told anyone I got a D in science.

Her homecoming was a big deal to him and my mom. They missed her. I missed her. We all did. They invited their families to surprise her when she'd walk through the door. Both sides of my family didn't come together often, only for our birthday parties. But every time they did, it was split: Mom's side clumped together around her in the kitchen, while Dad's all gathered in the living room. Two different languages were spoken, oftentimes about the other side, but I understood both. I was always listening to each side's judgments of the other. I remember an aunt on my dad's side talking shit about my younger cousin on my mom's side once because he was eating a stack of chips out of his hand rather than a bowl. It pissed me off, but at the same time, my mom's sister mocked them about how they were all overdressed at the same party.

That night, they were all in their usual spaces, but as the front door opened underneath the crystal chandelier, they all came together for a second to holler out, "Welcome home!"

Dad walked in first, holding two big suitcases, with his unlit cigar held loosely in his smile. He was beaming. I couldn't say the same about Raneem. Her smile looked fake and forced as she gave a few shallow hugs, with her oversize and overfilled purse under her arm.

Her highlights were grown out, which made her hair look more oily than it was. She wore a big red zip-up over her flared jeans and a baggy blue shirt. It looked big on her, like the crowd around her. My dad's mom held on to her forever as she told her in Arabic how happy she was to see her, commented on how she looked thin, and asked her what she was eating there.

"Welcome home, Raneem." My mom walked out of the kitchen to greet her and take her out of my grandmother's arms.

"Hi, Mom." She barely looked at my mom and put her purse on the first chair she could find.

I stood back before approaching her with my younger cousin Asma. We were standing against the French doors in the kitchen underneath a banner I made that read, *Welcome Home!* with balloons on both sides.

Asma grew up with us like a little sister. We were always together on the weekends, playing dollhouse and making music videos. But as I got closer to my girlfriends, I had less time to hang out with the cousins on the weekends. Asma was the oldest in her family; she was obedient, much like Raneem was; and she excelled in everything she was involved in. She'd had a focused head on her shoulders since she was little, and she made the right choices, always. Asma never wanted to hurt anyone, especially her parents.

"She doesn't look good," I told Asma.

"Why do you say that?"

"Look at her. She looks uncomfortable."

"It's probably because there are too many people here."

Our family was big, so it was easy to get lost in the crowd. There were times I'd find myself talking to nobody even though there were forty plus people in the room.

I walked over to give her a hug while my aunts gawked over how skinny she was. She put one arm around me while I grabbed on to her.

"I'm so glad you're home," I said to her. "You okay?"

"I'm tired," she said.

She looked worn out, with no energy to talk to anyone. Eventually, she excused herself to go and take a shower. Everyone made small talk while Mom made both American and Arabic coffee, and we waited for her to come back downstairs.

"Leek, can I talk to you for a minute?" my cousin Waleed said to me.

"What's up?" I asked him.

"Let's go outside."

We walked out to the front porch; the back porch was occupied by the men drinking whiskey and talking about Middle Eastern politics. My mom had a swing installed on the porch with a matching side table and chair for the summer nights. I plopped on the swing while Waleed stayed standing.

"Why are you acting so serious?" I laughed at him.

"Maleeka, I've been hearing things." Waleed and I were the same age and went to the same school, but we didn't have the same school experiences. He was an academic jock who spent time on the weekends studying textbooks and playbooks. His friends were his teammates or science group partners; we didn't hang out in the same crowd.

"Oh yeah? Anything good?"

He didn't laugh or smile. He didn't even look at me. "Nothing good."

I stayed quiet and let him elaborate.

"Maleeka, people are saying you're sleeping with that guy." He finally turned to look at me. "Marc is his name?"

"That's bullshit." I shook my head.

"Is it?" Waleed wasn't anything like Rasheed; he had a calm demeanor but worried eyes.

"I'm not sleeping with anyone."

"Why would anyone say that about you if it wasn't true?"

"People like to talk shit, Waleed."

"Promise me it's not true. I can't stick up for you if you're lying to me."

"I swear I'm not sleeping with him." I looked him in the eye. "But, Waleed, I like him. Like, a lot. He's a good guy."

He shook his head. "That's not what I hear."

"Don't believe everything Rasheed says about him. Rasheed barely knows him. I know him! He's a good guy. He has a good heart."

"He's not a stoner?"

"He smokes, but he's not a stoner," I said with a straight face, knowing he was considered a stoner.

"Maleeka, you know you can't ever be with him, right?"

I nodded my head.

"Stay away from him, Leek. I don't want you getting hurt or getting in trouble."

I wanted to scream. I didn't think Marc was capable of hurting me. I knew I would get in trouble, but I didn't care.

"I really like him."

"More than your family?" He looked at me with his chin down and his eyebrows raised.

I didn't say yes or no.

"Maleeka, it's not just about getting in trouble. You will break your dad's heart."

"Why do I have to care about him? He doesn't care about me."

Dad opened the front door. "Maleeka, go check on your sister. She hasn't come down yet."

"She's taking a shower, Dad," I said.

"Go, Maleeka." He walked back inside.

Before I opened the front door, I looked back at Waleed. "Please don't tell anyone what I told you tonight, especially Rasheed."

"I would never do that, Maleeka."

I knew he would never rat me out. Waleed always looked out for me. When we were eleven years old, playing at my grandparents' house, I went to the bathroom and stayed in there for half an hour crying, and Waleed was the only one who noticed. He knocked and asked me if

I was okay. I cried through the door and told him I was bleeding. He gave me his sweatshirt to wrap around my waist so I could walk home without anyone finding out I got my period.

I walked upstairs to find Raneem in her bed wrapped in a bathrobe with wet hair. She wasn't sleeping. Her eyes were wide open, staring off at the wall.

"Raneem?" I said, and got closer to sit at the edge of her bed. "Raneem, everyone is here for you. You have to get up."

She kept her head nestled in her freshly cleaned pillow and ignored me.

"Should I tell them to leave?"

Raneem nodded but still didn't say a word.

"Fine." I got up. I hated when Raneem would check out. She could fill a room with her energy when she was on, but when she wasn't, she sucked the life out of it.

I walked back down the stairs to find everyone looking at me, waiting to hear what was going on.

"She's tired. She wants to go to sleep," I told them.

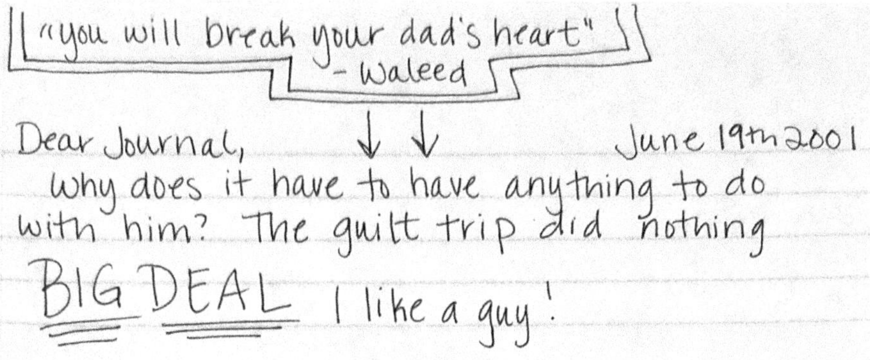

Dear Journal,   ↓ ↓   June 19th 2001
   Why does it have to have anything to do with him? The guilt trip did nothing

<u>BIG DEAL</u> I like a guy!

Guilt trips are part of their game. The family does it to all of us. Rasheed and Raneem fell for it. Obviously Waleed does too.
   It's normal to have a crush on people. It's normal to date people.
   I'm not doing anything wrong!!!

· · · · · · · · · · · · · · · · ·

Play me, sway me, tricks to see your lies
Maybe, you'll get me, if you keep on trying
I know that I'm not wrong
I've seen it all play out for way too long
Using fear and guilt to prove me wrong
I've lived this way confined for ~~way~~
         too long

     I'm done!

Who cares what your family thinks

...be the girl you wanna be

SHE NEEDS you

Raneem and I used to share a room, shared a bed really. I was devastated when she told my mom she wanted her own room and for me to move into the guest room. I was only nine, and I cried because I was losing her in a way. No more late-night laughs or comfort while my parents would be fighting downstairs. She got me to stop crying about the move by promising she'd put her bed against the same wall my bed was against. That way there was just a wall separating us, but she was still right there sleeping next to me. A few years later when she moved across the country, I cried again knowing she wouldn't be behind that wall anymore. But again she promised me she was just a phone call away, and she'd always be there for me. That summer, though she was back against the shared wall again, I lost her.

Mom told me Raneem was depressed. I had heard the word *depression* in passing before. It didn't feel heavy when Lauren would say, "I'm so depressed they killed off my favorite character," or when Emiko would tell me, "God, this movie is so depressing."

It was a short-lived feeling—almost like excitement for a planned event or a kind of fear over an unknown setting. But Raneem's depression wasn't like anything I'd ever seen before. It wasn't going away anytime soon. A couple of weeks after she got home, she was still in bed where I had left her the night of her homecoming. She'd get up to use the restroom or to get a cup of coffee, but that's it. When she'd walk past me, there was no acknowledgment or connection. She looked blank and empty, even scary.

I sat on my bed one night after coming home from watching *Crazy/Beautiful* with the girls. I leaned against our shared wall and listened in as Dad told her, "We are not depressed people." She sobbed as he continued: "It's okay, it's okay, you're going to be okay." He probably said the word *okay* twenty times until finally Raneem screamed, "I'm not okay!" Then the wall between us shook.

I jumped out of bed and rushed to her room. Mom stormed off past me, shaking her head, saying, "This is too much!"

I peeked in to see Raneem on the edge of the bed where the headboard met the wall. She held on to her knees, rocking back and forth. She looked more scared than I was. Dad grabbed her head and pulled it into his gut, stroking her hair, staring at the hole she had kicked through the drywall. "It's going to be okay," he told her.

I didn't know what to do; I didn't want to walk away like my mom had, but I was scared to get too close. I went back to my room and lay on my bed with only the wall separating us. I couldn't imagine how it would ever be okay like Dad said it would be.

I woke up early the next morning and sat on the curved staircase. That was my spot growing up. I spent countless nights on the wide step at the peak of the curve with my knees up and my back against the wall and listened while they'd tear up the kitchen with nasty words and violent outbursts. It was heading in that direction that day.

"This is a private matter, nobody needs to get involved!" I heard my dad say.

"I told your brother, he asked me what was going on."

"It's none of his business! Telling everyone will make it worse!"

There wasn't much awareness or acceptance of mental health issues in our family, especially Dad's side. It carried a stigma of weakness and madness, neither of which my dad wanted tied to Raneem. Because of that, Dad kept the issues hidden from our Syrian family. I think he knew they would use Raneem as a topic of gossip and put her and our family under a microscope. He thought it was better to keep it under wraps to protect Raneem from any judgments or assumptions that she had lost her mind. Her mind that he always held high on the charts, her brilliant mind. He didn't want anyone to know. Mom, on the other hand, told her sisters all about it.

"This isn't going to go away, Karim, she's depressed. She needs medicine."

"She's going to be fine."

"Oh my God. You think you have a relationship with your children? They're all scared of you, she doesn't want to let you down!"

I heard his chair screech against the kitchen floor, which made me assume he jumped out of his seat. "God damn it! I am protecting my daughter!"

I got up off the stairs to intervene. I hated hearing him raise his voice to her, and I knew she wouldn't stop until he lost it. "Dad, stop." He didn't stop; neither of them did. They kept going back and forth about what each of them did wrong raising us. They didn't even see me.

"I won't stand back anymore," Mom insisted. "I am going to start speaking my mind," she yelled before storming out.

My dad stood at the kitchen sink, dumping out his coffee. He looked defeated. I didn't know what to say, and before I could figure it out, he shook his head and laid into me.

"You need to be there for your sister." He turned his head back, with his body still facing the sink.

"What do you want me to do?" I asked him.

His whole body shifted. "Spend more time with her. Talk to her. Be there for her!"

"I don't know how to help."

He shook his head and walked away from me. "You spend so much God damn time with strangers. You should put your sister first." Funny he thought my friends were strangers; they knew more about me than anyone in that house did.

"What about Rasheed?" I asked, overwhelmed by the pressure to be my sister's savior.

"You're her sister!" He turned around to reprimand me with his finger pointing me out. "She needs *you*."

I made a strong cup of coffee for Raneem the way she always said she liked it: black like her soul. I hesitated to knock on the door. I tried to figure out what to say to put a smile on her face or, better yet, to get her out of bed. I knocked a couple of times.

"Raneem?" I said quietly. "Can I come in?"

She didn't answer me. I knocked again and turned the doorknob to walk in. The room was dark with the lights off and the shades shut. She had a black blanket tucked in the curtain rod to block the sun out. My eyes adjusted, and I saw a shape on the bed covered in blankets. I pumped myself up with compassion and energy to try to be there for my sister.

I sang her the good morning song trying to put a smile on her face, not like I could see her smile if she did.

Raneem didn't laugh. Her hair was all over her face. She turned her back to me and covered her head. I sat on the bed and reached over to move her hair aside.

"I made you a cup of coffee."

She didn't move.

"Please wake up, Raneem. Let's go do a puzzle and watch a movie. Please, I'm bored."

"Leave me alone, Maleeka."

I had to figure out a way to get her out of bed. But I couldn't do it alone. I turned to music. My sister had a fat crush on Tom DeLonge from Blink 182, so I turned her CD player on to "I'm Sorry," that way she could hear his vocals versus Mark Hoppus's. Raneem always pulled more toward what some considered the less exposed, introverted bassists rather than the attention-seeking lead singers I favored.

Tom's voice worked. She turned around and looked at me with a blank stare on her face. It was something; I got her attention.

"I see that smile," I told her.

She did smile a little, showing no teeth, but it was still a smile. She grabbed the cup of coffee.

"Do you want to do a puzzle?" I asked. "Mom got us a new one with five hundred pieces."

"Sure," she told me, moving her hair out of her face.

"Let's go downstairs."

Raneem went along with me after pulling back her greasy hair and putting on a bra. We sat at the big coffee table, and I sorted out the edges of the puzzle while Raneem sat there.

I mustered up the courage to pry. "What's going on, Raneem? You're so down lately."

"Mom thinks I'm possessed," she said, looking at the puzzle piece in her hand.

"No, she doesn't."

"I heard her telling Aunt Pat she sees evil in my eyes. It's fucked up to hear your mom say that about you."

"She didn't mean it, Raneem," I said to her, even though I also thought it was fucked up.

Raneem kept looking at the puzzle, in deep thought, with no movement. She stared at the table for a while.

"Do you feel loved unconditionally by them?"

"By Mom and Dad?" I looked at her, but she kept her head down.

"Yeah, like, no matter who you are or what you do, they'll love you."

"I guess I don't care enough to think about that." I got back to the puzzle.

"You wouldn't have to; you have enough friends, you don't need to worry about Mom and Dad. They are disappointed in me. I can see it all over their faces."

"They just want you happy, Raneem, that's all we want."

"Oh yeah, and what if I can't be happy?" she snapped at me, and finally looked up with anger in her eyes. "Do you know how hard it is to be fucking happy?"

"Raneem, wait." My voice cracked as she stormed out to go back to her room. I didn't want her back up there. Mom and Dad didn't even see her out yet. I knew it would make them happy to see her out of her room; that's all anyone wanted, to see her living again. But she couldn't force herself. She had no control of it. That was when I realized there was a big difference between feeling down and depression. She couldn't force herself to feel happy, not even to please them.

Dear Journal, July 1, 2001

You would think watching their daughter suffer would bring mom and dad together. But they aren't capable of that.

All they know is <u>FIGHT</u>.

I hate seeing her like this. She has no life in her eyes, they look empty. It scares me.
I feel like I've lost her.
I feel so bad knowing that she is hurting so much inside.

I wish I could fix it somehow. Snap my fingers and bring her peace. I hate not having any control and watching her struggle knowing I can't do shit about it.

MY beautiful
SISTER AMAZING
Special
Brilliant

Smoke Session & Deep Conversation

As summer went on, the house became darker and more unbearable every day with Raneem's depression. But my nights were an escape. I knew every online chat and late-night meetup was risky, but the risk made it exciting. It became my new norm. We would do our own things during the day, spend time with our separate friends, and meet at night when the world was sleeping. Our hookups, though not sex, were powerful. We'd see each other and instantly, without any words, physically connect, knowing we were both ready. Marc was much more advanced in his rebellion with drugs, but when it came to being physical with each other, I had no problem keeping up. I pushed the boundaries; it made me feel confident and sexy. And I loved the power I had enticing him. It made me feel like a big girl with control.

At the end of it all, we'd put a cap on the night with a smoke session and deep conversation. I was better about smoking. I figured out how to be high and enjoy it. Especially when I was with him. I loved listening to him talk, and he made me feel like I was worth getting to know. I got off on the undivided attention he gave me.

Marc handed me a loaded bowl on the bleachers we now referred to as our spot. It wasn't easy or comfortable to fool around on those bleachers, but the field would be too obvious. It was lit up, so if anyone walked by, they would see me. I tried to hit the bowl but struggled to keep the flame going.

He grabbed the lighter to help me out. "Where are your friends tonight?" he asked.

I took a hit and pointed to my head while I blew out my smoke without coughing.

"'Lithium'?" He smiled at me.

"I had to say it." I leaned back against the seat behind me and looked up at the stars. "Did you know that Kurt Cobain would sometimes throw up before performing live?"

He shook his head while exhaling his hit. "I didn't know that."

"Yeah." I grabbed the pipe. "I guess even the biggest stars can get stage fright." I took another hit without his help. "Did you ever get nervous?"

"A little, but once you're out there, you're on this wave of adrenaline. I sure as hell didn't have a following as big as Kurt Cobain, but even being cheered on by a hundred people was a rush. Hearing them scream out my name and call out words to songs I wrote felt like I was some sort of inspiration or gravitational force. It's something I'll never get over."

I couldn't help but lean toward him as he spoke. He didn't need a stage for me to feel his energy pull me in. Just listening to him talk on those cold, empty bleachers with a spark in his eyes captivated me. "It sounds like you miss it."

He turned his head to look at me. "Yeah, I guess I do."

"So get the band back together!" I sat at the edge of my seat and grabbed his knee.

He shook his head. "It's not the time." He took another hit and blew a big cloud of smoke before looking back at me. "How do you know so much about Kurt Cobain?"

"My brother's obsessed with him. His bedroom walls are covered with Nirvana posters."

"What's your room like?"

"My room? Try to guess." I smiled at him. I wondered what he'd think I was into based on what others did, because of my popular girlfriends and name-brand clothes.

"I'm sure you don't have Kurt Cobain all over your walls, though if you did, I would think that was pretty fucking cool."

"Not Kurt Cobain, but close."

"Close? What, you got Dave Grohl up there?"

I shook my head and smiled. "Eminem."

"You think Eminem and Kurt Cobain are similar?"

"They're both dark and sensitive masters of their individual art."

He cocked his head to the side and smiled. "I can see that."

"Eminem is the only artist I've ever loved enough to post on my wall. It's a commitment to put someone's poster up on your wall. It's a reflection of who you are, or who you identify with. My brother has Kurt, and my sister has pictures of John Steinbeck and Sylvia Plath, which says a lot about her."

"So you identify with Marshall Mathers?"

I sat up and turned my body to face him. "I admire him. He says whatever he wants. It's like he isn't scared to lose anyone, he's speaking his truth. And the way he uses metaphors and emotions to tell his stories takes it to a whole new level. I can feel everything he is feeling."

"I don't disagree, his wordplay is off the charts. What's your favorite Eminem song?"

"'The Way I Am.'"

"Not 'Stan'?"

I shook my head. "I love how angry he is in it. It's empowering to sing along with him. I make a point to memorize his lyrics."

"Damn, I didn't know you were a gangster." He laughed.

"I wouldn't say that." I leaned back against the cold bleacher. "I mean, I'm not gonna pretend to be hard. I pretty much have the entire Destiny's Child CD memorized." I laughed. "I'm sure you're not bumping Beyoncé in your headphones."

He laughed. "I have a poster of Beyoncé up in my room."

"No way!"

"Yeah, I mean I don't own any of her CDs, but I have her poster hanging on my wall."

"She *is* sexy," I said. "Can we also agree on Eminem being equally attractive?"

"Oh come on, Maleeka, I will admit Eminem is cool, but you're not going to convince me to call him sexy." He laughed.

"You mean to tell me you'd turn him away if you had the chance?" I laughed.

He shook his head. "Nah, I'd probably let him stay. I'm sure he'd have a ton of drugs with him."

"Of course you would say that!" I pushed him with my shoulder.

It was easy to talk to him about everything that mattered to each of us. He told me about his family and how close he was with his parents. He talked about his little sister like he was her biggest fan. *Rasheed would never talk about me like that,* I thought to myself. His family was open and honest with each other, not like mine. I told him about my family.

"So you think you'll have an arranged marriage someday?" He laughed.

"I would hope my dad would want more for me. But we don't talk about guys at all. It's forbidden. All he wants is for me to get good grades and go to college."

"That's cool he pushes school and college on you. Knowledge is crucial."

"Yeah, I don't know if college is for me. I mean aside from getting out of the house. I have other dreams."

"Dreams, huh?" He grabbed his pack of cigarettes out of his pocket. "What are they?"

"I don't want to say."

"Why not?" He smacked the pack against his palm and pulled one out.

"It's kind of stupid."

"No way, don't say that. Come on, tell me."

My heart pounded in my throat. The only person I told my dreams to was Lauren. She helped me prep for a talent show in seventh grade to read a poem I wrote, and the day before, I dropped out.

I took in a deep breath and stared at the bright lights on the field. "I write a lot."

He sucked his cigarette to light it and blew out his first hit. I loved the smell of the first hit of cigarettes. They smelled like a match burning before smelling like shitty nicotine the rest of the time. "You do?"

I grabbed my journal out from my purse and flipped the pages quickly so he couldn't read the words, but he could see how much I did write. The pages were covered.

"Jesus, you do," he said, with his cigarette in between his lips. "What's up with the magazine cutouts?"

"It's art." I smiled at him. "I have this dream to someday write a book," I told him as I stroked the words *Don't Read* on the front of the journal with my thumb. "But I also have all these ideas for songs." I looked up at him. "Like they come in my head sometimes. Rhymes to tell my story. I'd love to turn them into songs."

"That's badass, Maleeka, do you sing?"

I nodded my head. "Alone."

"Sing for me!" He tried to make eye contact with me.

I looked down and laughed. "Never."

He leaned back and nodded his head. "You'll sing for me one day, I'll make sure of it. Will you share something you've written with me?"

"It's not really your style." Marc was the songwriter for his band. He wrote about issues like mental health, society's rules, and drugs. I put the journal back in my purse. "I don't want you to laugh. It's different from the way you write."

"I had no idea you were a writer." He smiled. "Does your family know about your dreams?"

"I can't tell my family."

"Why not?" He was confused. His parents knew all about his art. They'd often be in the audience, videotaping.

"It's not an option," I told him.

"But your brother's in a band."

"He's in a band, but they don't have anything to do with it. It's something he does for fun now, but he'll be a doctor someday. That's how it is in my family. There are three options for future endeavors. Do you want to hear them?"

Marc laughed. "Go for it."

I turned my entire body to face him and sat crisscross on the bench. "Option number one: you can go to school for four years, get your bachelor's, and get a job straight out of school, making forty thousand a year as an engineer. People will think highly of you because the degree is math based, giving it prestige."

"An engineer? How boring."

"So boring." I shook my head and laughed before going on. "Option two: if math isn't your thing but you still want to prove yourself to the family, you study law. It's a professional degree with a great title and an even better salary."

"A lawyer, huh? I couldn't see you as a lawyer. You're too nice."

"Yeah, you're probably right." I laughed. "On to option three, the highest honors you could get in our family: dedicate yourself and go to school for, like, twelve years and be a doctor. You can save lives and make bank and everyone will address your Christmas cards as Dr. Marc Osbourne. It's a pretty big deal."

"Respect among your peers sounds great. But being a doctor, a lawyer, or an engineer is hard work. You have to like it to be able to do it the rest of your life."

"You don't have to like it for shit. You bust your ass to make your family look good. It feeds their ego. They brag about you and how amazing you are. If I told my family I wanted to write or sing, they'd all laugh in my face. They would never take me seriously."

"Damn."

"They have a set standard of what is right and what is accepted. But I know there are other ways to make it big. There are other ways to live."

"Sounds restraining," he said.

"It's my dad, he's the tyrant." I laughed.

"Your mom isn't strict?"

"She just goes along with my dad's rules."

"What are the rules?" he asked.

"Well, let's see." I looked up at the sky and numbered them on my fingers. "No makeup, no tank tops, no short skirts, no sports, no friends, no calls from boys, no boys in any manner. Not as friends, and of course not as boyfriends." I put my hands down on my lap and looked at Marc, who nodded his head. "He wants my focus on school and family, that's it. I don't know what my dad would do if he knew I was with you right now." I laughed a little. "Or if he knew about every night we've been together. He would lose it."

"Lose it?" His eyes got big. "God, that sounds intense."

"You wouldn't believe the scenes he's made."

"Wow." He looked off into the distance. I wondered if I had said too much and freaked him out. I didn't want Marc to hate my dad. I backtracked a bit.

"Don't get me wrong. He has a good heart deep down, but he's always mad at me. Rasheed tells me I'm raising his blood pressure and I'm going to kill him."

"You're not a bad kid, though. I mean, shit, I know bad kids. You're far from it."

"They aren't used to having a kid push the limits. My brother and sister never rebelled. They always follow the rules."

"Tell me more about your sister," he asked as he brushed out his cigarette.

"What do you want to know?"

"Well, I know enough about Rasheed, but what's she like? Raneem, is it?"

I couldn't help but smile a little, maybe because he asked about someone I loved so much, or maybe because of how much I loved her. "She's beautiful. Seriously, she is the most beautiful person I've known in real life. And she is smart. Smarter than you even." I laughed.

"Not possible." He laughed along.

"I don't know, I would put my money on her."

"Well, that's funny 'cause I'd put my money on you," he said back. "The most beautiful, that's all you."

I grabbed my hair to put it behind my ears and shook my head. "You don't understand; Raneem has always been the beauty in our house. Beauty and brains too big for anyone to handle, even herself."

"What do you mean?"

"There's this part in *The Great Gatsby*, when Daisy wishes her daughter to be a beautiful fool, because a fool wouldn't be capable of living a miserable life. Ignorance is bliss, you know?"

"Ignorance is ignorant."

"Maybe, but it can save you from heartache or discomforts to play stupid. I feel like those who are brilliant are more in touch with truth, and truth can be pretty depressing. Raneem is brilliant, she knows and feels on a level most don't. I wonder if her brilliance contributed to her demons."

"What kind of demons?"

"The doctors say she has manic depression." I had never said those words out loud, never wrote them out in my journal. I would refer to them as her demons, or say she's "down," but those words slid out of my mouth easily with Marc sitting next to me.

"Oh shit, that's serious."

I told him how it had torn apart our family, and I told him how much worry, fear, and shame surfaced with the diagnosis.

"There is nothing to be ashamed of, for her or for your parents."

"I know, but nobody talks about it."

"Sometimes I think your family is too sheltered. It can be endearing, but it's not real life. There are so many people out there that struggle with mental health. The ignominy behind it all is only going to make it worse."

"I'm sorry, I want to be smarter than this, but what does *ignominy* mean?"

"Shame." He smiled at me.

"Gotcha." I nodded my head. "You're right, Marc," I agreed wholeheartedly. "The ignominy makes it worse. I wish more people thought the way you do."

I loved his acceptance and understanding of such a taboo subject. And I loved that he wasn't too hard on my family, who were different from what he was used to. Depression is a heavy subject, but he got it. I loved his mind, how open it was, and how easy it was for him to accept and understand things.

Dear Journal,   July 10, 2001
   My favorite thing about myself
is my depth and it's so easy to share
that with him. But I'm scared to
show him my writing.

They're just drawn out sloppy words
Verses kept not heard
My dreams seeping through the page
Keeping me engaged

To my heart ♥

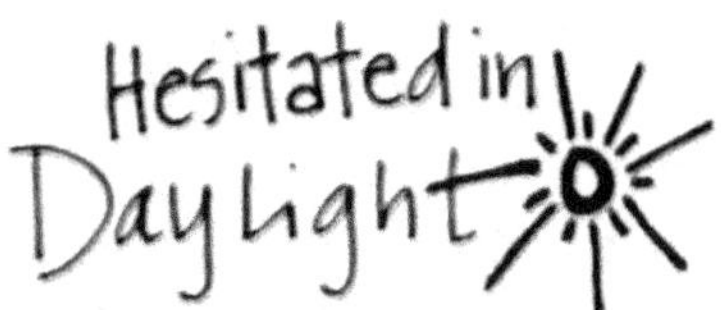

I was grateful for Marc; he distracted me from the chaos at home. And I held close to my friends; they kept me busy during the day so I could avoid the depression and the turbulence from my parents, who were at each other's throats.

I met the girls at Freedom Café in downtown Maskin after leaving Raneem in her room with the lights off. I put my head down and walked past her room quickly so she wouldn't see my full face of makeup and the cute new outfit I wore to go meet my friends. I didn't want to rub it in that I was living life while she was stuck in her bed.

We girls sat with our feet up on the sofas, sipping on our Italian sodas, when I heard a guy say, "What's up, Maleeka."

I looked up to see Rasheed's best friend at the table next to us.

"Hi, Brian," I said. Brian was at our house all the time, but he never spoke to me when he was there. Rasheed wouldn't let his friends talk to me. "Is Rasheed here?" I asked him.

"He's supposed to meet me."

I nodded my head and turned to the girls. "Let's get out of here."

We walked up the street and took up all the width of the sidewalk with curbside appeal up the ass. They were overly done with hanging flower baskets and big potted plants. Even unnecessary statues of elk and bears. I almost ran into one as I stared off at the parking lot down the street, packed with a ton of people standing around watching a group of guys skate over curbs and handrails.

"Guys, wait, Marc's over there," I told the girls.

"Let's go say hi. Maybe he'll smoke us out," Samantha said.

"There are so many people over there." I shook my head and looked back at Freedom Café.

"Who cares, don't you want to go say hi to him?" She walked in their direction and looked back at me. "Come on, it'll be fun!"

I couldn't move, my feet were planted on the ground. "Rasheed is coming," I told Lauren.

"He's going to the café."

I looked over my shoulder again, down the street to see if his truck had pulled up.

Lauren grabbed my hand. "He's not going to see you in that big-ass group of people."

"Maleeka! What's up?" Marc called over the crowd. He dropped his skateboard and walked up to me to give me a hug. Normally I'd be all for that hug to turn into a kiss and more. But I hesitated in the daylight with all those people. Even if Rasheed didn't see me there, other people did. And I didn't know who would tell who what.

"Hi," I said, with one arm around him. I patted his back and moved away.

"Can I introduce you to the girls?" he asked me.

I didn't answer or move. I could see Rasheed's baby-blue Chevy pull into the parking lot two blocks down.

"Maleeka?" He snapped me out of my stare.

"Sure." I nodded with my eyes on Rasheed as he walked into the café.

Amelia and Karen were Marc's childhood friends, both gorgeous, with tough exteriors in their black bomber jackets and torn jean shorts. Karen even had a cigarette in her hand. It looked like an accessory; she looked hot with it.

Karen blew her smoke out. "So you're Maleeka?"

"Yeah." I put my hair behind my ears and looked back at the café again.

"We've heard a lot about you," Amelia said, looking at Marc.

I also looked at Marc. He had a big smile on his face like he was showing off an award. I couldn't smile. A normal girl would be flattered if a guy told his friends about her, but not me.

"Nice to meet you both," I said with a forced smile. I wanted to get out of there. "Girls, are you ready?" I called out to get their attention.

"You okay?" He got closer to me to keep it between the two of us. "You're acting weird."

"I'm fine." I nodded my head, backing away from him. "I have to go."

"That girl likes you, Marc?" I heard Amelia ask as I walked away.

"I guess." Marc laughed it off.

"Be careful, Marc," I heard her say, and I cringed. I didn't want them to hate me, but I knew I didn't give off a good first impression either.

Dear Journal,   July 16, 2001
   It's hard to see him in daylight. I can't
hide the obvious connection.
Kissing him at night feels so natural
Saying hello during the day felt so wrong

Darkness is easy
Nobody sees me
I'm free to be, selfishly
Darkness is peace

Daylight is scary
Eyes are all on me
Consuming me
Confusing me
Scaring me

Take me to your shadow
Pitch black with just the stars
There's ~~freedom~~ in our darkness
I feel free light wrapped in your arms

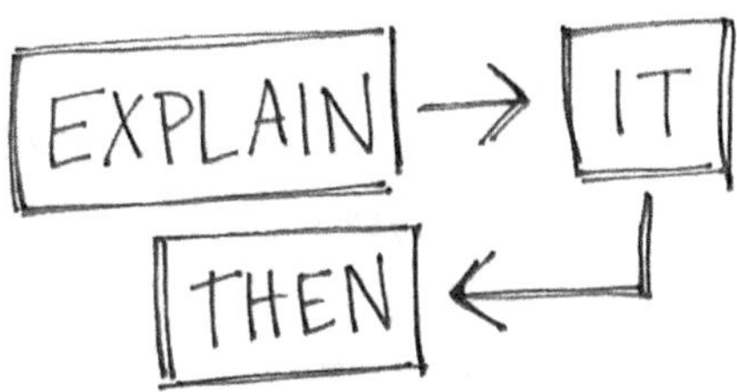

It took a while for him to log on that night. He stayed out with his friends skating and smoking pot. He didn't have a curfew like I did. I sat in the office with the lights off and the only brightness coming from the screen. Everyone was sleeping at home. It was late. Finally at 1:11 a.m., I saw his name appear online. But he didn't say hi to me. I knew I'd have to initiate this chat.

Leek55: sorry about tonight

Marco83: Oh you mean for acting shady in front of my friends

Leek55: what's shady mean?

Marco83: I thought you listen to Destiny's Child

I couldn't tell if he was trying to laugh it off or pretend like he didn't care.

Leek55: use another word

Marco83: I don't know, you just acted like you don't know me

Marco83: I figured you're embarrassed to know me, but whatever fuck it

Fuck it? He was pretending like he didn't care.

Leek55: I wanna explain it to you

Marco83: Okay explain it then

Leek55: you have to know I like you Marc . . . like more than friends, but I know no matter how much you mean to me or how close we are I'll always have to hold back . . . if they ever found out, especially my brother, I would be killed! seriously I don't know what would happen

Marco83: Well that's cool, I didn't think I was such a fuckin piece of shit that your family would kill you for talking to me

I hated that what I said had to make him feel like he was anything less than what he was.

Leek55: it's not that you're a piece of shit, it's that you're a guy, a guy I messed around with and Rasheed knows about it

Marco83: Fuck that I'll kick your brother's ass

Leek55: why are you talking like that? you can't kick my brother's ass and have everything be fine . . . he is my brother

Marco83: It doesn't mean you have to be an asshole when you see me in public

I couldn't be mad at him for calling me an asshole; I was. I couldn't stop thinking about how I turned around like I didn't give a shit about him and his friends he wanted me to meet.

Leek55: I'm sorry I don't know what else to do. I've never dealt with this stuff before

Marco83: It's cool, like I said, fuck it

Leek55: I don't want to "fuck it" this is a big deal. I like you Marc . . . did you read that before?

Marc and I had fooled around several times by now and gave each other compliments left and right. But neither one of us had come out yet to say, "I like you." It was assumed; yes, we liked each other, but saying it and saying it first was hard. He let a few minutes pass, putting me on edge.

Leek55: Are you going to say anything???

Marco83: Cool

Leek55: cool?

Marco83: Well I don't know what to say, you care so much about what everyone fuckin thinks

Leek55: I don't care about everyone!

Marco83: It seems like you do

Leek55: you don't understand . . . you don't know my family

Marco83: You're right, I don't

Silence.

Leek55: so what happens now?

Marco83: I don't know whatever fuckin happens

Leek55: okay

Marco83: You continue ignoring me because of what your family thinks, and I continue being the pothead nobody would want their daughter with

I had never heard him get angry or frustrated with me. I hated his tone through the computer, but I understood it.

Leek55: I'm sorry, what can I do seriously?

Leek55: it's a constant battle I've liked you for a while now and it seems like every day we get closer, and I'm so glad . . . but at the same time it sucks cause there's always a voice in the back of my head saying I can't have what I want . . . that being you

Marco83: Well, fuck . . . I don't know what to say

Leek55: I want you to know that when I act shady or whatever I'm not trying to be a bitch I'm just trying to figure this all out and make everything work the best way it can

Marco83: That's cool, Maleeka, I get it

His attitude changed, I must have gotten him to see my perspective the best way he could.

Marco83: Maleeka, you're a good person. I think you need to do what you want and say fuck your family

Marco83: Not fuck them, but they need to know you're your own person

That was a big suggestion. I couldn't "fuck my family." Sure, I wanted to be able to do that. But it was drilled into me that family was supposed to be everything to me, even though it wasn't.

Leek55: I don't think I'm strong enough to do that . . . I need them

Marco83: I get it, look as long as we still hang out and talk, that's all I want

Leek55: I'll work on my public demeanor

Marco83: Honestly, I'd rather see you privately anyway, it's more fun that way

Leek55: Haha you just like getting off

Marco83: I like YOU getting me off, Maleeka

Was that his way of telling me he liked me too?

Leek55: I can't believe I said all I said to you tonight

Marco83: Ha that was dope, you're something else, Maleeka

Marco83: I don't really need a girlfriend in my life right now, but if I did, you're fuckin up there

Leek55: well I can't have a boyfriend in my life right now, but if I could you're fuckin up there too :)

Marco83: Let's keep it going then, maybe the stars will align in our favor

Leek55: I'm cool with that

Leek55: we can leave it up to the stars :)

Marco83: Hey, babe, I'm gonna go to bed

Leek55: okay sleep well

Marco83: You too, we'll talk soon

Leek55: can't wait :)

Marco83: Good night, babe

Marco83 signed off at 1:43:09 a.m.

He was right; I should have been strong enough to be my own person. But he was also right that he was such a piece of shit by my family's standards. They would never approve. They would kill me, and I hated that I cared. He made me feel better than any of them ever had. They would never see him for anything other than what Rasheed thought he was, but in my world, he was everything. I grabbed my journal, relieved he wasn't mad at me anymore, but feeling shitty that it had to be such a struggle. Especially for him. He deserved a girl who could be everything to him, a normal girl.

Dear Journal, July 17, 2001

FINDING YOUR Truth
fight FOR Your FREEDOM

Under Firm Control

I'm not strong
enough to face them.
It's easier to hide. But he deserves
more than that.

You deserve better than what I'll ever be
someone that wont hold back
or hide from their family
I cant keep this all a secret
I want to scream outloud
Cant have you as my boyfriend
God knows I'm not allowed
I want to keep you close to me
But I want no one to know
I probably should give you up
But I cant let you go

a MONSTER

Dear Journal, July 19, 2001
 "Maybe the stars will align in our favor"
  - Marc ♥
I love the idea of leaving it up to the
stars. In a way it takes the pressure off
of me. If I leave it up to the stars, I can
fall blissfully without any responsibility.

Leave it up to fate, blame it on destiny...
Then nothings my fault.
That sounds like it could be a song 😊

Indulged in the stars
~~hide~~ outshined by their glow
emerged between clouds
the fates are in control
Feel fire in the flame
They're responsible to blame
As you follow the plan
It's out of your hands

I pulled my curtain back to be able to see the stars, knowing he was under the same sky. But the stars weren't the only things fuming. Dad paced in the driveway in his robe as he spoke expressively to the police officer. I should have turned my light off and tucked under the sheets to dodge the scene, but I was too nosy. I slid my window open a bit to hear them.

"You sure everything's okay, sir?" the officer asked Dad.

"Yes, I'll take care of it from here," he said.

"Ma'am, if you need anything, you let us know," he called out to Mom, who was unable to respond.

The police officer handed his card to Dad and left for the night so they could settle their domestic dispute themselves. It wasn't the first time the police had to intervene in their blowouts. I guess the behaving-in-a-way-so-people-won't-talk-about-you rule wasn't applicable to them and law enforcement.

"It's your fault! You've destroyed her," Mom said as she stumbled inside the house from the driveway. I prayed that Raneem was sleeping through this.

"She's not destroyed, she's just having a hard time," Dad said, shaking his head as he walked up to his truck. Mom had the truck that night. I don't know why; she never drove his truck.

"She is destroyed. She hates us. Your precious angel hates you. And I do too." I heard Mom's voice crack.

"You're drunk!"

"I drink because I hate this life! I hate what you've done to us."

"Me?!" he screamed. "I do everything for this family."

"You put too much pressure on them, on her especially. You've always been too much with her. And you're too close to her. It's not right."

"What's not right!?"

She lowered her voice. I couldn't make out what she said, but I heard Dad scream hysterically.

"Are you crazy!? Are you calling me a monster? What are you implying?"

"You've ruined her!" she yelled at him. "You ruined my daughter."

"You're drunk! You don't know what love is. Your accusations are disgusting! You're the monster!"

The screaming stopped finally when the front door slammed shut. Mom went to bed while Dad stayed outside to clean the truck.

I wasn't sure what he was cleaning or what she insisted wasn't right. Whatever it was, it infuriated him, he scrubbed the seat so hard and threw the floor mats on the driveway. Dad got out of the cab to grab more paper towels. He looked up and caught me in my window, watching. I tried to back away, but I wasn't quick enough.

"Maleeka, come here. I want to show you something."

I didn't want to go down, I was scared to know what was going on, but I knew he needed someone to talk to. Luckily Mom was in her room. She wouldn't appreciate me hearing him out. The truck looked worse the closer I got to it. There was a broken bottle, and red wine spilled everywhere.

"Your mom got drunk and took my truck out to destroy it."

"Why would she do that?" I looked around and tried to make sense of the scene.

There was a picture, previously hanging from the rearview mirror on a lanyard, lying on the floor. Mom had ripped the image and the mirror down and smashed the windshield with it. When we were young, Dad took us on vacations most could only dream of. We went to

France, Turkey, Spain, and Ireland. The picture on the floor was taken in Germany. Mom was holding her three babies, all under the age of five, with cheesy smiles while riding a ferry. Dad took the picture; I can imagine it was a happy moment. I'm sure he had that picture up to remember the sweet, simple times we shared together, when all he had to do was pull out a camera and say, "Smile," and we'd all do it.

"Your mother doesn't love me. I do everything for that woman. I give her luxury. But she doesn't love me," he continued, scrubbing the floor mats covered in red wine. Mom used wine as an outlet; Dad used me.

"Maybe Mom doesn't believe you love her, Dad. Maybe she needs more than luxury to know it."

"She doesn't know what love is. Her mother never loved her. Her father was always drunk. She never knew love, so she doubts mine. And she makes my love for my children feel wrong," he said, shaking his head, and looked at me with tears in his eyes. "You know what she thinks of me? She thinks I am a monster. She's implying I have molested your sister."

I took a couple of steps back, shaking my head, confused and disgusted. *That's* what wasn't right. I hated my mom for accusing him of that, and I hated him for telling me.

When babies are born in our Syrian Christian world, after they are dressed, they are pinned with a tiny blue bead. It's attached with a safety pin, sometimes a small cross with it. It's meant to keep the evil eye away, to protect them from a curse. They believed so much in evil that they held on to the old tradition. If you compliment the child, you have to end it with a prayer for God to watch over them, that way nobody would think your compliment carried hate or jealousy. So nobody would think you're cursing their child.

Raneem was a beautiful baby and became a gorgeous teenager. She had it all, and my parents knew it. She had the right amount of both of our parents' best features. And her intellect was well known by all. The family called her their princess growing up. There were plenty of reasons for one to be jealous of what they thought was perfect about her. I didn't think Mom bought into the evil-eye theory, but she told me as much as she believed in God, she believed in evil. I think she was getting desperate for an explanation for Raneem's depression, and it was easy to assume someone had put a curse on her "perfect" daughter.

Dad was out of town again. It was good timing after the cop showed up to the house. The space gave them enough time away from each other to pretend it never happened. It was hard for me to look at my mom after Dad told me what she accused him of. But like every other fight, I had to go on as if it never happened.

"What's going on?" I asked my mom, confused to see a man in the front fancy room on the sofa against a lace pillow. I didn't know who he was.

"I am getting the house blessed." She looked up at me.

"What for?" I asked her. The man stayed quiet.

"Someone has cursed your sister. I want to bless this house. I want all the evil out of this house. I want the evil out of her."

"Evil? Mom, how could you say that? She isn't evil."

"I want her to feel light. I want her to have a life like yours. You do whatever you want, and you're happy," she said.

I hated that Mom thought my life was easy and light. I knew it was nothing to Raneem's pain, but it wasn't always easy. Sure, I wasn't doped up on medicine in bed all day, but the depression affected me too. Watching my sister hurt was devastating; being dragged into my parents' issues was intense. It broke my heart that everyone struggled, but it also made me feel alone. How could she honestly think I was completely fine? There was no talk of what each one of us felt; we all grieved the depression separately.

Dear Journal,   July 23, 2001

How could she think I am fine? There has to be some sort of motherly instinct to know your kid isnt fine, watching all this. Not even a check in to say "hey, are you okay dealing with all this?"

It's probably easier for her to assume I'm fine. That gives her one less thing to worry about. I know she is worried sick about Raneem. I am too.

· · · · · ———————————— · · · · · ·

I know you're hurting, I am too, but it's
    not as crystal clear
Mom and Dad don't notice, it's not for me
    they fear
They worry about your health, they worry
    about your mind
They never ask if I'm okay watching
    from behind

I wonder what you think when you see
    me standing there
Do you notice me or think I might be a
    little scared

I'm sorry that you're struggling, I don't
    want to make it worse
I pray God gives you peace and takes
    away this curse

(No) Stereotypes

A couple of weeks after Mom got our house blessed, I told the girls to come over to stay the night. My bedroom window faced the front of the house and had a flat roof outside above the garage. The girls and I would sneak cloves out there at night. It was far enough away from my parents' bedroom that they never heard what was going on. That night after the house went to bed, we sat on the roof with a pack of cloves, taking swigs off the oversize bottle of red wine we got from my garage. My mom was a stock-up shopper. She always had a bulk of everything in our garage, including her favorite discount wine.

"Doesn't your mom notice when we take these?" Lauren asked.

"She hasn't yet," I told her. "She buys so many and drinks so much. She loses track, I'm sure."

"Well, it works out for us that your mom has a secret drinking problem." Samantha laughed.

"Yeah, I've learned to make the best of it." I took a big swig off it while I shook my head. I hated the way my mom drank; it wasn't for fun, she did it to cope, and it would often end up giving her liquid courage to attack my dad, which would turn the house into a disaster.

I passed the bottle to Emiko as headlights hit our faces. I covered my eyes as Samantha stood up.

"Sit down, Sam, you're drunk!" Lauren told her.

"Oh my God, is that Carson?" Samantha said, hunched over with her hand blocking the beam of light. "It is!" She waved and looked back at us. "Jake and Marc too."

He flashed his high beams, and I jumped up.

"Em, tell them we'll meet them at the corner, he can't be outside my house!" I ran into my room. "And tell Sam to lower her fucking voice!"

We sneaked out and approached the guys, led by the girls as I trailed behind them, looking back to make sure it wasn't my uncle's truck that drove by.

"What's up, girls?" Marc said as he pushed through them, wearing a big smile. I turned around to find him right in my face, he grabbed me with one hand on my waist and the other on my neck, ready to kiss me.

"Hi," I said, startled by his grab as he pulled me in and kissed me hard.

"Hey," he said, attached to my lips as he finished the kiss.

"I wondered if I would hear from you tonight," I said as I backed away.

The girls, Carson, and Jake were all standing against Carson's truck, staring at us, but I didn't care. I knew Carson would keep Marc's secret because he did the last time we hung out, and Jake would keep mine.

"We have to get out of here," I told them all.

"What do you girls wanna do?" Carson pulled his keys out of his pocket.

"Let's go to Brandon's!" Samantha said.

Brandon was one of what we called "the young crew." He was the youngest with three older brothers, all handsome varsity athletes who liked to party. He followed right behind in their footsteps.

"Brandon Camp?" Carson asked. He knew the Camp house had good parties often. "Yeah, let's go."

The girls and I volunteered to ride in the bed of the truck. We couldn't all fit in the cab. Our hair blew all over the place, with the wind smashing into our faces. Marc would check on us from time to time, looking back at me through the window with a smile on his face, and I would smile back.

It was my first time bringing both worlds together, the young guys and Marc. But I knew they'd keep my secrets. They saw me do inappropriate things, and nobody ever found out. I trusted the guys; they were my boys. We pulled up to the beautiful mansion out in the country. Marc helped the girls out of the bed, ending with me. He grabbed my hand with his left hand, and with his right he handed me a pipe.

"Aren't you going to smoke?" I asked him.

"We already did on the way here," he told me. I took a hit and handed it back to him.

"Give it to the girls," he said. I appreciated his generosity.

"I can't light it," Samantha said, struggling with the wind and the lighter.

"Here," I said, cupping one hand around the pipe and lighting it for her with the other. "Hit it," I said. I could see Marc smiling at me, almost as if he was proud I knew what I was doing. I wasn't much of an amateur anymore.

"You good?" I asked her.

"Yeah," Samantha said between coughs.

"It's okay to cough, that means you're going to get really high." I smiled at Marc, who was still smiling at me. "Here, Lauren," I said, passing it to her.

She hesitated to take the pipe.

"You have to let loose, Lauren!" Jake told her. "Who cares what Zach thinks? He's not here."

"You're not allowed to smoke?" Carson asked her.

"He doesn't like me to do it when he isn't around."

"He seems a little controlling," Carson told her. We all looked at Carson with big, uncomfortable eyes. We all thought it, but we never told Lauren that.

"Let's not get involved, Carson," Marc said, and loaded another bowl for us girls to get high before we walked around the side of the house. Marc grabbed my arm to talk to me in private.

"I don't like that guy."

"I don't either," I whispered. "I try to get along with him, for her, but I hate him."

He looked at me with big eyes. "I didn't know you hated anyone."

"I hate him. He is so fake. He pretends he is perfect around her family, but he's an ass, especially when he's mad. He talks to her like she's a guy he's going to beat the shit out of."

"Wow," Marc said. "What a piece of shit."

"I wish I could talk her out of dating him. But she wouldn't listen. I hate what love will do to a girl."

"She's a big girl; you can't talk her in or out of anything. All you can do is be there for her."

"Leek, come on!" Lauren yelled out, interrupting our shit-talking fest about her boyfriend. I ran up to walk with the girls as Marc caught up, with Carson and Jake behind them.

"I'm fucked up, guys," Emiko said as she struggled through the gravel in her wedge sandals.

"Jake, she's all yours!" Samantha said as we girls laughed. "You know how horny Emiko gets when she's stoned."

"Holy shit, you came!" one of the guys yelled out as we turned the corner to the backyard. After getting tied up with older guys, we didn't spend as much time with the original crew. All our guys were out there, drinking and listening to Wu-Tang. But no girls; girls in our grade were having slumber parties with movies and popcorn.

"You stoned, Leek?" my friend Chase asked me, muffled in my hug. Everyone knew what was up when you walked into a room with Marc Osbourne, and most of them wanted in on the action. I laughed, proving him right as he laughed too and looked over at Lauren.

"Hey, Ren," he told her with a smile on his face, happy to see her like always. Chase and Lauren dated before Zach came in the picture, he still loved her.

"Hi, Chase." She looked down.

The girls all said their hellos as Chase still stared at Lauren. "He let you out tonight, huh?" he asked her.

"Be nice, Chase," I answered back for Lauren. "Where's Brandon?"

Brandon was a generous host. His parents had money and a beautiful home, with an in-ground pool outside, a basement with pool tables, and refrigerators full of drinks. He shared his wealth, always wanted everyone to have a good time, and he was always smiling. He ran up to us.

"Maleeka, baby! I'm so glad you came!" He grabbed me, picked me up in the air, and circled around. Within seconds, he had a drink in my hand and his arm around my shoulder. Marc stared at me as I laughed at Brandon's tipsy ramble. I looked over at him to find a smile on his face. Carson saw it too.

"Be careful, man," I heard him tell Marc. "She's got her arm around another guy."

"She's not that kind of girl, Carson. Look at how beautiful she looks with that smile on her face."

His smile gave me relief. Lauren stopped hugging all our guy friends when she got together with Zach. I didn't want to lose friends over a guy.

"I want you to meet Marc," I told Brandon. "Marc, this is Brandon," I said, still under Brandon's arm.

"What's up, Brandon?" Marc put his hand out to shake.

"It's good to finally meet you, Marc," he said, receiving his handshake. "You've got quite the pull on one of my favorite girls." He laughed.

Marc smiled at me and looked back at Brandon. "You smoke?"

"Yeah, I'll smoke," Brandon said, gesturing for Marc to sit next to him on the luscious patio set.

Marc told me once there were no stereotypes when smoking weed. He said it brought people together. Marc was different from my friends. He wore a black Bad Religion shirt with a flannel unbuttoned over it. He had on baggy cargo pants with trashed skate shoes. My friends were all in polo shirts, board shorts, and bright-white hardly worn shoes. A couple of them had their ears pierced with fake diamond studs in them, and Brandon wore his brother's letterman jacket. I wondered what he thought of them, if he thought they were a bunch of mindless jocks, or douchebags. But within minutes he was nodding along with the others to Wu-Tang Clan's "Ain't Nuthing ta F' Wit."

The guys gravitated to him as he rapped along to the words not everyone knew, and they listened to him while he went off on the track "Triumph" with no chorus. I didn't know he knew anything about Wu-Tang, or even that he liked rap music. But Marc loved the best of everything, and like all he was interested in, he knew more about it than anyone else. I sat back and watched him with the crowd; he owned it like he did the stage I first saw him on; he was charismatic and engaging. I was grateful for Wu-Tang; they connected the dots and brought them all together, like that bag of weed.

"You guys ready to head out?" Carson said as he stood up.

"It's still early," Samantha said.

"It's twelve thirty in the morning, Sam!" Lauren said. "By the time we get home and get back in the house, it will be one."

Samantha didn't want to leave. She was having fun with all the guys. She sat on the love seat of the patio set with her feet up and her shoes off. Lauren, on the other hand, sat at the edge of her seat the whole time we were there. She put her beer on the side table and met Carson in the grass.

I followed by standing up and helping Emiko out of her spot. She was so tiny and sunk into the cushions and under Jake's arm.

"Thanks for the smoke out, Marc," Brandon said as he walked us to the side of the house.

"Anytime, man. Thanks for having us," Marc said.

Brandon gave the girls each a big hug and ended with me. With his arms around me, he told Marc, "You got the best one here. She's true. She's a real friend."

Marc smiled with a cigarette in his mouth, about to light it, and nodded at him.

"Love you, Brandon," I told him with a kiss on his cheek.

We walked up to the truck, and I grabbed Lauren's arm.

"Ren?"

"You want to hang out with him longer, don't you?" She smiled at me. "I'll take the girls back to my house," she said. "Go enjoy your night, Leek."

"I love you."

"I love you too, Leek." She put her arm around me. "Girls, let's ride in the truck. Leave Maleeka and Marc in the back."

Marc looked back at me.

"Are you okay with that?" I asked him.

"Of course."

We jumped in the back, and he got close to put his arm around me and keep me warm. It was a warm summer evening, but the wind was cold, and the faster Carson drove on those back roads, the colder it got.

I leaned my head back and yelled, "It's so cold!"

Marc laughed and took his unbuttoned flannel shirt off to put it around me. He grabbed my jaw that shivered and turned it closer to him.

"You're true?" He put his forehead against mine, holding my head still.

"He was just talking me up." I laughed a little before he kissed me.

"Maleeka." He pulled away and looked at me as if there were a sweet song playing while he did so. Every kiss before would lead to immediate making out, top off and pants undone. But this kiss was more like a rom-com kiss.

"Marc, just kiss me."

He shook his head. "You're something else, Maleeka." He grabbed the back of my neck and kissed me. And that, of course, took off. He ran his hands down my chest and into my pants.

"Oh my God!" I heard Samantha yell through the open window. "They're making out back there!"

I ignored her as I lay on the hard metal truck bed with Marc on top of me. I finally warmed up with the pressure from his body on mine and his hot breath all over me.

"You're such a slut!" She laughed.

Both Marc and I laughed, knowing they could see us. I took my hand off him for a second to put my arm up and flip her off.

The truck parked; we were outside Lauren's house. I buttoned my pants and fixed my hair before I sat up.

"Marc Osbourne?" I heard.

"What's up, Quinn," Marc said, jumping out of the truck to tell him hello. They were reminiscing about the last time they got stoned together when they ran into each other at a party. The girls got out to give me shit.

"You can't keep your hands off of him, can you?" Lauren laughed.

"You guys, it was freezing, I had to keep warm."

I jumped out of the truck to gather around them all at Carson's window.

"You girls coming in?" Quinn asked.

The girls nodded as Emiko gave Jake a kiss good night through the rolled-down window.

"Will you walk me home?" I said quietly to Marc with my back to Quinn.

"Of course."

"Good night, girls," I called out to them as they walked through the back gate.

"You guys dating?" Quinn asked Marc.

Marc didn't say anything.

"We're just hanging out, Quinn," I answered for him.

He shook his head with a smile on his face. He knew better. He saw the way my hair looked when I got out of the truck. "Be good, Maleeka."

We got to the corner of Lauren's street, where you could turn right to get to my house or left to get far away.

"Are you ready to call it a night?" he asked me. I was glad he did.

"Let's go to our spot."

I grabbed his hand and took him in the opposite direction of my house. He didn't let go, and neither did I. We were interlocked, like we were plugged together, more intimate than anything we had ever done before. And as we walked down the dark street, I realized I had never held his hand before. I had sucked his dick, but never held his hand.

We were alone on the dimmed bleachers with one last bowl. My heart pounded, waiting to see what would happen next. We already fooled around; were we going to do it again? He put his hand over mine on the bleachers. "Come here," he said, and kissed me. It wasn't a rowdy kiss. It was sweet and soft. A kiss I assumed a real couple would do.

He pulled away and grabbed his pipe to load. "Greens?" he asked as he handed me the first hit to his last bowl.

"You're such a gentleman." I laughed, taking a hit.

"You're becoming a pro with that pipe."

"You taught me all I know," I said after blowing out my smoke.

He laughed. "I take full credit."

"Thanks for coming tonight and being so cool with my friends." I watched him take a hit with his eyes squinting while he sucked in the smoke and nodded his head.

"I had a good time, your friends are cool."

"I scored big with the friend game. I'm lucky to have them."

"I'm surprised none of those guys have snagged you up." He handed me the pipe.

"Every guy there has either dated one of the girls or confessed their love for them to me." I laughed and took another hit.

"Don't get me wrong, your girlfriends are all beautiful girls, but they have nothing on you."

I coughed and shook my head. "You're crazy."

"You've said that before." He smiled at me while wrapping his hand around mine to grab the pipe.

"Is there anything you don't like about yourself?" I asked him as he finished the bowl and tossed the ashes out. I wondered if I was the only one who carried insecurities.

He put his hands in his pockets and shook his head. "Not a God damn thing, I am sexy!"

I laughed. "You *are* super cute, but there isn't anything about yourself you wish you weren't?"

"That's a big question," he replied, and paused for a minute, leaning back on the bleachers and staring at the sky. "I can have a little bit of an addictive personality."

"What do you mean? Like you were born to be an addict?"

He shook his head. "I have a moral compass, but when I love something, I love it hard. Good or bad."

"Like Johnny Cash?" I smiled at him. Marc told me he related to Johnny Cash with his morals, his religion, and his reputation. How he always juggled his moral code with having fun.

"Yeah, like Johnny Cash." He grabbed his pack of cigarettes.

"There can be a balance; there's a time and place for everything."

"Not for me. I'm impulsive. When I want something, I want it all. And when I love something, I love excessively. I become obsessed with it. It consumes me."

"Don't you have a hard time letting go of your control?"

"Not at all. Control kills passion."

"I don't think you should ever love anything too much. You give up control being obsessed. My dad always told me never to get too close to anything or anyone. He says it will control me and take away my power."

"Power? Jesus, Maleeka. What kind of mob family are you in? There's no power in love."

"So you've heard those rumors too?" I laughed. He looked at me with a question mark between his eyebrows. "My dad and uncles showed up to my eighth-grade promotion in leather jackets, shiny loafers, and unlit cigars in their mouths. After that, everyone started saying my family was in a mob."

He laughed. "I've never heard that before."

"No way, come on."

"I don't hang out with a lot of people that know you, Maleeka. But if I heard that, I would think it was fucking cool. I love a good mob story."

"What's your favorite mob movie?"

"*Carlito's Way.* Yours?"

"*The Godfather.*"

"Oh yeah? Which one?"

"Number one. Sonny's my favorite."

"The hothead?"

"*He* was impulsive." I smiled at him. "But he had such a big heart. I loved how he stood up for his sister."

"That got him killed."

"True." I laughed.

Dad raised us on *The Godfather.* He thought there were lessons to be taught, in the midst of killing and corruption, for family ties and sticking together as one unit. He'd often pause it after his favorite line of the film. The camera is focused on Vito when his son Sonny walks in the study after fucking the bridesmaid at his sister's wedding. Vito looks back at him then at Johnny Fontane, who's asking for assistance to get the lead role of a movie he's already been denied.

Vito asks Johnny about whether or not he spends time with his family. The camera doesn't even focus on Johnny; it's obvious the question is asked to put Sonny on the spot, and Sonny knows it too. Vito then goes on to state that the measure of a real man is whether or not the man spends time with his family—that was Dad's favorite line.

It was well past 2:00 a.m., and though I could have sat there forever, I couldn't stay up as late as Marc did. He never got tired. He walked me home, and I was so caught up in conversation that I didn't realize we had passed the corner I'd normally get dropped off at.

"Is someone up?" he asked me as we walked up to my driveway. Raneem's bedroom light was on.

"It's just my sister."

"Will she rat you out coming home this late?"

"It depends on her mood." I looked up at her window and back at Marc. "Thank you for walking me home."

"Anytime, babe. Let's hang out soon, okay?" he said.

He kissed me good night, and I walked inside the house, feeling brave. His kiss made me feel indestructible. I could face anything. Even Raneem.

"Where were you?" Raneem asked me. Her bedroom door was open, so we made eye contact as I walked past.

"The girls wanted to go to Lauren's. I went for a little but decided I wanted to come home."

"You walked home alone?"

I didn't want to lie to her. I thought if I opened up to her, it would bring us close again. "My friend Marc walked me home."

She bit her lip and shook her head. I thought wrong.

"Is that who you're writing all those Dr. Seuss rhymes about?"

My face went numb. "You read my poems?"

She let out a mean breath from her nose. "Real poems don't rhyme, Maleeka."

I hated her for saying that more than I did for her reading my journal. She threw my intellect in my face. To her, girls like me, who cared about clothes and makeup and boys, weren't smart. I told her once I wanted to move to New York when I grew up, and she laughed and told me I'd end up in Nebraska with a bunch of kids, baking pies.

"Are you dating him?"

I grabbed both elbows and shook my head. "Are you going to tell anyone?" I begged her with my eyes not to.

"I don't give a fuck." She reached over to turn on her reading light and got up to turn off the main light. She was done with the conversation.

I sat on my bed and cradled my journal in my lap. I opened it up to look through all the things she could have read. And everything I read made my heart race faster.

The next morning, I woke up to "4am" by Our Lady Peace blasting in Raneem's room. My initial reaction was relief she was up out of bed, but right after, panic set in. Why was she up so early? Who was she with? What was she telling them? I jumped out of bed and ran to her room. She sat at her desk, writing in her journal. My big sister was another reason I started writing. She was a writer herself, inspired by her favorite authors, John Steinbeck and Fyodor Dostoevsky. She told me once their understanding of inter- and intra-human psychology was why they were her favorites. I didn't know what that meant, but in an effort to get close to her one night, I watched the 1955 movie *East of Eden*. God knows I'd never read the book.

"Raneem," I said, standing in the doorway.

Her head shot up from her journal, but she kept her back to me as she looked out the window. "Did you know when I was a junior in high school, Johnny Page asked me out in speech class?" She shut her journal. "And I wanted to date Johnny Page."

"Why didn't you?" I sat on her bed behind her.

"I wasn't allowed."

"So you told him no."

She finally turned her body to face me. "Yeah, I told him no, and he didn't understand. I couldn't tell him my dad wouldn't allow it. He would think I was weird. I thought he liked me enough not to like anyone else. But by the end of first semester, he asked out Amy True. They won the cutest couple our senior year."

"Raneem, I'm so sorry."

Raneem always acted like she didn't care about the lifestyle I wanted. I thought I was the only one. She was the golden child, and I thought she was happy in that role.

She got up off her chair and put her journal on her bookshelf. "I can't wait to get the fuck out of here again. Mom and Dad are toxic for me."

"Did you ever tell Mom?"

"Mom will never be an ally, all she cares about is herself. She plays dumb all the time, and acts like she had no idea I'd want to be a normal teenager, like you."

"I'm sorry, Raneem, I had no idea. I thought you were fine being the perfect child too."

She sat next to me on her bed. "Fuck being perfect. I'm proud of you for being brave, Maleeka."

Raneem cared way more than I did about pleasing my parents. It was almost as if she was addicted to their approval, and that kept her away from the things she wanted. I didn't want to be like Raneem, but I also didn't want them to know anything about me. I didn't care enough for them to stop me, but I did care enough to want to keep it from them.

Dear Journal,   Aug. 5, 2001
    I feel bad Raneem wasn't able to
live the life she wanted. I feel guilty for
all the good times I had that she had to
miss out on.
    She thinks I'm normal. I wish I was.
Instead I have to sneak around with a
guy I like and worry about them finding
out. And what they would do to me if
they did.
    I wonder what it would be like to
have a boyfriend and have him over to
meet my parents, and have happy parents.

    I wonder what it would be like to be
a normal teenage girl.
    I live my life in secret, growing up
in a web of lies they know nothing about.

Make Him Jealous

"Here's the single one!" Samantha hollered out as I opened the gate to Lauren's backyard. She sat next to Quinn's friend Caleb, who was well manicured, like Quinn. He wore a polo shirt with dark faded jeans, and his hair was iced with gel.

I looked at Lauren. "Why is she saying that?"

"Caleb is looking for a good time tonight." Lauren laughed as she handed me a shot. I knew I had catching up to do, I could tell the girls were tipsy.

"I thought you're dating Marc Osbourne," Quinn said to me.

"We're just hanging out," I told him as I took the shot and grabbed a soda to chase it.

"Right." He nodded his head.

"He's her booty call." Samantha laughed.

I hated that Samantha said that, I knew he was more than that, but I also knew how it appeared. We never hung out during the day, we didn't have a title, he didn't even have my phone number. We weren't in a normal relationship.

"He's not a booty call," Emiko said. "He's a—"

"Don't make it too easy for him, Maleeka," Quinn said before Emiko could finish.

"I'm not allowed to date," I told him.

"But you're allowed to fool around with him in the back of a truck."

He tilted his head at me with a little attitude. "If he wanted you, he would ask you out. He wouldn't want anyone else to have you."

Marc never came out and told me how much he liked me, but the way he kissed me and the way he talked to me was enough for me. Until Quinn said that. Maybe I did make it too easy for him.

As the night went on, I couldn't shake what Quinn said out of the bottom of my gut. The last time I was with Marc felt different, like we were going somewhere. I grabbed Lauren's phone to call him. I thought if I heard his voice I would get Quinn's voice out of my head.

"Is he home?" Samantha said to me after I hung up the phone.

I shook my head, looking down at the phone.

"You want to be his girlfriend?" Samantha grabbed the phone from me.

"I can't do that, I can't be his girlfriend. But I guess I want to make sure he likes me."

I wanted him to confess his love for me, I wanted him to want me as much as I wanted him. But how do you ask for that?

"Make him jealous. That will show you how much he likes you."

"You think?"

"For sure. His true feelings will come out."

"How am I going to do that?" I said, watching her pour vodka into a shot glass. She handed me another shot of the cheap liquor, and I took it. "Caleb, come here!" she called out.

He walked over with his beer. "You girls getting fucked up?"

She gave me another shot, and again, I took it. "Maleeka wants to make out with a guy tonight," she said.

"Sam!" I laughed as she gestured with her eyes for him to have at it.

Caleb grabbed me. He was a terrible kisser, too eager, and his tongue did something weird inside my mouth.

Samantha walked away, laughing to the others.

"What the fuck is she doing!?" I heard Quinn say.

"She's making it hard for him." She laughed as Lauren's phone rang.

"Oh my God, perfect!" Samantha said. "Hi, Marc, it's Sam . . . Yeah, hang on a sec." She walked over to my make-out session. "Caleb, get off her for a second. The phone's for you, Maleeka. It's Marc," she said, loud enough for Marc to hear.

I pushed Caleb off me to look over at Samantha. "Sam?" I looked at her before looking at the phone.

"Make him jealous," she whispered, handing me the phone while Caleb kept kissing my neck.

"Hi," I said, trying not to be too apparent there was a guy on me.

"What are you doing, Maleeka?" he asked. I could tell he held back from jumping to conclusions.

"Nothing, you?" I pushed Caleb away from the receiver.

"Maleeka, Samantha told a guy to get off of you. What are you doing? Who's on top of you?" He sounded frantic.

"Nobody, Marc. Why? Would you care if there was another guy on top of me?"

I finally got Caleb off me for a minute to walk away. Heading to the other side of the back porch, I caught eyes with Quinn, who shook his head.

"Maleeka, you know I have feelings for you."

"Okay, cool. You have feelings for me. What the fuck are they? Tell me," I said with attitude; those shots got to my head quickly; all I had eaten that day was a handful of peanuts and a few pieces of beef jerky. "I want to know how you feel."

"By fooling around with another guy!?"

"I'm not fooling around with anyone," I lied. "And anyway, I'm not your girlfriend, we aren't together. So who cares if I am?" I told him as Caleb was up my ass again from behind with his arm around my waist.

"You want another drink?" he asked me.

I rolled my shoulders back to break loose from his grip and walked away to continue on with Marc.

"Maleeka, who the fuck is that?" I could hear his breath get heavier, like he was ready to brawl. "What are you doing to me right now?"

"I don't know what I'm doing," I told him, burying my head into my hands. I was playing a dirty game.

"Is there a guy on top of you right now?"

"No, Marc. I swear." It got quiet.

"Maleeka," he finally said. "Be my girlfriend?"

My head shot up. Samantha was right. The game worked. But what the hell was I doing? I couldn't say yes to that. "Marc, I can't—"

"I want you, I don't want anyone else to fucking touch you. Please, babe, be my girlfriend."

I sat on the bench and rested my head against the wall. "I can't be your girlfriend, Marc, but I'm so glad you asked."

Towel Heads

In September, Raneem was well medicated and flew back to Harvard. My mom suggested she stay home, but she insisted it was better to leave. Rasheed was now a senior, planning his future with Dad by his side. He was so caught up in college applications and volunteer hours that he had less time to jam with his band. It was easy to avoid him in the summer, but now that we were back in the same halls again, he could keep a closer eye on me. Sophomore year was upon me, and I wanted a new look. I took the soft highlights out of my hair and colored it dark burgundy. I looked hard with my new hairdo. Less like Baby Spice and more like Ginger.

"The dark hair suits you," Brandon said to me in first-period honors English. "You look punk rock."

"You think so?" I laughed while our teacher was preoccupied on the phone.

"Oh my God! Oh my God. Okay, I'll take them there," she said before hanging up the phone. "Class, I need your attention," she said with a tremble in her voice. "Gather all your belongings. We won't be coming back to class. We are all going to the library. There is breaking news."

"Do you think someone has a gun?" Brandon said as we grabbed our things.

"Why would they have us leave class if someone had a gun?"

We arrived at the library and turned toward the roll-out television to read the headlines—"America under Attack."

I couldn't take my eyes off the television. What the fuck was going on? Why was this happening? All of a sudden a dark cloud of panic fell over everyone.

"If anyone needs to call their family, please do," the guidance counselor told the group.

"This is so fucked up," Brandon said, looking at me.

"Yeah, no shit," I agreed.

"Fucking towel heads," I heard a guy yell out from the front of the room, glued to the television. He was angry, and he had every right to be, but I cringed. I only wore a turban when my dad would dress me up for Halloween, but still his comment hit me.

The broadcasters reported the story with the same haunting image of the second plane crashing into the building on repeat. People were freaked out, standing still with no expression or emotion. It was eerie.

We watched it over and over. It was the first conflict of our generation, the first glimpse into everything we read about or learned about in school. Everyone knew this invasion would declare war, which brought up a question: would there be a draft?

"There's no way, people aren't forced to do things the way they once were," I said to Brandon.

"There has been no reason to be forced to do anything until now," Brandon told me. "Even if we're not forced, there is going to be pressure once we're eighteen."

It grew us up within minutes after hearing what happened. I had never had such worldly conversations with my classmates; everything until now was relevant to our high school politics. Boyfriends, breakups, and best friends. Not real life.

By the second period, people were saying ridiculous comments throughout the corridors. Until then, I could tell people I was Syrian, and they'd ask me where that was. When I told people I spoke Arabic in middle school, they asked me if I was Arabian. Now all of a sudden, everyone knew what an Arab was and where the Middle East lay. Before September 11, they had no idea what I was, and better yet, they had no negative feelings about it.

"Aren't those your people? I could see your dad as a terrorist," Kalvin said to me, laughing.

Kalvin Stump was friends with us all, but he was one of those guys who acted like a dick to get a reaction out of people. He was wealthy and good looking, and he knew it. He called girls hoes and guys pussies. Nobody wanted to be on his bad side. I didn't know what to say, I was uncomfortable. I laughed along with them all. I wish I had told him to shut the fuck up.

I grabbed the pay phone in the commons at lunch to call Marc.

"It's fucking crazy, huh?" he told me.

"So messed up, I can't believe it all. I mean, I know war is real, but I guess I never thought it would be something that we'd deal with."

"Maleeka, there's war going on all over the world. Every day, everywhere."

I was relieved he didn't say a word about Arabs, or about me being Arab. He wasn't the type to joke about shit like that. And he loved that I was Arab. He always asked me to speak to him in Arabic; he said it was sexy.

"Yeah, you're right." I leaned against the wall. I didn't want to talk about it anymore. I wanted to talk about us. I wanted to talk about things I could control. I turned to face the wall and pressed my forehead against it. "I miss you." I hadn't seen him since the school year started.

"I miss you too, babe."

"Maleeka?" I heard Rasheed's voice and turned around to find him right behind me. My instincts made me hang up the phone without another word to Marc. "Who are you talking to?"

All my friends were in those halls. Whose name could I use?

"I was trying to get a hold of Raneem."

"Did you? How is she?"

"She didn't answer."

"Dad called, he wants us home. Now."

"But I have class."

"I don't think he cares about class right now, Maleeka."

Rasheed gave me a ride home from school. I had never walked those halls with my brother. I never rode to or from school with him, but he followed my dad's orders. Rasheed seemed rattled by it all too.

I wondered if people were giving him shit. But I didn't ask, we didn't speak on the way home; the bass from Nirvana's "Lounge Act" filled up the truck so we didn't have to.

Dad was already home from work when we got there. He and Mom sat on their chairs in the living room, watching the news without speaking.

"Are you guys okay?" my dad said to us. I wondered why he was concerned with us. We were a couple thousand miles away from ground zero.

"We're fine, Dad," Rasheed said. He and I sat on the sofa next to them, he on one side and I on the other. We sat in silence watching the news report. I waited for someone to say something. I couldn't keep looking at the smoky-haze coverage of panic.

"Maleeka." My mom lowered the volume and looked over at me. "I think you need to color your hair blond again."

I was confused. What did my hair color have to do with a terrorist attack?

"You look more American when your hair is blond."

I laughed a little bit until I realized my mom was serious.

"Raneem's and Rasheed's skin isn't as dark as yours. I don't want people to give you a hard time," she said as she got up off the chair and walked out to the garage to grab a bottle of wine to open before preparing dinner.

My dad turned off the TV and looked over at me and Rasheed. "People are going to start asking you questions about your ethnicity, about your religion, and even about our family. Always be proud of who you are, you understand me?" he insisted. I nodded.

"People are ridiculous," Rasheed said.

Dad sat at the edge of his seat and shifted his body to face us head-on. "Maybe, but they're mad. They will become angrier as time goes on with anyone or anything of Arab descent. Look what happened to Japanese Americans in their own country after Pearl Harbor. They were tormented and seen by their neighbors as the enemy."

"I can't believe that would happen nowadays, Dad." I looked at him.

"Believe it, Maleeka. When people are angry, they don't see clearly. They can't reason with their anger. They unleash it on anyone they consider their enemy. But I don't want you to ever deny who you are." He pointed his finger at us.

"We'll be fine, Dad, don't worry about us," Rasheed said before he left the room.

I wanted to think it was a joke, or not real, but it was. My dad had faced the stereotypes of an Arab man the minute he came to America. He couldn't hide behind blond hair or green eyes. He was dark skinned, with jet-black hair and an accent that gave him away within seconds of a conversation. He sounded like those people from another country who answer when you call your cable company that everyone complains about not understanding. He had to prove himself to coworkers, strangers, and even his in-laws. He was mocked and ridiculed, called a "sand ni**er," a "camel jockey," and a "towel head." He'd heard it all before, and he knew now it would be said more often. He wanted us prepped for ignorance. He wanted us as strong as he had to be. I bit my lip and looked around the room. I didn't know what to say or how to get out of the heavy conversation. I got up to follow Rasheed out of the room.

"Maleeka." My dad got off the chair as I turned back to look at him. He put his hand on my ear and pulled me in to kiss me on the top of my head. "Leave your hair, I like it dark. You look more like me." He smiled.

September 11th 2001

A DAY
I WILL NEVER
— FORGET —

God be with all those who have passed and the families they've left behind.

Scary to think of what will come from all this. It won't end here.

Dad: "Always be proud of who you are."

Marc: "You should be proud of who you are."

Sometimes I think Dad and Marc would get along really well.

CHANGE THE SUBJECT

A couple of weekends after September 11, my dad's niece was getting married. Family members flew in from all over, with heightened security measures. It was all they talked about, how they were uncomfortable and judged. I felt for them. I knew firsthand what it felt like to be looked at differently for what I was. Sure, I wasn't getting searched and groped by security guards, but I was often on edge around my dad's family because I was different. I didn't feel like I was one of them.

The morning of my cousin Dunia's wedding, everyone was outside my uncle's house on the warm September day. The family all looked like celebrities on a red carpet. The women wore fancy dresses with beads and embellishments and got their hair and makeup professionally done. The men were in suits, and the bride was gorgeous. I stood back and watched the photographer snap photos and the florist pass out corsages to the aunts and uncles. I wanted to make sure Mom got one. Asma's mom was in the kitchen, putting trays of handmade Arabic sweets, finger food, coffee, and champagne out for people to have a bite before the festivities began. My mom stood out in the yard alone, wearing her big Audrey Hepburn–inspired sunglasses.

There were times I envied Asma. She was the daughter of a full-blooded Syrian mom who spoke Arabic and made lavish Middle Eastern dishes. She fit in with the family, probably because she was related to my uncle distantly. They always like when you take one from the family or community.

Dunia was not, however. She was marrying an American she had met in college. She must have really loved him to deal with everyone's loudmouthed opinions about it. The first time the family met him, my grandfather laid in on her (in Arabic, of course) about how she was better than he was. And how she hurt her father by being with an American. Her poor fiancé looked like a fool being put down without even knowing it. I always hated when those who spoke English spoke in Arabic around Mom. I translated it into their way to tell her, "You don't belong here."

"Maleeka?! Is that you?" I heard my cousin yell out to me in the front yard. She wore a beautiful navy blue Ralph Lauren gown with a shiny Tiffany & Co. necklace.

"Hi, Lydia." Lydia was a couple of years older than Raneem. She always looked perfect, with lined lips and penciled-in brows. And she wore the most expensive designer clothes.

"Red hair?" She ran her fingers through the ends of my hair and looked at me with wide eyes as if it were a sin to color your hair. Every girl on Dad's side of the family had dark, virgin hair up to their shoulders, with or without bangs. I had rocked that look all my life until I got my hands on a few style magazines.

"Aumo Karim, you let her color her hair red?" she called out to my dad, who stood on the other side of the driveway with a cigar in his mouth.

He didn't say anything, but some of the other ladies joined in her cattiness. I stood among them like a piece of shit getting swarmed by pesky flies.

"This is the new Maleeka," my cousin Antoinette said, coming from behind me. "She never comes around anymore. She's too busy with her friends."

"Oh yeah?" Lydia looked at me with a sneaky eye like she wanted to know more. "Are you getting yourself into trouble, Maleeka?"

"No," I said, "it's not like that."

"Of course she is. She is spending time with a bunch of American kids," Antoinette's mom said in Arabic, also swarming me.

I looked at my dad. He had his head up in the air, exhaling his cigar and shaking his head.

"I am American." I looked back at my uncle's wife.

She shook her head with her lips pressed together like she wanted to spit. "You're Syrian!" she told me with her finger in the air, and walked away.

"I'm not doing anything wrong," I told the cousins.

"Let's ask your dad. Aumo Karim, is Maleeka getting herself into trouble?" Antoinette laughed. I hate when people laugh after saying a remark they know will upset or embarrass you, as if laughing means they don't mean it.

Dad didn't laugh. He took another puff off his cigar while shaking his head. "Change the subject," he told them.

"We are joking, Aumo."

He kept eye contact with his niece and pointed his cigar at her. "Change the God damn subject."

Boom! The drum echoed inside. The bride was ready. *Boom ta dat boom, boom ta dat boom dat ta ta.* They call that drum a *tubal*; it carries enough bass and vibration to induce chills up your spine.

Dunia came down the grand staircase in her beautiful ball gown, followed by her sister. Her mom waited for her at the bottom of the staircase, chanting Arabic blessings. I was so relieved that conversation was over and we could focus on the bride.

Family is *love*

Arabic music is full of life and spirit. Language barriers cease to exist. That was one activity my mom always participated in—dancing. She learned the steps to what is called the *dabke*, a choreographed circle dance led by the tubal. Everyone had the same step and flow that followed the drum. The tubal could make anyone feel Arab.

Dunia and her new husband were in the center of the circle, dancing while the family hovered, throwing hundreds of dollar bills at them. The dance floor was the safest place to be since it was too loud to have a conversation. There wasn't an opportunity for passive-aggressive comments or snide remarks. The music was the only thing that connected me to the family because I knew those steps too. I stayed on the dance floor as long as I could, but given the height of my impractical heels, I eventually had to give my feet a break.

I grabbed a vodka cranberry from the open bar and headed out to the lobby. *Shit,* I thought to myself as Antoinette approached me. I didn't want to hear any more nonsense.

"Can I sit?" she asked me. I scooted over on the leather bench in the hotel lobby.

My cousin, Antoinette, had everything they thought she should. She had a law degree, a hot body, perfect skin, and expensive handbags, and all the most handsome guys in our community wanted her.

"You think Dunia made a good decision?" Antoinette asked me. Obviously, she didn't.

"She looks happy," I told her, and took a drink without looking at her.

"We all want our freedom, Maleeka, but we can't be selfish. Our parents do everything for us. We have to respect and honor them. We owe it to them."

There was a rumor in the family that Antoinette was engaged to an attorney at work but ended it once her parents told her they wouldn't support her with an American. How sad she had to be to let go of a guy she loved for the sake of making her parents happy. He was probably devastated.

"She loves him. Don't you believe in love?"

"Family is love, Maleeka."

Dear Journal,   Sept. 29th, 2001
Don't they care about the fact that I am American? I guess not since they won't even acknowledge that I am.

I don't blame Mom for the walls she puts up while around Dad's family. They don't go out of their way to be nice to her the way they do with each other.

I hate seeing her sit alone.

"Family is Love. We owe it to them."
— Antoinette

I can't tell you how many times I've heard that. It's like propaganda to control us!

Sometimes I think this family is a cult!

If she did leave someone that she loved because of her parents, that's on her. She made that choice. I would never do that.

But then I think about Marc...

I hold back so much because of them

under their
control

The weekend after the wedding, I left my house through the garage while my parents were terrorizing the kitchen. They always fought after spending time with the family. It worked out best for me, as I was able to grab a bottle of wine on my way out without anyone noticing. Samantha was the first one of us to get her driver's license, so she picked me up for the varsity football game, with Lauren and Emiko already in the car.

We had no interest in watching the game; we were there to hang out with our friends. We sat with our fast-food cups filled with my mom's merlot. I held on to my cup and sipped my wine out through a straw until I heard Samantha say, "Look who's here."

Marc approached us with two of his friends: Carson and a guy named Bruce.

"What's up, babe?"

"Babe" was now my official name to him. *Hi, babe; good night, babe; I miss you, babe; babe, be my girlfriend.* Every time he'd say, "Babe," my stomach would drop. Babe meant I was special to him. A name he only used for me. But when he said it there, my stomach clenched with nerves. There were people all around us. What if they thought babe meant girlfriend? He put his arm around me. I appreciated it, but I was a wreck inside.

"What are you doing here?" I smiled at him. I tried to keep my distance while I contained my excitement at seeing him.

Before he could answer me, Samantha, Lauren, and Emiko gave him a hug without any hesitation. I stayed back against the concrete wall and let him charm my friends. I could tell he was buzzed, but I couldn't judge; so was I.

He paused long enough to look at me. Now that I knew Marc wanted me to be his girlfriend, I couldn't stop staring at him, trying to figure out how it could ever work, if at all. He got closer to me, and as he did, I took inventory of everyone around me. Rasheed was at a speech tournament, and Waleed was in the front row of the bleachers, watching the game with his JV team.

"So what are you doing here?" I asked him again.

"What do you mean? I always come to these games." He laughed.

I rolled my eyes. "Before or after you got kicked out of school?"

He didn't laugh; he was busy staring at me like I was the most impressive thing he had laid eyes on, and he couldn't laugh about that. "You look beautiful tonight, Maleeka."

Before, when Marc looked at me like that, I'd break through the intensity by closing my eyes and kissing him. But I couldn't kiss him there. I put my head down and played with my straw. "Yeah, right."

He bent down to pull my attention back up. "You're joking, right? You don't feel like the most beautiful girl in this fucking stadium tonight?"

I loved hearing him insist he was right. Especially when it went against what I thought. "I do now."

"Mission accomplished." He smiled and grabbed my cup. "What do you have in here?" He smelled the wine through the straw.

"Have a drink." I smiled.

"Maleeka Munir . . ." He shook his head with a smirk before he took a sip. I could tell he found it amusing I was getting drunk at a football game.

"Marc!" Carson yelled over the heads of everyone around us. "Let's get out of here."

"I'll meet you at the truck," he told the guys.

They agreed and headed out.

"Come with me," he asked with a sparkle in his eyes. "Bruce is having people over, and I want you to come."

"I can't, I'm going to Lauren's house after this."

He got close and grabbed my hand for a hot second. "Please come. If you hate it, I'll get you back to Lauren's."

I pulled my hand away and put it in my pocket. "I can't, Marc, really. I can't."

I wasn't ready to say good night to him, but I couldn't be at Bruce's house with him. And I couldn't ask him to stay and watch the game with me with the entire school surrounding us. It was best for him to leave with his friends and for me to stay with mine. I walked him to the gate that led out to the parking lot without getting too close to him.

"Call me later tonight," I told him.

"I will, babe," he said as he walked away to his friends.

I stood at the gate, with a smile I couldn't wipe off my face. I knew it was a big deal that Marc came. He put the planned evening with his friends on hold and got them to swing by the game so he could see me.

He got about halfway to the car when he turned around and smiled at me with all his friends watching. I was like the girl I wanted to be the first time I saw him at his show, his girl. His pause and smile halfway to his ride said it all.

Our connection was brutally interrupted by his friend Bruce. He yelled across the parking lot, "Hurry up, man. You're taking forever with that slut."

I cringed, but it didn't take more than a second for Marc to get in his face and shove him against the truck.

"Watch it, Bruce!" he said as he pushed again harder. "Don't ever call her that again!"

Bruce stumbled back to balance on his feet. "What the fuck, Marc! What, you love this girl?!"

I could see Marc nod a couple of times before he let Bruce go. He ran back to the gate where I stood, grabbed my hands in front of everyone and looked into my eyes. "I love you, Maleeka," he said, and kissed me right on my lips.

I was caught off guard and didn't have a chance to push him off. So I let him kiss me; it was quick, with no tongue, but full of energy. He let me go, smiled at me, and turned to walk back to his friends. Nobody out there in that parking lot expected Marc to fall in love, let alone with a girl like me.

Dear Journal, Oct. 6, 2001

Having a guy like Marc love me is so flattering. He loves the best of everything

You're brilliant.
   and deep
and you **Love** me

trust
him

I love your taste in music
I'm inspired by your mind
Convinced of all your theories
See truth run through your eyes
So when you say you love me
I know it's a big deal
Cause I trust your thoughts
believe your heart
and everything you feel

P.S. FUCK Bruce! that guy
           is a bitch

WE'RE PARALLEL

More people saw the kiss than I would have liked. Even my English teacher asked me if I was dating Marc Osbourne. I panicked, and of course denied it, hoping she wouldn't say anything to Rasheed. I knew I had to pump the brakes, and I had to figure out a way to keep him at arm's length, close enough to feed off his love but far enough away so nobody would know.

That fall, Mom decided the house needed a second phone so the internet wouldn't tie up the main line. I convinced her to set it up in my room; that way we wouldn't have any more scenes. My own phone changed everything. Marc could call me whenever he wanted. He promised never to leave a voicemail in case my parents or Rasheed would hear his voice. So instead of leaving me a message to call him back, he would leave me recordings with whatever song he was listening to. Whether it was Built to Spill, Radiohead, or the Beatles, he was always listening to good music. That evening after school, I came home to find Weezer's "Falling for You" playing on the recording.

Every song before this had been good, but with this one, he was telling me something. Shaking at my touch, and liking me way too much, and he'd rather settle down. Settling down sounded official and grown up, something I couldn't do with him.

When I called him back, he told me about his new schedule as a busboy and his first day of college classes. He was doing all he could to save enough money to move out on his own.

"Sorry, I didn't even ask, how was your day?"

I sat at the edge of my bed and went off. I stuttered as I told him I couldn't see him in public anymore. I wanted him but I needed more privacy. He stayed quiet and let me talk.

"You probably think I sound ridiculous," I told him as I heard his lighter flicker before he took a hit. It could have been a cigarette or a joint, I wasn't sure. But I knew he smoked to help him process what I told him.

"I don't think you're ridiculous, babe."

"It's not that I don't want to see you, it's just easier for me this way."

"I want to spend time with you in any capacity possible. If the phone's all I got, I'll take it," he assured me.

"You make everything so easy." I lay back on my bed with the phone on my ear while I heard another puff of smoke blow out of his mouth.

"I'm not letting you go that easy. Don't you remember what I told you the other night?"

"I wasn't that drunk." I laughed.

"Well, it's true, Maleeka, I have fallen in love with you."

"I know." I smiled and nodded my head. "Rivers told me."

"Well, how do you feel?"

"I told you a long time ago I like you, Marc."

He chuckled under his breath. "You *do* say 'like' too much." Referencing Weezer.

He wanted more than "like" right then. I didn't know how to say love, I could write all day about how much I loved him, but I had never said it out loud.

"I know, I'm sorry, I just don't know how to say—"

"Tell me this, are we parallel?"

"Parallel?"

"Yeah, our figures in the backdrop, are they parallel?"

I nodded my head as if he could see me.

He continued. "Regardless of the untouchables on the forefront."

"Sounds like you're on to a great song there."

"I have to write this shit down." He laughed.

"Are you going to write a song about me?"

"I already have."

I was flattered to have someone with his depth and his ability write a song or even a passage about me. Was I worth the writing of a song?

"When was the first time you knew you liked me?"

"I love you."

I laughed. I knew he loved saying those words now that he'd released them.

"I know, but when did you first decide, 'Hey, I like Maleeka'?"

"I didn't decide, I felt it. I didn't tell myself, 'Go like Maleeka.' I decided to hang out with you and to spend time with you. But I didn't have any control over falling in love with you."

"Okay, when did you uncontrollably fall in love with me?"

"That night you were at Lauren's house when I thought you were with another guy. I've never felt anything like that before. The pain made me realize I would give anything never to feel that way again. I never wanted to let you go or lose you."

I didn't say anything. But fuck, I felt like shit about that.

"Did I freak you out?"

I turned on my side and played with the edge of the bed sheet. "Have you ever seen *The Wizard of Oz*?"

"Why are you asking me that? Who hasn't seen *The Wizard of Oz*?"

"There's this part where the wizard tells the Tin Man that hearts aren't practical because they are breakable."

"So you're afraid of heartbreak?"

"It's a scary thought to fall in love with someone, or something. To lose your control."

"You have to trust, Maleeka. Didn't the Beatles ever tell you, 'All You Need Is Love.'"

"The only love I've ever known has been chaos. Nothing is appealing about it. I don't ever want love like that."

"Your parents?"

"Yeah, I know I'm safe, and I'll always be taken care of. But this house and their love . . ." I rolled over onto my back and let out a breath before saying, "When it's bad, it's devastating."

"It's hard to imagine someone who smiles the way you do would have such a destructive home life."

I nodded. "Not many people can."

Dear Journal,   Oct. 9, 2001

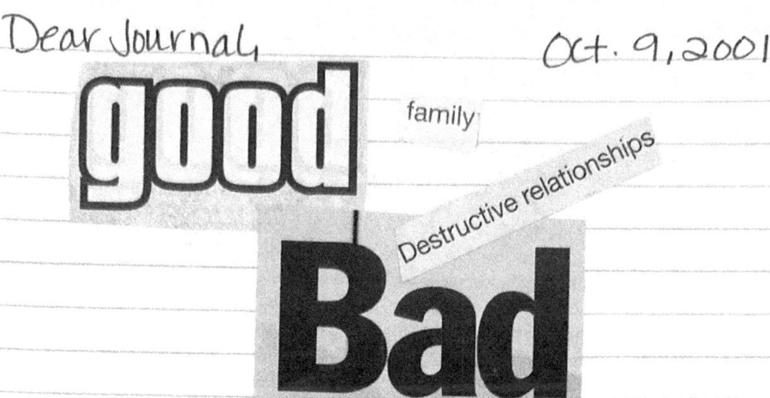

On the outside it seems that I am fine
and your the one that's the bad guy
now you're starting to see the truth
I'm the one fucked up, not you

Your presence strong, your eyes so bright
my twisted world is our biggest fight

Your heart holds so much peace
my mind's filled with insecurities
your home full, topped with love
mine has me guessing if I am enough

SUBSTANCE TO BRING Bliss

"Swear on your children!" my dad screamed at my mom and pointed at me and Rasheed in the kitchen. He stormed to her and threw her Bible at her feet on the living room chair. "Swear on your Bible that you didn't do this on purpose!" I wasn't a strong believer like my mom was, but throwing the Bible on the ground had to be a sin.

"You're so dramatic, I was cleaning the room," she said as she took another drink.

"You were trying to poison me!" he yelled.

Mom was always against chemical cleaning products; she didn't like the toxins, so she always used vinegar to mop the floors, dust, and clean the windows. That day, she doused the guest room Dad slept in with the harshest cleaning products she could use.

"This is too much," I said, and turned to walk up the stairs.

"You're just going to walk away?" Rasheed asked me as he stood in front of me on the staircase.

"They're crazy. And she's obviously drunk," I told him.

Dear Journal,   Nov. 1st, 2001

  Dad is SO dramatic, and I hate
Mom when she drinks. She scares
me when she sits in that chair, her
face all red and she doesn't speak.
  She scares me more than Dad does
what is she thinking? Why can't she
express herself? What the fuck is
really going on?
She drinks to find peace, but it tears
the house apart.

I can't wait to move out of here to
start my own life and my own peace.
That's all I want is peace.

I closed my journal and grabbed the phone.

There are so many substances in the world that give relief. They provide peace, though they aren't always good for us. Marc was my substance, my coping mechanism that brought me peace after the chaos.

"Are you okay, babe?" he asked me. All I said was hi to him, but I had little life in my voice.

"Yeah, I'm fine. I'm just tired," I told him. I didn't want to tell him about the "poison." "How was your night?"

"It was good, we were slammed. But it was good. I feel good, I'm good." He said *good* so many times.

"It sounds like you've been drinking."

I heard his lighter hit the crackling weed. I was starting to catch on to what each one of his vices sounded like based on his breath and the length of his inhale. "I had a couple drinks after my shift."

"Sorry, I didn't mean to call you out."

"Don't be, I love how you can tell by my voice." I knew he was smiling through the phone. "I miss you. I couldn't wait to get home and hear your voice."

That was all I needed. I didn't need to tell him about the drama downstairs, or about my crazy parents. All I needed was to hear his voice and feel his love to forget about the house. He could take away the confusion and noise in my head with his words. I felt good like he did, though I didn't have any substance to bring me bliss; all I had was him to feed me affection.

I heard his window creak open, knowing he went back into his room, and I heard his box spring bounce, assuming he lay on his bed. "Babe, be my girlfriend," he said abruptly, strong from his substances.

I shot my head up, taken aback by his question. My bliss was interrupted. "How much have you had to drink?" I said. "You know I can't be your girlfriend, why are you asking me?"

"Because I love you!" he said. "Everyone asks me why you aren't my girlfriend. It's what normal people do when they love each other, they date."

I was shocked to hear him give pushback to my boundaries. I knew his buzz encouraged him to do so, he wouldn't have brought it up otherwise.

"I'm not normal, you know that! Tell them that."

"I didn't mean to say normal, fuck being normal. Maleeka, I love you and want you to be my girlfriend. Or at least be able to see you."

I looked up at my shelf with a framed picture of the family. My crazy family, that preached family values, but also broke shit, threw things, and even tried to "poison" each other. I hated their love; it was uneasy and confusing. How could I value their opinions on what I should be doing and fear what they'd do if they knew who I loved when their love was full of contradictions? Why was I affected by them? I certainly didn't respect them, but I was scared of them.

"I understand, but I can't. And if it's too much for you, I get it."

I wanted to give him an out if he wanted it, but prayed he didn't.

"It's not, I'm sorry I brought it up, forget I said anything," he told me.

I nodded my head, relieved, but didn't say anything to him.

"Babe, I have to do something. Can I call you back?"

"Call me back? What do you have to do?"

"Please, stay awake. Leave your light on so you won't fall asleep."

I wondered what the hell he might be doing. I assumed one of his buddies was there to smoke him out. I grabbed my journal and sat on my windowsill, waiting to hear back from him. I couldn't end the night with the idea of my situation being too much for him.

Dear Journal,

(10:15pm)
Nov. 1st, 2001

Will he stay my secret forever?
I wish I was strong enough to tell everyone
in this house how I feel about him
and not give a shit.
I don't know if I fear what they'd
do to me or what they'd do to marc
more. Is forbidden love even a
thing anymore?

There are movies out there
Old stories ~~that~~ been told
Of star struck love
in opposite worlds

It doesn't seem real
now a days to be true
but there is no way
I can be with you

HOLD ON.

in the name of

FORBIDDEN. LOVE

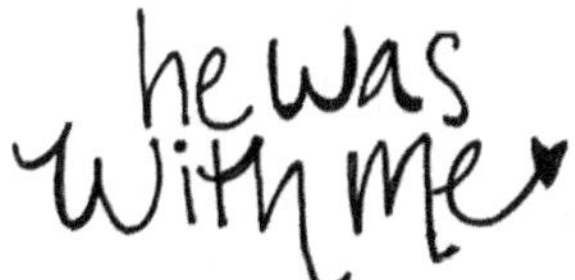

As I taped the last cutout in my entry, my bedroom door opened without a knock. I didn't even hear footsteps approaching. I assumed everyone was sleeping, it was past ten o'clock.

"Do you know how much hell I go through daily being married to your dad?" Mom said with a red face and bloodshot eyes. I closed my journal and let out a deep breath.

"Mom, I know Dad's crazy. I know that. But I know you're not easy either."

"You'll never know what I go through."

I raised my voice. "Then leave him, Mom. I don't know what else to tell you."

She shook her head and glared at me. "You live a charmed life, Maleeka. I hope you marry a man someday who loves you, a man who puts you first before his family." She turned her back to me.

"Do you?" I called out as she turned off my light, shut the door, and walked away to leave me alone in the dark.

I threw my journal off my lap and got up to turn my light back on. Before I did, I felt a presence. I couldn't figure out where or why, but I didn't feel alone, and it didn't scare me. I walked to the window with the lights off so I could see outside clearly. There was fog surrounding the streetlights and moisture on the bare asphalt. Everything was still, like nothing had been there. I shook my head and turned on the lamp on my nightstand that was covered with shit: makeup, Post-it notes, and a couple of cups with condensation on the outside. I kept ice handy late at night. Crunching the ice cubes helped keep me awake without consuming any calories.

> "You live a charmed life Maleeka."
>   — mom
> She has no idea....
>
> Every time they fight, he's all
> I want. Every time I hear Dad raise
> his voice, I want to hear marc's.
> He separates me from them.
> He gives me my own life.
> I hate being tied up in their issues.
> I hate having to worry about them
> so much.

About twenty minutes later, I was still awake, crunching on ice and doodling in my journal as I waited to hear from him. My eyes were heavy and my shoulders weak. The only relief would be to rest them on my pillow and close my eyes, but I wanted relief more than sleep. I wanted him. I got out of bed to wash my face with cold water to force a surge of energy. When I got back in my room, I pulled my hair into a tight, high ponytail to help keep my eyelids open.

"Come on, Marc." I got in bed and stared at the phone under my pile of pillows so nobody in the house would hear it but me. Finally it rang.

"Hello?" I said quietly.

"I'm back, babe."

"Where did you go? I almost fell asleep."

"I had to go see someone."

"You went to go get weed, didn't you?"

"No, I had to see you."

"You were here?" I sat up in bed. I knew it, I felt it in my gut. I was grateful he didn't hang up with me to go get high.

"You looked beautiful writing in your journal," he said. "I want you however I can have you, babe, I'm sorry I brought all that bullshit up to you."

"Don't be sorry, I know it's not easy."

"I left you something in the mailbox," he told me.

I jumped out of bed with more energy than my ponytail or cold water could give me.

"I can't believe you were here," I said, smiling. "Hold on, I'll be right back." I crept down the stairs and grabbed my care package.

There was a folded-up piece of paper that sat underneath a pack of cupcakes and a worn-out plastic bag with a couple of hairy green nuggets inside. His care package told me he was going to make the best of our situation.

"Weed." I laughed at the drug drop-off when I picked up the phone. "You came to bring me weed?"

"I brought you cupcakes, and I'm on to you, Maleeka. You won't eat 'em unless you're stoned."

I grabbed a pipe he had let me borrow the summer before that I never gave back to him. I hid it in my makeup bag, under my compact bronzer, a few tubes of lip gloss, and mascara. "You wanna smoke together?"

"Let's do it."

I opened my window to sit on the sill and loaded the bowl. It was my first time smoking a bowl by myself, even though he was with me the only way he could be.

"Did you read the poem I wrote to you?"

"Oh shit, I forgot. Is it a poem?" I grabbed the piece of paper and opened it.

I read it out loud. "'The figures on the backdrop are parallel.' Oh my God, you finished it."

Everyone talked about Marc's talent in writing music, which all stemmed from his poetry. People gave him props for being a fantastic writer, and I agreed with them all wholeheartedly, but this poem was better than anything he'd written before. He wrote it in metaphorical terms about the galaxy and equations that he helped me understand by cracking the codes to explain how it was all about us.

"Marc, thank you. Thank you for understanding my situation, thank you for loving me regardless."

"Do you like it?"

"I love it. It's written so well, and I love how it's not obvious to anyone else that it's about us," I told him as I flattened out the folds and placed it in my binder cover.

I didn't care if anyone saw it. They would have no idea who wrote it or what it meant. Only he and I knew how much it had to do with our love. The metaphors were safe, like our phone calls. They were inconspicuous, something I could hide behind. As much as I missed seeing him, it was easier to not have to worry if anyone found out. I was free and safe. And I never wanted to hang up. He could stay awake forever; he told me he was an insomniac, and I tried hard to keep up to get as much time with him as I could.

"Radiohead has to be my favorite band. I'm going to make you a CD so you can love them like I do," he told me as it was pushing two in the morning, and he was still full of energy.

"Radiohead loves me like you?" I mumbled into the receiver with my face nestled in my pillow.

"What? No, I said you can love them like I do."

I didn't say anything. I fell asleep for a second, but it felt like hours. I was tired.

"Babe? Are you there?"

"I love you, and I love Radiohead too."

"Did you just say you love me?" he said. It was my first time doing so.

I woke up, I knew I said it, even though I was half-asleep. It made it easier to say it to him before drifting into slumbers without control.

"Maleeka, are you awake? Did you say you love me?"

I didn't answer. I was scared to say it again.

"I'm going to let you go so you can sleep," he said.

"No, please don't go. I'm awake, I'll stay awake."

"It's okay, babe, we'll talk tomorrow."

"Marc," I whispered.

"Yeah?"

"Please don't hang up. Stay with me tonight."

I didn't want to hang up, I wanted him with me all night. Even if I was sleeping. I wanted to know he was there.

$* Nighttime Escape *$

Dear Journal,   Nov. 15, 2001

MARC   OSBOURNE

MALEEKA MUNIR

TRUE   LOVE   86%
0 3 2 3   1 2 0 3

He writes me poetry and
reads me beautiful quotes by Henry David
Thoreau. He plays me music and comes
to visit me, leaving me sweet gifts in the
mailbox. Last night he left me a
Radiohead CD with a rose.

Your spirit takes me on your trips
Your mind inspires me with no limits
Play me a track, a piece of your world

*read me a passage to last and to hold
onto forever until we get past
all of this noise and constant backlash
♥ ♥ ♥ ♥ ♥ ♥*

*God, science is hell and so boring!
I can't wait until I'm done with
high school so I'll never have to take
a science class again!!!*

I was exhausted all day every day, but I kept a smile on my face, unable to erase it. The girls noticed my aura, but also the bags under my eyes.

"Maleeka, wake up!" Lauren said.

"Sorry." I sat up, rubbing smudged mascara from under my eyes. "I wanted to rest my lids." I struggled to stay awake at the lunch table with the crew. The guys were all gathered around the table we sat at as we girls talked quietly together.

"She fell asleep in science today!" Samantha told the girls.

"So what do you do, spend all night on the phone with him?" Lauren asked me.

"Yeah, we talk until we fall asleep. I didn't go to sleep last night until one. And woke up to the phone dead by my head."

"You fall asleep together on the phone?" Samantha looked at me funny.

"Well, I normally fall asleep first."

"What a creep!" She laughed. "He just listens to you sleep?"

"Well, yeah, until he falls asleep or the phone dies." I smiled.

I loved to fall asleep while he stayed awake on the line and listened to me sleep. When I'd wake up in the morning to find my phone dead on my pillow, it energized me knowing I was loved and adored. I was exhausted but also happy.

"How romantic!" Emiko said with a smile on her face.

"Romantic?!" Lauren said. "You're going to kill yourself staying up so late every night. Don't you run out of shit to talk about?"

"No, we talk about everything, and we pretend we're hanging out, only through the phone. Last week he ate dinner in his room while we were on the phone together, and he helped write my English paper."

"Why don't you go and hang out with him for a couple hours and go to bed at a decent time?" Samantha laughed.

"I'm not like you guys. I can never have a normal relationship."

"Well, do you ever see him? I mean, you can sneak out and see him."

I shook my head. "We just talk on the phone."

"I don't care what they say, Leek," Emiko said. "I think it's romantic as hell to have him all to yourself all night. He's like your nighttime escape from the world." She nudged into me.

"Yeah, he is. It just sucks because we don't get to hook up like in the summer." I laughed.

"Do you have phone sex?" Emiko asked as they all laughed together. I smiled.

"Oh my God! You're having phone sex!" Samantha laughed.

It was true. We told each other what we would do the next time we'd meet. He was graphic in his explanations and would tell me how to touch myself while he got off listening to me moan. It was easy for me to give vivid affection over the phone; there was nothing in the way. I was comfortable and confident with him, letting him know how much he meant to me and how much I missed his touch.

a night OFF

Dear Journal,   Nov. 17, 2001

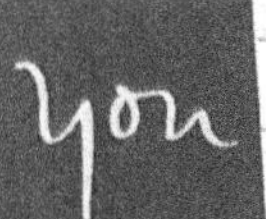

YOU WAKE UP TO THEIR TUNES IN THE MORNING and fall asleep to them at night. **AND STILL** you want **more**

I know I am doing something I shouldn't be, but at the same time, I can never get enough of it. I want more. I need more. Is it only drugs that you can get addicted to? Can you be addicted to a person, or the way someone makes you feel? He's a hit to give me life and to make me strong. Like a drug.

Give me a drag, let me inhale your love
Light me up burning to clouds up above

Coat me with pleasure, block out the pain
dose it up higher, enough to sustain

You're bad like the worst
    good like the best
give me a hit so my soul can rest

Every night we'd spend time on the phone together, I became more dependent on him. I hated it when he wasn't home. I didn't know what to do with myself. It was Saturday night, and he was out. Rather than going to sleep, I decided to log online.

Carson84: what's up Maleeka?

Leek55: Hi Carson are you with Marc?

I assumed that would be the only reason he'd reach out to me. I had never talked to Carson online.

Carson84: No I'm not with those guys tonight. I needed a break

Leek55: a break?

Carson84: Yeah, a night off to be sober

Leek55: oh okay

I didn't know what to say, except okay. I was about to tell him good night, but before I could, he wrote me.

Carson84: so tell me what a girl like you is doing with a guy like Marc?

Leek55: come on Carson he's not so bad

Carson84: ha! Marc not so bad . . . you have no idea

I didn't say anything. I felt trapped, stuck in a conversation I didn't feel good about having behind Marc's back, but also intrigued to know why Carson thought that.

Carson84: he's too much Maleeka, he's way too into drugs.

Leek55: everyone smokes weed Carson

Carson84: weed isn't half of it

I grabbed my cup of ice and crushed through my nerves about where this was heading.

Carson84: has he told you about his prescriptions??

Leek55: what does that have to do with doing drugs?

Marc told me he was diagnosed with ADD and was given Adderall to help with it. He also told me he had a hard time sleeping, and the weed helped, but he took "stuff" to help with that too. I didn't think twice about anything prescribed to him. Those were things he had to take.

Carson84: do you know what adderall is?

Leek55: all I know is that it's supposed to help you concentrate

Carson84: yeah if taken as advised . . . It's like speed otherwise

Again, I didn't know what to say.

Carson84: can you keep something between us?

Leek55: sure

Carson84: I'm worried about that guy he has no boundaries

Leek55: he seems to have it all under control

Carson84: is that what he tells you?

Leek55: he's having fun like everyone else

Carson84: trust me he isn't like everyone else . . . he's too much

Leek55: I don't know what to say

Carson84: I'm not telling you this to talk shit about my best friend. I'm telling you cause maybe you can talk to him

Leek55: and say what?

Carson84: he seems to really like you maybe you can get through to him . . . keep him on the right path

Leek55: I don't know Carson

Carson84: talk to him . . . but don't tell him I said anything to you

Carson84: I got to get to bed I'll see you around

Leek55: okay good night

Carson84: Remember keep this between us

Leek55: yeah I will

Carson signed off and left me with a bombshell in my lap. I could brush off Zach's or Rasheed's opinions about Marc, because they didn't know him like I did. But for his best friend to tell me he was out of control was different. Marc had the ability to make everything he did seem harmless to me. He had a way of brushing things off, like the acid he had told me about a few months before.

Dear Journal, Nov. 18, 2001

"He's too much" – Carson Meyer

I know Marc is extra. That's what makes him so passionate. Everyone likes smoking weed, Marc loves it. Everyone loves music, Marc lives for it. Everything he feels is extreme. He told me himself when he loves something he loves it hard. Good or bad.

And like he loves music, art and drugs, he loves me. And that feels good.

TOO MUCH

After Carson told me he thought Marc was out of line, I started to pick up on things more than I had before. Carson wasn't the first person to warn me about Marc, but the fact that he was his best friend made it resonate. I didn't mention anything to Marc about it, other than maybe one passive-aggressive comment about how he was always drunk on Tuesday nights after he closed shop with his coworkers. He laughed, and I laughed, to make it less awkward after I said it.

It was well over a month since I had seen Marc after I told him I couldn't see him in public. We sneaked out once, but with him working late on the weekends and my school schedule, it was hard to see him. We talked every day, but I missed him. Especially when I'd spend time with the girls and their boyfriends. We went to City Parlor Pizza the night before Thanksgiving. I rode with Lauren and Samantha, and as we approached a group outside the pizza joint, I could see Emiko under Jake's arm, smiling at me.

"Oh my God, guys." I pulled them back to me. "It's Marc." He had his back toward me, but I recognized his posture in his usual center-of-the-group spot, with a cigarette in his hand.

"What's up, girls?" Jake said to us as we got closer. Marc turned around immediately, his eyes scrunched together with his smile.

"Hi," I mouthed with reserved excitement in public like that.

He put his cigarette out on the steel handrail he leaned against. "Hey, babe." He walked past the guys and put his hand on my face like he wanted to kiss me. I rolled out of his palm and up on his shoulder to give him a hug instead.

"What's up, Maleeka?" Carson said while I was still under Marc's arm. Apparently Carson's break from Marc was over.

I took a couple of steps away from Marc to our safe-zone distance while Samantha gave him a hug.

Carson used his eyes to get my attention quietly. He gestured his head toward Marc.

"Did you talk to him?"

I shook my head, reading the instant message in my mind.

Carson84: so tell me what a girl like you is doing with a guy like Marc?

I looked over at Marc, who stared at me, at every inch of me. He wasn't engaged with any conversation. He stood back and burned holes into my hesitant demeanor.

"You look beautiful tonight," he told me, loud enough to interrupt Lauren asking everyone what kind of pizza she should order.

Everyone stopped and looked at us. I wanted to get mad at him for being obvious in front of so many people, but how can you get mad at someone for calling you beautiful?

"Thank you," I said, and tucked my hair back behind my ear. The tunnel between us closed in and felt more intense.

He got close to me and put his arm around my waist from behind. He was well aware of the rules I had, but they didn't appear to matter to him at the moment.

"God, I fucking missed you," he said, with his breath against my neck. The whisper was quiet, but the vibration was loud. I felt it, and I wondered if everyone else did too.

Carson looked at me, and again I remembered what he said.

Carson84: he's too much Maleeka

I turned toward him with my back facing Carson. I had to think of a way to make him stop, to remind him of my boundaries, to keep things undercover. Did he forget? Was he fucked up? Or was he infused with passion so he didn't care? Carson's message ran through my mind on repeat.

"Want to get away from everyone?" I asked him quietly.

"Fuck yeah," he said, thrilled by my request.

He reached out to grab my hand to lead me to Carson's truck, but I was quick to dodge him by pretending to look through my purse. "I'll meet you there," I said quietly.

I waited long enough so it wouldn't look like I was following him. As I got closer to him, he approached me, ready to kiss me.

"Is it unlocked?" I asked him.

"Yeah." He smiled and opened the door for me.

I jumped in the back seat of the truck and turned to kiss him.

"I missed you so much," he told me with a heavy breath. I could taste the whiskey in his mouth.

I didn't say a word, but I grabbed him with passion to show how much I missed him too. I didn't think twice about keeping up with him—until I couldn't. He couldn't resist. Our desire had built up over the phone, and in no time both our shirts were off and his hand was inside my pants.

"I am going to fuck you right now," he said.

"We can't do that," I told him. I assumed he only said that to try to turn me on. But he was serious. He pulled his pants down while I lay back and shook my head.

"Marc, we can't."

He grabbed my face to kiss me again and started sucking on my neck. "You said you wanted this."

I did say I wanted it. I told Marc often on the phone I couldn't wait for him to "fuck me," making nothing about it sound sweet and romantic. I told him I couldn't wait to have his dick inside me, to turn him on, and I had promised him he could have every bit of me the next time we saw each other.

"What are you going to do, fuck me in the back of Carson's truck?" I laughed while he kissed the spot almost at my collarbone.

"I'll take what I can get. God knows when I'll see you next," he said, panting, pulling my pants past my knees and lying back on top of me. I had never been so naked in front of him. His body was heavy against mine.

"Marc, stop."

But he didn't. He knew better. One night on the bleachers, he had his hands down my pants, and I told him to stop. He did, and I asked why. I didn't mean it. I took the words about not stopping right out of the Foo Fighters song "Everlong." I thought it was sexy.

"Marc." I let out a big breath. His kiss on my neck did feel good, it made my shoulders fall back and my chest puff out. "Please, stop."

I could feel his dick between my legs, and I knew it would be inside me within seconds. Carson came back to mind.

Carson84: he's too much

My insides were hard and tense. "Marc," I gasped. "Please stop, I can't breathe."

Carson84: he has no boundaries

I couldn't get Carson out of my head. I couldn't make it stop, and I couldn't make Marc stop.

I turned hysterical. "I said stop! What's wrong with you?" I used all my anger and energy to pull myself up and push him back against the car door.

He shook his head like he was lost. "I thought you said not to—" I didn't let him finish.

"Stop!" I pulled my pants up and grabbed my shirt off the floor of the truck.

"Babe, what the fuck is wrong!" He looked at me like I was an alien. "You told me you wanted this."

"Just leave me alone." I grabbed the door as he buttoned up the shirt I'd ripped off him.

"Babe, wait!" He let go of his shirt and grabbed my arm.

"Don't touch me!" I stumbled out of the truck.

"Maleeka, please!" He lunged out to grab me but missed.

I walked as fast as I could through the parking lot to find the girls. They weren't outside anymore. My heart pounded through my chest, I was scared to look back in case he followed me. When I got inside, I saw Lauren; her face gave me immediate relief. I turned around to make sure he wasn't there. He had let me go.

I stayed close to the girls; I didn't know what else to do. I felt gross and dirty, and I tried to explain to them without the guys catching on.

"I thought you were down to have sex?" Emiko asked. "What changed your mind?"

"You don't get it, something's up. I've never seen him like this before. It was weird. He was so aggressive, he's too much," I quoted Carson to the girls.

Samantha laughed. "Don't act like you don't like it, Leek." She handed me a plate with a slice of greasy pepperoni pizza. "I thought you liked it rough."

I pushed the pizza across the table at my insensitive friend. "I didn't like it. I mean, I do, but I don't right now. I don't know." I rubbed my face and pulled my hair back. "He was so aggressive."

"Isn't that part of your rape fantasy?" She chuckled.

I told the girls I liked it when Marc initiated our hookups and took control with force. They laughed and told me I was weird, and Samantha mocked it by calling it a rape fantasy. Lauren and Emiko said it made sense, considering guys were taboo in my world, they said I could blame it on Marc and not be held responsible.

"Shut the fuck up, Sam, you're so annoying!" I snapped at her. "Can we go?" I said to Lauren, who nodded quietly.

"Come on, guys," she said. "Let's go."

Dear Journal,   Nov. 21, 2001
  I hate how he grabbed me
  He was fucked up. He didn't care.
  He wouldn't stop. He was so fucked up!
  God what the hell have I gotten
  myself into?   I hate him

  I can feel his sweat still on me
  I can smell it in my hair
  His lips were full of power
  His ~~breath~~ whiskey shivered in my ear

  His fingernails were dirty
  as they dug into my thighs
  there was pressure on my chest
  fear screaming through my eyes

  Is it wrong to want him days before
  But push him off tonight
  Is it wrong I ripped his clothes off
  then suddenly changed my mind
          He scared me!

Carson was right. I hate ~~him~~ Marc for proving it
to be true. He was right.

HE WARNED ME:
everyone did

I woke up the next morning to five voicemails on my machine. I had turned off my ringer after coming home the night before, knowing he'd call. I didn't want to talk to him. In his first message at ten forty-five, he sounded sure of himself, calm and confident like he assumed I wasn't home yet. His voice was well paced, and he didn't stumble on any words, and he made sure to leave his name out.

He said, "Maleeka, it's me. When you get this message, please call me."

In the next message, I could hear nothing but him light up a cigarette, take the first pull, let it out, and hang up. That was at eleven thirty. The one after came a half hour later, and he didn't sound good. His voice cracked as he called out, "Maleeka, please. I'm so sorry," and hung up.

At one in the morning, the fourth message was nothing—no words, just empty, cold air filled with heavy, jagged breath. I could hear his tears run down his face. It was the longest message yet. Maybe he was trying to figure out what to say or didn't realize he hadn't hung up. It was nineteen seconds of confusion I translated by his breath.

In his last message at two thirty in the morning, he tried a different tactic to help me remember who he was and what we had. It was Sonny & Cher singing "I Got You Babe." A song I told him I loved because he called me "babe." Before Sonny could finish singing his famous line, I pushed delete. I was mad at him for proving Carson to be right: he *was* too much.

Thanksgiving was beautiful, with a clear blue sky and bright sun that roasted my room. I got up to shower; I wanted to get rid of anything left on me from the night before. Anger, sweat, frustration. I wanted to wash it all away.

"Good morning, Maleeka," my mom said as I walked past her room to grab a towel from the linen closet.

"Hi, Mom," I said to her, with my shoulders slouched and a heavy sigh. She didn't pick up on it. She was busy cleaning off her vanity, throwing her lipstick in the drawer and slamming it shut. As flustered as she was, she looked beautiful. Her blond hair hit her shoulders and gave a whimsical wave to her ends. She wore a true blue sweater with black high-waisted pants and a gold chain with a one-inch cross Dad had bought her while we were in Syria a couple of years back. Mom only wore real gold. She said the costume shit turned her green. I stared at her chain. My poor mom; she did have loads of luxury, but also lots of pain.

"Is everything okay?" I asked her.

"I'm leaving soon to go to Aunt Pat's. Your dad isn't going, so you'll have to ride with Rasheed."

"Oh, okay. That's fine." I didn't question why my dad wasn't going. In all honesty, I liked it more when he wasn't there. I wasn't on edge, wondering if relatives on my mom's side offended him. He told me once Mom's side always treated him differently because he was a foreigner, and after he told me I'd watch for it. I could tell when he'd tense up, or shake his head. Just like I could tell when Mom wasn't happy around his family.

Dear Journal,   Nov. 22, 2001
   Her pain is so obvious. It shines
brighter than her jewelry. It weighs
more than her chain.
   I see it and feel it.

I wonder if she notices mine.
Even if she did ask me what was
wrong, I would have told her
        nothing

I can't tell anyone in this house
what's going on in my life. But still,
I wish someone would notice.

It had been weeks since I spoke to Marc. He tried calling a few more times and even left me a pack of cupcakes in the mailbox to get me to call, but I didn't. I told my mom the cupcakes were from Lauren and threw them away so I wouldn't be tempted to eat them or call him back. I knew I had to be done with him. Eventually he gave up and quit calling. I thought it was what I wanted.

Dear Journal,   Dec. 11th, 2001

It's easier to distract yourself from reality when you keep busy. It's easier to say you're done and put what you're feeling in a box in the back of your brain when you have shit to do. But the distractions are wearing off. He hasn't called me in a while, and even though I have been avoiding his calls all this time, I still can't help but wonder why he stopped.

I should call him, but I don't know what I would say to him.

I devoted my time to my friends again during winter break. Staying out of the house kept me out of my room and away from my phone. I tried to keep up with the beers, the bowls, and the laughter one night around a bonfire at Brandon's house. The girls were cuddled with their boyfriends to stay warm while we all gathered around the fire in clumps of conversations and Jay-Z's *The Blueprint* played loudly.

"You need to have fun, Maleeka," Emiko told me from under Jake's arm. They were always attached to each other.

"I'm having fun," I told her, finishing off my beer. Even though I wasn't. The crew was fun, but as close as I was with them all, I felt alone. I didn't have anyone to cozy up to. They were all my friends, but only my friends. I missed the depth I had with Marc. I missed the undivided attention, the connection, and what Emiko told me he had for me, the obsession. Carson was right, he was too much, but I needed his intense love. I wanted it all back. I grabbed another beer and joined the crowd. Everyone drank to have fun, but I drank to get past my thoughts. I played my own drinking game as the night went on, taking a gulp every time I felt lonely and unseen.

"Maleeka's got the biggest tits of all you girls," Brandon hollered out, drunk, approaching me and getting himself a grab as he put his arm around me.

It was the only compliment I had heard in a while, and though he crossed the line by grabbing me in front of everyone, I let him get away with it, it flattered me, degrading or not. Unfortunately, even if it was scummy, it still felt good.

"Do you want another drink, Maleeka?" he asked me. "Kalvin, give Maleeka a shot!" he called out over my head.

"I'll give you a shot if you show us how big your boobs are!" Kalvin said.

I pulled down my tank top under my zip-up. "They're not that big." I laughed as the guys all got a show of my new pink lace bra.

"Maleeka, stop," Chase said, getting close to me. "What are you doing?" He pulled up my top.

"Relax, Chase, they're just boobs." I pushed him away and took the shot from Kalvin.

"Maleeka, you're fucked up," Jake called out to me from the log he sat on with Emiko.

"So what?" I laughed. "I'm having fun."

"Are you? Or do you want attention?"

That wasn't the first time Jake said that to me. It took me back to when I was thirteen years old in eighth grade. I sat in a car with Jake and two of his friends. One named Charles. I took off my top to let them see and touch my boobs. Jake sat in the front seat, shaking his head, telling me I needed attention as the other guys grabbed and touched me and I let them. I had a crush on Charles, and I would do anything to get him to notice me. But after that night, Charles asked Lauren to the Valentine's Day dance, and I never talked to him again.

I knew Kalvin didn't like me; he just wanted to see my boobs.

"Fuck you, Jake. I love you, but fuck you." I walked away, stumbling through the gravel.

"Where are you going?" Lauren yelled out. "Chase, stop her!"

"I'm fine. I need to go home." I walked into the distance, away from the crowd.

"Maleeka, stop, don't be dramatic. You can't walk home," Chase called out, and caught up to me.

I hated being called dramatic. My mother called me that all the time growing up when I'd get emotional over my parents' fighting, or the rules I had to live by, or the time I cried and told her I thought I was fat.

"Maleeka." Chase grabbed my arm. "Are you okay?"

"I need to let it out, I'll be fine." I got on the ground.

"What are you doing?"

"Cover me, so nobody sees." I squatted by the bush and shoved my fingers to the back of my throat. Chase put his arm around me as I heaved in and out.

"Is she okay?" Lauren shouted out.

"She's fine," Chase yelled to her. "You're fine, Leek, I got you," he whispered, pulling my hair back. "Give me this." He grabbed the hair tie off my wrist and wrapped my hair in a sloppy ponytail to keep it off my face.

"Chase." I looked up at him with tears and sweat on my face. "I don't belong here." I hated the way I acted in an attempt to get attention. I didn't want to be that girl.

"What the fuck, Maleeka, of course you do. You're our girl. I always tell you, you're one of the guys."

"Exactly," I said to myself. I knew my role with my friends: I was an accessory. I wanted to be more than that. I stood up off the gravel and wiped the tiny pebbles off my knees. "Will you take me home, Chase?"

He nodded and put his arm around my waist to help me to his car. I loved that I was close to them all, but there was a big piece missing by being friend-zoned. There was a level of love that wasn't touched, a depth of love I needed.

Dear Journal, Dec. 15th, 2001

Jake is right, I do need attention.
But not from those guys!
I can't do it anymore, I need Marc.
Nothing else matters. I don't care anymore
about that night in Carson's truck.
I don't hate him. I want him back the
way I had him before.
I want to call him, but I'm scared.
What would I say to him?

You Are too much — but it doesn't matter
You're not here — that's what's wrong
You have no boundaries
I don't either
When it comes to you, I'm too far gone

Who am I to think I'm better
There's no better than you
empty eyes
shallow guys
none compare come close to you

TOO MUCH

It's what I need

I sat in my bed, still feeling a little buzz, and grabbed my phone. I don't know if it was the last shot I took or the desperation that pushed me to call him that night, but I had to talk to him.

"Is this Maleeka?" his mom said before I told her who I was.

I had no idea she knew my name, or knew I existed. But it made sense. Marc wouldn't have to hide me or my name from his parents.

"Yeah, it is." I straightened up my slouching shoulders immediately as if I were meeting her in person. "I'm sorry to be calling so late, I thought Marc would have the phone."

"Don't worry, you didn't wake anyone. Marc isn't home yet, but I will have him call you as soon as he gets home."

"Okay, thank you. Again, I am sorry it's so late." If our house phone rang at eleven thirty at night, Dad would be losing his shit. It was crazy to me that she was so chill about it all.

"Don't sweat it. Have a good night, Maleeka. I hope to meet you in person soon," she said.

"Thank you, Mrs. Osbourne."

"Call me Suzy," she said.

I nodded my head, again as if she could see me. "Good night, Suzy."

I stayed up as long as I could, waiting for him to call me back. I figured he would be thrilled to hear I had called. I fell asleep without a call back and woke up in the morning without a missed call or voicemail.

I Feel ♥ Your Heart ♥

I made a well-explained excuse the first night he didn't call me back. I told myself maybe his mom fell asleep before he got home so he didn't know I called. But the next day he didn't call either, or the next. Not the entire week leading up to Christmas.

I told Marc once that Christmas Eve was my favorite holiday, not Christmas. Christmas meant it was over, but Christmas Eve was filled with hope and anticipation for the next day. I loved looking forward to occasions more than living them. He laughed when I told him that; he said, "But you don't get gifts on Christmas Eve." And he promised he'd deliver a gift for me on my favorite holiday, not the day after. When I woke up that morning, I had to check the mailbox. As I walked downstairs I pictured a cupcake, a CD, maybe even a poem. I was confident that it would be the perfect way to reconnect and slip the night in Carson's truck and the avoidance after the fact under the rug. I even went so far as to think maybe he wasn't calling me back so I would be that much more surprised to find the gift Christmas Eve morning. How romantic.

It was empty.

That hurt more than the unreturned call. Did he forget? Or was it a promise he couldn't keep since I pushed him out of my life? Whatever the reason, the empty mailbox on Christmas Eve morning told me he was done with me, and I knew it was all my fault. I wished more than anything I could go back to that night, to those five voicemails I deleted. Had I answered, we could've resolved the issue together. But I didn't know how to handle the conflict; all I knew was taught to me by my parents. Avoid it long enough until it blows over. Marc was not like my parents. He told me once that conflict can create connection. I cut that cord.

I walked back upstairs to take a shower. I turned on the water and let it run until it was warm enough and pushed play on my CD player. It was the Destiny's Child album *Survivor.* I skipped to the track "Emotion" and let myself cry in the shower. My tears didn't feel as big as they would otherwise; they blended in with the warm water washing them down as if they weren't there. I put my arms up on the wall under the showerhead, with my eyes closed, wondering where the hell he was, and what he was doing. I needed him.

When "Brown Eyes" came on, I remembered the first day he smiled at me while on stage. I remembered the first time he called me, the first time we hung out, the first time he told me he loved me, and the time I told him this was our song, but "*Blue* Eyes" instead of brown. He laughed. I knew he loved it.

I sat on my bed on top of the covers, wrapped up in my bathrobe, with a towel in my hair. I couldn't take my eyes off my phone. I hated that I had deleted his voicemails. I wanted to hear his voice; I missed his raspy tone, his upbeat hellos, his soft good-nights, the way he'd tell me, "I'm stoked on you, babe."

I could hear commotion downstairs between my parents. Something about "I don't care if you don't come." And the front door shut. I looked out the window to see my mom pull out of the driveway in her Lexus they bought a few summers before. Everyone was happy that day, especially Dad.

"Maleeka?" I heard my dad's voice before he knocked on my door. My dad didn't come to my room often. I don't think he appreciated Eminem staring at me on the wall or the pictures of all my friends. I hung those pictures up on purpose to show my family that regardless of the rules, I cared about those people.

"Come in," I said softly.

"Hi, *habibti.*" That means sweetheart in Arabic. "Are you okay?" His interest immediately brought fresh tears to my eyes.

"What's going on, Maleeka?" he asked me, taking a couple of steps into the room.

I didn't say anything. I sat on the edge of my bed and wiped a tear off my face with my hand. I couldn't tell my dad what was wrong. I couldn't tell him how much I missed Marc even though he had crossed a line and almost fucked me in the back of his friend's truck. I couldn't tell him I flashed a bunch of guys in hopes I would feel better about myself, but it made me feel stupid. I couldn't tell him how heartbroken I felt to find the mailbox empty.

"Maleeka, if it's because of your mom and me—"

"Dad." I looked up, taking a deep breath in. "It's not about you or Mom."

"Well, what is it?"

I shook my head and grabbed the towel wrapped around my hair to bury my head into it and cry harder.

He came up to me and knelt down at my bedside. I didn't know what to do. I hadn't been consoled by my dad in a long time. I wasn't a little girl anymore who would let him wrap his dark hairy arms around me while I cried over falling off my bike. I was tangled up in hurt and heartache he would go ballistic over.

"I want you happy, Maleeka. I want to see you smile. Do you know how beautiful your smile is? It lights up this whole house," he said, stern like he was lecturing me. He got up to point at the picture of Raneem, Rasheed, and me on the shelf behind him. Raneem and Rasheed were posing politely for the camera, and I was hugging Raneem's waist with a big, cheesy smile on my face. "Look at that picture of you three. I feel your love through that picture. I feel your heart coming out of that picture. You should always be happy. You're my heart. You are the heart of this family. If anyone ever helps this family, it will be you, Maleeka."

My dad was the emotional parent between the two of them; just as he expressed his anger, he also expressed his love. It was stern and forceful but real. But I knew I could never be close to him, being close meant being honest, and I couldn't tell him anything about me that wouldn't disappoint him. I kept things surface and told him he didn't have to worry about me and I would be fine. Always.

2 different Holidays

Aunt Pat and Uncle Stewart's house was staged like a Christmas movie. They had a massive tree decorated with delicate ornaments next to the grand piano Aunt Pat would play "Silver Bells" on. She'd bring out her fancy china and set the dining table centered with poinsettias and candles. There weren't many of us, so we could all fit at one table.

I could tell they were talking about a serious subject when we walked in. Everyone stopped and looked up at us, and Mom's face was a little flushed.

"Pour me a drink, would you, Maleeka?" my grandma told me after I gave everyone a Christmas Eve hug. All my aunts liked their wine like my mom did, but Grandma Rowe, she loved her vodka.

I poured the vodka over fresh ice into her glass and counted to three in my head—*one Mississippi, two Mississippi, three Mississippi*—then threw a splash of orange juice over the top. Screwdrivers were Grandma's thing. It was a well-known joke among my cousins that the orange juice in Grandma's fridge was spiked. It was almost as if the vodka was part of her personality. She was a spitfire, and I found her comebacks and callouts amusing, unless she talked shit about Dad.

Uncle Stewart was the only adult man at our functions, unless Aunt Linda brought a date. He sat at the head of the table to give grace and carve the turkey. I picked at the small portion on my plate; I didn't have much of an appetite. Raneem was home from college and told us about a guy who worked at the bookstore on campus and their awkward encounters.

"I think he's catching on to my daily visits." She laughed.

Raneem's laugh and chatter about a cute guy brought life to the table; she had everyone engaged. I wasn't sure if it was the medicine that helped or the therapist she was seeing in Boston, probably both. I looked over at Rasheed. He didn't laugh, but he also didn't tell her to shut up. He would never sit quietly if I talked about a boy at the dinner table. I wondered if he was relieved to see her talk with energy again. I think everyone was.

"You've got to quit wearing those baggy clothes, Raneem," my grandma called out to her. "Show him what you got. If you got it, flaunt it."

We all laughed at Grandma.

"I prayed while I was pregnant with Raneem that if it was a girl, all that height from me and her dad would go to her tits." My mom laughed.

"And it sure did, for both of them," Aunt Pat said.

"Okay, I'm done eating." Rasheed put his fork down and shook his head.

Grandma laughed. We all did as she told Rasheed to relax.

"Are you going to Sitto's for dessert?" I asked my mom across the table.

She shook her head.

"Maleeka," Uncle Stewart said. "You need to start sticking up for your mom around them."

"You mean the sands?" I said, looking at my plate. Uncle Stewart was a Vietnam vet who wore an American flag shirt every time I saw him. I couldn't help but translate his pride into hate for those who weren't American. Especially since Dad told me that he referred to Dad and his family as "sands."

"What was that?"

"Nothing." I got up and put my plate in the kitchen.

I wished Dad had never told me about the "sands" comment. It was hard to be around Uncle Stewart knowing he thought that way about them. About us.

"Brenda made her bed with those Arabs," my grandma said as I walked back to the table. "She has to lie in it."

I hated the way my grandma said *Arabs*. She made the first *A* a long one, like she was mocking them. I could talk shit about my Arab family, but I hated when someone who wasn't Arab did.

I looked at my mom, who didn't say anything. I understood why she wouldn't want to go. There was no place for her to be at my dad's parents' house. She wasn't involved in the Syrian food prep with the women, and the men wouldn't let her play cards with them. She told me once when she first married my dad that she asked to play cards, and they all looked at her like she was crazy. Women didn't play cards with the men. I understood why she'd want to stay at my aunt's house and play Trivial Pursuit with them all.

"Ay huh!" my grandfather yelled as we walked in, slamming his cards on the table to show off his royal flush.

Sitto and Jiddo's house was different from Aunt Pat's. It was two different holidays. There were way more people, so we couldn't all fit at one table. The men all sat at the dining table, and the women catered to them. The only thing I'd see an uncle or older guy cousin do for themselves was pour their own glass of whiskey. There was no Christmas music playing, but rather old cassette recordings of music from the village they're from.

I circled around the table and gave them all my cheek while they kept their eyes on their cards and leaned in to kiss me. Nobody asked where my mom was. I wondered if they cared.

"Salim, you want a piece of baklava?" my aunt called out to her husband, who sat at the table, staring at his deck. He didn't answer her.

"Salim?" she said again. I looked up at her and back down at my uncle, who still didn't say anything.

She brought a plate over to him and hesitated before she asked again, "Do you want a piece?"

He clenched his teeth. "God damn it just put it down!" he said with his eyes still on his hand of cards.

I took a piece of baklava and told my aunt how delicious it was. She looked defeated and worn out. She had slaved in the kitchen and over that tray of baklava. Nobody told my uncle he was an ass to talk to her like that. That was just the way it was. I hated the dynamic between men and women on my dad's side. I didn't want that for myself. I wanted a man who appreciated me, who encouraged me, and who praised me.

When I got home that night, I ran to my phone. Still nothing. I hated that I had pushed him away.

I called him Christmas morning, assuming he'd be home. Everyone was home on Christmas morning. His mom told me he wasn't; I didn't believe her. I felt stupid picturing him shake his head as Suzy said, "Hi, Maleeka." I felt sick knowing he wouldn't want to talk to me. Every day he didn't call me back hurt more than the day before. By New Year's Eve, the girls all had opinions on what I should do about him.

"Maybe it's time you let it go, I mean, there are so many other guys out there," Lauren told me as she did my makeup for the annual Syrian Club New Year's party. Dad insisted we all had to go as a family, sans Raneem, who had left that morning to go back to Boston.

"Like who?" I opened my eyelids she had applied makeup to and closed them again. "I'm not like you, Ren, I don't have guys falling at my feet."

"What are you going to do, keep calling him?" Samantha said, and flipped through a magazine on my bed. "You have to stop, for your pride if nothing else."

"I do feel pretty stupid," I said as Lauren backed away and handed me the mascara to put on myself.

"He's confused, Maleeka, and hurt," Emiko told me, leaning up against the wall. She had the inside scoop from Jake on how Marc was doing.

"He could at least call her back," Samantha said.

"It took Maleeka weeks before she called him back," Emiko told Samantha.

I didn't say anything. She was right.

"I'm sorry, Leek. Try to understand where he's coming from. I know he still loves you."

I got up to get dressed and let out a sigh of relief. Hearing that reminded me of the poem he wrote me, our love was parallel, and I still loved him. I put on my dress in my closet and came out.

"Damn!" Samantha threw the magazine down. "Maybe you'll find a Syrian guy tonight in that tight-ass dress."

"Yeah right, I would never." I shook my head.

The extension of our Syrian family went out even further to other Syrians referred to as "the community." A bigger group of people we had to behave around. They filled their days with idle gossip and searched for imperfections to highlight with rumors, and they ousted anyone who lived an alternative lifestyle. I was not excited to be spending New Year's Eve with them.

The rented hall was dimmed with low lights on the ceiling and a big balloon drop hanging. There were shiny silver tablecloths and streamers you'd find at a dollar store and what were supposed to be balloon weights used as centerpieces with tiny stars at the end of each wire. The background music played low enough for people to mingle before the live band took over.

"Why did we have to come here tonight?" I asked my mom as we walked in behind Dad and Rasheed.

"What else are we going to do?" my mom asked as she waited to say hello to a distant cousin of my dad's. Dad made us say hi to every person at the party. We would follow behind him as he showed us off like a prize.

"I could think of a million other things than to hang out here, Mom."

"Just play along, Maleeka. That's what I do."

My mother reminded me of Princess Diana as she walked through the crowd. Not only did she resemble her, but she "played along" and did her best in a world she didn't belong in. She shook the man's hand and turned to me as she told him what grade I was in. He took my hand, and I smiled politely, giving both cheeks to him to kiss before we walked over to the next table behind Dad and Rasheed.

"Brenda, I want your youngest for Jamil," I heard a woman tell my mom while they pressed cheeks together in front of me. "She's beautiful. I want my son to marry her."

I walked up to her with a forced smile on my face to say hello. Growing up, this woman had always made it clear she wanted Raneem for her only son, Jamil. He had a crush on Raneem, and his mother approved because Raneem was beautiful and came from a good family.

"You're beautiful, honey," she told me after the kisses she gave me.

I kept my lips closed without a word and maintained the same forced grin.

"How's Raneem?" she asked my mom.

"Good, she's back in Boston."

"You sure she's good?" She tilted her head and looked at me with her arm still around my waist. My shoulders rolled back in defense. I knew from the side-eye she gave me she had heard something. "I heard she's seeing a therapist."

"She's fine," I said as I slithered out of her grasp.

Mom nodded. "She had a rough patch, but thank God, she's doing well."

"Good." She looked back at me, and I put my head down. "Be a good girl, Maleeka." She pinched my cheek. "I want you as my daughter-in-law someday."

I didn't say anything. Everything I wanted to say would go against the "respect your elders" rule we had to abide.

"I thought Jamil had a crush on Raneem," I told my mom as we walked away.

"Well, if he did, he doesn't anymore. Nobody here will go for your sister now that they know she's not perfect."

I hated that they knew about Raneem. I hated that they thought she wasn't good enough anymore. I also hated that I cared what they thought. Everyone in that hall pretended to be perfect, and I knew they pretended because we did too. Mom and Dad sat together, mingled together, and played nice in front of everyone, and God knows they weren't perfect.

They asked everyone to take their seats so the Arab band could get the party going. Instead, I went to find Asma. She stood in the lobby by the bar with Waleed. All the young teens hung out in the lobby. I got a drink while Rasheed chatted it up with a cute Syrian girl who was not following the rule that you weren't to talk to a guy alone so rumors wouldn't get started. I stayed close with Asma and Waleed since they were the only people I liked at the party.

"You're looking pretty hot, Asma." I smiled at her and handed her a drink.

"Oh, thanks." She looked down.

"Be careful in that dress. You're going to get a lot of looks tonight."

"Me? What about you? Michael is totally checking you out." She raised her eyebrows to a guy standing behind me. I knew he was. I saw him staring at me in my tight black dress while I ordered our drinks.

"Whatever. Let him."

"Go talk to him. We'll go with you so it doesn't look obvious to everyone."

"I'm not going to talk to him. He's just scoping out any available Arab girl to snatch up because he has to. He doesn't like me."

"Yeah, you're probably right." Asma laughed. All the guys in the Arab community were expected to only marry within their culture. It didn't give them many girls to choose from.

"We're in a fishbowl. A handful of girls for them to pick from. I'd like to be more special than a one-out-of-ten ratio." I grabbed my straw and took a drink of my Jack and Coke. Getting drunk was the only way I would have fun there.

"Is there whiskey in here?" Asma looked at me after taking a sip of her drink.

"Yeah." I smiled. "Have fun, Asma, you deserve it."

"Don't force her to drink," Waleed said.

"It's fine," Asma said. "It's actually pretty good."

Waleed shook his head.

"What did you do last night? We called you to come over to Sitto and Jiddo's," Asma asked me.

"I know, but I was out with friends."

"I told you, Asma, her friends come first. She doesn't care about us," Waleed said.

"Of course I do, but I had plans."

"You always have plans, Maleeka." Waleed rolled his eyes.

"We decided these are your lost years." Asma laughed.

"Why do you say that?"

"You don't have much to do with the family. You're lost, but you'll come back." She smiled.

"There's more to life than the family, Asma, or this community."

"What, like partying?" Waleed said.

"Oh, shut up, Waleed. It's not like all I do is party!"

"That's all you do," he snapped back. "These *are* her lost years."

I did feel lost, but not because I didn't hang out with the family. Rather lost while I was with them, and the community. It felt phony and forced. Marc was real, and I was my most authentic self while I was with him: seen and understood and valued. He accepted Raneem's story with compassion, and he didn't want me because I was a good girl or came from a good family. He loved me for me. I knew in my world he was taboo, but after spending time with the family and the community, I was convinced *that* world didn't know what was best. That world thought my sister wasn't good enough, which was complete bullshit.

I had to do something big to show him how much I loved him. Something bigger than a phone call, I had to go out of my comfort zone to take away all the confusion Emiko told me he felt.

Dec. 31, 2001

THESE ARE YOUR
Lost Years
—ASMA

Lost in the chaos
Lost in my heart
Torn up without you

I know it's my **Fault**

It's hard to know I've hurt you
But I have to say
It does make me feel better
knowing you're not okay

It reminds me that you love me
even though I cut you out
It butters up my heartache
that you're hurt and filled with doubt

You still care

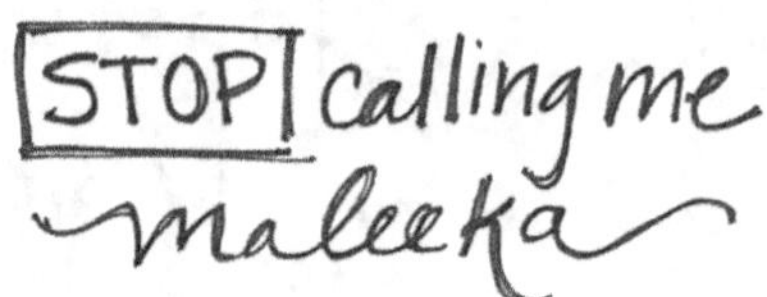

The next evening after my hangover wore off, I walked up to Marc's house alone. I had never been to his house before. I was nervous. I kept what Emiko told me on repeat in my mind. *He still loves me, he still loves me*—God I hoped he still loved me.

His mom opened the door in a long bathrobe over her pajamas, with a cup of tea in her hand. "Maleeka?" she said.

"Hi, Mrs. Osbourne." I smiled and looked down. I was surprised she knew it was me. I had never seen her before.

"You look just like Marc described you." She smiled.

I wrapped my hair behind my ear. I was sure Marc exaggerated what he thought was beautiful about me. For her to agree made me blush. "Is he home?"

"Come in." She opened the door farther. Their home was different from mine; they had red walls covered with picture frames all over. It was cluttered but cozy.

"Marc, you have company." His mom walked me into their family room.

He sat on the sofa, wearing sweatpants, a hoodie, and thin-rimmed glasses. I had never seen him in glasses before. He looked soft like the fuzzy blanket he shared with his younger sister sitting next to him.

His eyes shot up at me, and he dropped the bowl of popcorn to his lap.

"What are you doing here?"

"Marc!" His sister looked at him with big eyes.

"No, I mean . . . I'm sorry, that was rude, I'm just shocked."

I nodded my head and held on to my hands that were shaking. "Can we talk?"

He threw his side of the blanket on his sister and got up.

"I'm Nora," his sister said to me.

"Hi, Nora, I'm Maleeka."

"I know." She smiled.

He walked me to the front door, past his mom, who smiled over the top of her teacup.

"She's pretty," I heard Nora say to her mom.

"Yeah, she sure is," Suzy said.

As we walked through the hallway out the front door, I noticed boxes piled up against the wall, with big words written in Sharpie: *MARC'S CLOTHES, BOOKS, DISHES.*

"What's going on, Maleeka?" he said as he took his glasses off and put them in his front hoodie pocket. I hated that he called me Maleeka, he hadn't called me by my name since we first started talking. It made me feel like I was nothing special to him, like a stranger, or a girl he just hooked up with because he was drunk.

"Are you moving out?" I asked him as we made it to the bottom of the staircase leading up to his house.

"Yeah, I found a place. I move in this weekend."

"Wow, that's big news. I had no idea," I told him.

"How would you, you cut me out of your life."

"I called you—"

He wouldn't let me finish. "Maleeka, I was going crazy!" he said, taking a few steps back with his palms out. "You cut me out! I lost my mind, I was sick—"

"I was mad and I didn't know what to say to you," I interrupted him.

He put his hands to his sides. "You could have at least heard me out, let me tell you how sorry I was."

It got quiet. We both stopped talking and took in a deep breath from the air between us. I didn't know how to have a conversation like that. I never heard the word *sorry* at home. After every fight or dramatic evening with my parents, sorry was never a thing. We didn't talk about it or hear each other out. We just moved on, or we were expected to.

I took a couple of steps closer to him. "I'm sorry I didn't call sooner."

He sat on the second step of the staircase, with his shoulders hunched over and lit up a cigarette. "I'm sorry if I scared you, or hurt you." He took a hit and blew the smoke to the ground we were both staring at. "You know how much I love you."

I shot my head up. "You still love me?" Hearing him tell me he loved me meant more to me than him telling me he was sorry.

"Of course I do." He looked up at me. "But I don't think I can keep doing this. I can't love someone I can't have."

That's why he wasn't calling me back; he was trying to fall out of love with me. That scared me. Losing his love scared me more than he did that night in Carson's truck. I knew he was too much, I knew he loved too hard, but I needed that love.

"You have no idea how fucked up I've been over all of this, Maleeka."

"Please, stop calling me Maleeka."

"What do you want from me?" His eyes looked lost, like he had no control. I hated seeing him look helpless. He took another drag and shook his head. "I can't do this, Maleeka."

I grabbed his cigarette from his hand and put it out. He smoked to help himself get through the conversation, but he didn't need that cigarette as much as he needed me. "Marc." I stood between his legs, looking down at him. "I love you."

"What did you say?" He looked at me with a highlighted tear in his eye from the reflection of the streetlight behind me. The only time I had told him I loved him was when I was half-asleep on the phone. I had never said it consciously to his face, looking in his eyes.

I put my hand against his cheek. "I love you, will you be my boyfriend?"

"But you're not allowed."

I smiled at him. "You can be my secret. God knows I'm good at keeping those."

He stood up and grabbed the back of my neck. "You sure about this, Maleeka?"

"Marc, please." I pressed my forehead against his. "Stop calling me Maleeka."

He pulled me in to kiss him. It was the perfect kiss, full of passion and relief. Even his tear dropped and rolled down to my lips.

"A secret is enough for me, babe."

That word *babe* made my shoulders fall back, and I collapsed on his chest. I got my peace back, wrapped in his love.

It was a quick journal entry, but it was the most confident and sure entry I had ever written. I did it for myself without the consent of anyone else. I knew it was best. I got in bed feeling different, like I had grown up. I felt independent and self-assured. I trusted in myself more than ever before and I felt normal. Like a normal teenage girl.

Marc getting his own place changed everything. After he settled in that weekend, he called me to come check it out, and I did without hesitation. It was a private space, so I didn't have to worry about anyone finding out.

The tiny two-bedroom apartment sat on the first floor of a building that hadn't had an update since it was built in the early eighties. The exterior was painted an old-lady yellow with white trim, and the interior only had lights installed in the kitchen and bathroom. The other rooms were lit with table lamps, giving little light through the beige shades. Samantha, Emiko, and I walked through the dark hallway, with Marc holding my hand.

"Finn, this is Maleeka," Marc said to his roommate.

Finn looked harmless on the couch in the dimmed living room, watching a Bob Marley concert on a twenty-seven-inch box TV. He wore a flannel button-up with baggy jeans and fuzzy old-man slippers.

He looked up at me with his sincere almond eyes and stood up to reach for my hand. "No way, this is Maleeka?" He smiled at me.

"It's nice to meet you," I said to Finn as we shook hands.

"Holy shit, Marc, you said beautiful, but I didn't think *this* beautiful," he said.

I looked at Marc smiling at me. "Isn't she?" he said as he leaned back against the wall.

"These are my friends Emiko and Samantha." I turned around to face the girls behind me.

"Damn, you're all gorgeous," he said. "Nice to meet you, girls." Finn shook their hands. "You're welcome here any time." He laughed as he patted Marc on the shoulder and walked to the kitchen to grab a bong and bring it over as we all got settled.

I sat between Emiko and Samantha on the couch. The couch was ugly; it was seventies brown with orange and red stitched into the plaid and the cushions worn. Like everything else in their apartment, it was a hand-me-down.

"Go sit next to your boyfriend!" Samantha pushed me away from her with her shoulder. Marc sat on a futon on the other side of the room, loading the bong.

"Oh, sorry." I got up to walk toward him.

I didn't know how to be a girlfriend. I felt clumsy in front of everyone, my body language inexpert. I didn't know how to show any public display of affection. My parents sure as hell didn't teach me any; I remember seeing their hands interlocked over the console in the car once on a road trip, and it was awkward.

"Don't worry about that shit, babe. You can sit wherever you want." He blew out a smoke cloud big enough to fill the space between us.

"Well, now I don't know what to do." I laughed, standing awkwardly in the middle of the room.

"Have you ever had a boyfriend, Maleeka?" Finn asked before taking a hit himself.

I shook my head. "I guess I don't know the rules of being a girlfriend."

"Sit with the girls, babe. That way I can stare at you." He smiled at me.

As the bong went around the circle, we girls dominated the conversation with our enthusiasm, and told stories. The guys listened to our chatter.

"Marc, you should have seen Maleeka last night." Samantha laughed, handing me the bong.

"Shut up, Sam. I wasn't that drunk." I laughed along and took a hit.

"Yeah, you were! She was going off about you and about your blue eyes. What was the song she made us listen to all night?" She leaned over to look at Emiko.

"Something about his eyes when he says he loves her." Emiko laughed, taking the bong to Finn. "It was pretty cheesy."

"It's a good song!" I said, putting my hand over my left eye. "Tonic."

"She must have been drunk." Marc laughed.

"What! Why do you say that?" I took my hand off my face and looked at him through the smoke.

"You aren't very open around people about how you feel about me."

"Just give her a few drinks." Samantha laughed. "She'll open up to anyone."

"Whatever." I wanted to change the subject. "We brought snacks!"

"Oh, now you want to eat?" Samantha said with a side-eye.

"She's eating 'cause she's happy." Emiko smiled at Marc.

"Or stoned." I laughed.

I passed the brown paper bag around to offer to everyone before I grabbed a yellow Laffy Taffy. I preferred fruity candy over chocolate while stoned. The juicy flavor helped produce moisture in my mouth.

"Do you guys want to hear my joke?" I said, chewing.

"Those jokes are so stupid." Emiko laughed.

"They're funny!" I said. "Why is a bad joke like a bad pencil?" I looked up at everyone.

"Just tell us." Samantha laughed and lay back on the sofa.

"It's good, are you ready?"

"Tell us!" Emiko reached for the wrapper.

"See, you're dying to know!"

"Oh my God, Maleeka." Finn laughed.

"Okay, okay, it's like a bad pencil because it has no point!" I laughed like a little kid.

"Damn, babe, you *are* cheesy." Marc laughed while the others shook their heads. I think Marc liked it when I was silly 'cause he could be too. And he looked lighter and happier when I was happy.

"It ain't easy being cheesy," I told them in my British accent, imitating the Spice Girls. I thought it was spot-on after spending my entire sixth-grade year pretending to be Ginger Spice.

"What was that?" Samantha laughed. "You sound like Forrest Gump's mom."

"The Spice Girls."

Finn laughed. "You are a spice girl, Maleeka."

<u>every</u> PART OF ME

The girls stayed longer than I thought they would, but I was glad they did and had fun. I walked them to the front door after they said their goodbyes to Marc and Finn.

"Have fun tonight, Leek," Samantha told me. It was going to be my first sleepover with Marc. "Remember, enjoy it and relax." She gave me a hug.

I nodded. I had told the girls earlier that I was nervous for our first night together alone in a room with a bed. We never had the luxury of a bed before, and I knew he would go down on me, and that meant his face between my thighs. I hated my thighs, especially the insides of them. That's where the dimples were.

Emiko grabbed my shoulders. "He loves you, that means every part of you."

"I know." I smiled as she shook my shoulders.

"Call me in the morning, and I'll pick you up," Samantha said as they walked away.

"Thanks, Sam, I owe you."

I went back to the living room and found it empty. Marc and Finn had gone out to have a cigarette on the patio. I fumbled through the stack of books on the side table next to the sofa and read names I recognized from Raneem's bookshelf: Hunter S. Thompson, Charles Bukowski, and Chuck Palahniuk. *God,* I thought to myself, *Raneem would love Marc.*

"You reading?" Marc said at the sliding door as I flipped through the pages of the novel *Choke.*

I stopped on a page that held his bookmark and smiled. It was our masterpiece we made in detention. I loved that he still had it.

"Read the back," he told me.

I unfolded the blue-lined paper and turned it over to find his scratchy handwriting with typewriter lowercase *a*'s and *g*'s. I read inside my head, *Her stare ignites my path. They guide me through hollows. The streak of hazel is my compass, leading me to landings obscure, immaculate, and longed for.*

I wanted to ask him what *obscure* meant, but I didn't want to break the romance—I knew what *longed for* meant, and that was enough.

"Man, you must really love this girl." I looked up at him.

"It's her eyes." He smiled and reached for my hand.

I closed the book and grabbed my purse to follow him to his room.

"You guys calling it a night?" Finn asked us.

"I'll be back out for a cigarette," Marc said. He always smoked a cigarette after we were done fooling around.

"I can't believe I'm in your room." I looked around while I put my purse by his bed in the middle of the room. It wasn't a real bed; it was a mattress and box spring with no frame or bedposts. He had a fitted sheet wrapped around the mattress and one blanket crumpled up on the edge. There was a dresser across from the bed, and a lamp shared the outlet closest to his mattress with a fan on high. They both sat on the floor next to more books.

He shut his bedroom door. "It's not much," he said, scratching the back of his neck.

"Hey, it's better than those hard bleachers."

"Come here." He reached out to me and put his palm on my face, but he didn't kiss me; he stared at me. I kept my eyes on his chest, wondering what he was doing. I wanted to know what he was looking at, what he was thinking, and why he wasn't throwing me on the bed like I assumed he would.

"I want to do this right," he told me. "No more fuckups, no more fights."

I nodded.

"Babe." He propped my jaw up to make eye contact like he was giving me a lecture and needed my full attention to prove his case. But the eye contact cut his lecture short. I bit my lip while looking at him with a grin. And he lost it.

"Fuck," he said, kissing me. His lips trembled, and we got down to his bed.

Just relax, I told myself as he unbuttoned my pants. Marc had had his fingers down there plenty of times, but never his mouth.

"Marc, wait." I put my hands over my crotch. He looked up at me.

"Are you okay?"

"Can we turn off the light?"

"Maleeka, you are gorge—"

"Please, it will be better with the lights off." The lights off meant less exposure.

He did as I asked and got back on top of me and kissed me. "Are you sure you're okay with this?"

I nodded my head. I was glad he asked.

He kissed my neck and my chest, and when he got to my hips, I put my hands over my eyes. Maybe if I closed my eyes, it wouldn't be as scary. He held on to my hips and squeezed my flesh with his fingers, which set off a wet sensation. It was one thing for him to feel it with his fingers, but to taste it with his mouth made me panic. What if I was too wet, would that gross him out?

"Babe," he said, and I looked down at him. "I love you," he told me before he kissed the inside of what I thought was my fat thigh. I took in a deep breath and nodded as I lay back and let myself enjoy it, knowing he did love every part of me, even though I didn't.

"Marc." Finn knocked on the door. "You still at it? Rob's here."

"Oh my God, Marc," I whispered as I grabbed my shirt off the floor. "He knows we were messing around."

"Babe, you're my girlfriend," he told me, like that was supposed to make me feel better.

"What if they heard me?"

"Who cares if they did?" He leaned in and kissed me on the cheek; I wouldn't let him kiss my lips after his tongue was inside me. "Give me a minute," he yelled out to Finn, getting up off the bed. "Come on, you have to meet Rob."

Rob was Marc's best friend. I'd heard all about him, but I had never met him. He dropped out of high school before I got there.

"I have to freshen up," I said, turning my face toward the fan. I needed a few minutes for the air to cool me off and for my heart rate to go down after what felt like my first orgasm.

"Take your time, come out when you're ready."

I opened his bedroom door with a freshly powdered face and a new layer of lip gloss. The hallway was dark, but the living room lamps were on, and I could hear girls laughing. Marc leaned against the wall, facing the sofa so only he could see me walk through the hall. He reached his arm out before I made it to the living room, cuing the crowd I was approaching. I was nervous to see who was there, who knew I was coming out of his room. As soon as I reached the living room, I put a smile on my face.

"Rob, this is Maleeka." Marc smiled.

Rob sat on a skateboard with his back to me, knees up and his arms on them. He wore baggy dark-blue jeans with navy plaid boxers showing. And his white Volcom T-shirt made him look tan. He got up off the skateboard and turned around with a big smile as white as his T.

"What's up, Maleeka? I've heard so much about you." He put his arms out and gave me a hug. I let go of Marc's hand and wrapped them around Rob like we had been friends for a while.

"Same." I smiled with my chin hitting his broad shoulder.

Marc spoke highly of Rob, so I loved him before I met him. I looked over his shoulder and saw Amelia and Karen on the couch. They didn't look too happy to see me. Amelia was Rob's girlfriend. I let go of him.

"You remember the girls?" Marc said to me. I nodded. I hadn't made a good first impression in the parking lot the summer before when I barely looked at them or Marc.

"Yeah, hi." I smiled as big as I could. I had to redeem myself.

I stayed close to Marc on the futon and didn't talk much. They all intimidated me—well, the girls. Not so much the guys. It was easier to be myself in front of the guys. But the girls were a tough crowd. I didn't know what to do when Marc got up to go have a smoke with Finn and Rob. Karen went with them, but Amelia didn't smoke.

She sat on the sofa and grabbed her purse to pull out an *InStyle* magazine. Maybe we could be friends.

It was silent for a while.

"How old are you, Maleeka?" she asked with her eyes on the magazine, flipping through the pages.

"I'll be sixteen in a few weeks."

"You're only fifteen?" She finally made eye contact with me and put the magazine in her lap.

"Yeah." I dipped my chin to my chest and picked at my fingernails. We sat in silence for a moment. I think she could tell she made me nervous.

"I like that color," she told me. "Where do you get your nails done?"

I told her the name of my salon, and she told me hers as the guys walked in. Marc sat next to me with a smile on his face and put his arm around me. I think he was as relieved as I was that we were talking. I wanted all his friends to like me.

PLAYING HOUSE

I loved being Marc's girlfriend. For the first time maybe ever, I was in control of my own life. I was able to have my own story. But I knew I was still different from my peers. Most girls dated in high school. Their boyfriends walked them to class, kissed them hello in the main hall, and saved them a seat at spirit assemblies. Dating Marc was nothing like that. Instead, we made out in his kitchen while he warmed up dinner, I had a designated spot on the sofa next to him while we watched TV, and, instead of walking me to class, he walked me to his bedroom to fool around. We fell asleep in his bed without worrying about anyone finding us—his parents or mine. We played house, and I loved it. I loved watching him make me a cup of coffee in the kitchen or bring me a blanket if I fell asleep on the sofa. Even watching skate videos with him, something I would never do alone, while I did my homework made me happy. We were like a grown-up relationship, not a typical high school love story.

Lauren dropped me off after school one day. She pulled up to the apartment and left her car in drive.

"Don't you want to come in?" I asked her as if it were my own house.

"I can't, Zach's coming over," she told me.

"Okay." I unbuckled my seatbelt.

"You're so lucky he has his own place," she said. "You can do whatever you want."

"Zach's always sleeping over at your house," I told her.

"But it's always awkward knowing my parents are upstairs."

"Your parents don't care. You can do whatever you want."

"And now you can." She smiled at me.

I gave her a hug and ran inside, through the pouring rain. I walked in through the sliding door like I owned the place. I didn't use the front door anymore.

"What's up, Maleeka?" Finn said in the kitchen, making soup, humming as he searched for a ladle while Jake played around on the guitar, tuning it.

"Hi, Finn." I threw my backpack on the floor and gave Marc a kiss.

"How was your day, babe?" he said.

"Good." I grabbed my notebook and pulled out my English paper. "You got me an A." I smiled.

"Fuck yeah." He laughed.

"You're doing her homework now?" Jake smiled as he shook his head. "Maybe you can do mine too."

"You can't pay him back the way I do, Jake." I laughed and gave Marc another kiss.

I got comfortable on the couch while Marc brought Jake a beer. I had been to my fair share of parties where there was weed on the tables and beers passed around, but their apartment was different. There was nothing to hide, no reason to go hard while the adults were out of the house. They were the adults. They could do whatever they wanted, even leave the bong out as if it were a decorative piece.

I put my feet up on the coffee table next to the bong to prop my journal on my knees while I wrote. Marc sat at the edge of the sofa, nodding his head to the chords while Jake played Sublime's "Marley Medley."

"I'm dating an artist," Marc told Jake, smiling at me.

"Yeah right." I laughed.

He grabbed a pen off the coffee table and took my notebook. He turned the page and wrote quickly: *In a world of peace and love, music would be the universal language." —Henry David Thoreau . . . Sing for us, Maleeka.*

"Never." I shook my head after I read his secret message.

Then he sang his own version of the song while tapping his foot:

"Baby you really gotta show us—Come on now stop your hidin'. Sing along, don't hide your voice—You know how much I love you."

He put his hand on my knee, his head shot up with his shoulders back as he belted out singing about the train that was bound for glory. He was handsome, proud, and unafraid. I envied his confidence.

Dear Journal   Jan. 25, 2002
   Marc is bound for glory. I know it! ♥
My fear holds me back
Tight like the strings on that guitar
not like you
you're all that I want to be
you're you
Vibrant and loud, you're beautifully you

Plucking at my visions
scratching at my fears
strokes in all directions
chords that pull me near
to you

You're all that I want to be
you're you
Vibrant and loud
beautiful you

I love listening to them play music, I love
sitting in a room w/ people that have ideas
and enthusiasm, dreaming of
expression and art with
so much depth.

When I'm at Marc's
or with Marc I am
inspired. Just his curious
eyes alone, they inspire me.

"IN a WORLD of peace and
Love, music would be the
universal language"
    - HENRY DAVID THOREAU
SING FOR US MALECKA!

IT WAS AN ACCIDENT

The day of my sixteenth birthday, I got everything I could want. Marc left me a rose in my mailbox with, of course, cupcakes, and the girls greeted me in the halls with a bouquet of balloons to follow me around all day, that way everyone had to tell me happy birthday. Mom got me my own cell phone and took me to the DMV after school. I passed my driver's test, and after work, my dad took me to get a brand-new car off the lot. He insisted we all drive new cars so they'd be reliable. My friends all teased me for being spoiled, and though I did always get more than most, I knew I also dealt with fulfilling more expectations than the rest.

"There are rules that come along with this car, Maleeka. I want you to prove yourself to us," Dad told me as we drove home. "I want your grades to improve and your involvement with the family to increase."

I nodded and played along with it all. I didn't care about the rules he ranted about. All I could think about was my new freedom. As long as they accepted my lies of where I was going, I could go anywhere. And I already knew exactly where I wanted to go.

"I want you to be home by eight, okay?" my mom told me in the kitchen as I grabbed my purse and CD booklet to head out for the first time alone.

"Mom, that's only an hour."

"Eight o'clock, Maleeka, don't push it. And remember, nobody in the car with you."

"I won't even be driving. I just want to show Emiko my new car."

"Please be careful," she said as I grabbed the keys and gave her a side hug to run out the door.

"I will, Mom, bye, love you!"

I was off on my first ride, but not my first lie. I was going to Emiko's, but only to pick her up to go to Marc's.

"You got it?!" He opened the front door. I told him I would call him if I failed and show up if I passed.

"I got it." I smiled as he kissed me.

We both knew this would change everything. I didn't have to rely on my friends taking me to see him. It was true freedom and would allow us to go anywhere we wanted. Marc had had his license taken away over winter break. He told me it was for too many speeding tickets, but I wondered if it might be something else.

"Finn, guess who's driving?" he hollered in the hallway.

"Oh yeah? Congratulations, Maleeka," Finn said, coming out of his room with a smile on his face and a jig in his step as Lead Belly sang "Midnight Special."

"Let's see your new ride," Marc said as he put on a jacket. It was cold outside.

"Your parents bought you a car?" Finn said and followed us out. Finn had never gotten his driver's license; he used public transportation because it was available. "Damn."

"Lucky girl, huh?" Emiko laughed.

"It's just a car." I was shy about my privilege, so I tried to play it down while the guys checked out my brand-new silver Jetta.

"A brand-new fucking car," Marc said, checking out the driver's seat.

"Whatever." I shook my head.

"Do you think I'm a spoiled bitch?" I asked Marc quietly as we made our way back inside.

"I wouldn't say 'spoiled bitch.'" He laughed a little. "But yeah, you get everything you want."

"I mean, yeah, I get a lot of things, but I don't even care about that stuff. Money, clothes, cars. It doesn't mean anything to me. I feel like people think I'm spoiled."

"Who? Finn?"

"Not only Finn, everyone."

"You have more than most, but you have a big heart, Maleeka."

We sat together around the coffee table while Finn took a call.

"Our ounce is ready," Finn said as he walked out of his bedroom, looking only at Marc.

"Oh, perfect," Marc said.

"Yeah, I'll go grab it; stay here with your company."

"Do you need a ride?" I chimed in.

"Would you do that?" Finn looked up at me.

"Yeah, where do you need to go?" I got up to get my purse.

"A guy named Shawn's house."

"You really want to go there?" Emiko asked me. "You have to be home soon."

"It will be fine, Em," I assured her.

I showed off on the way there, playing Bone Thugs-N-Harmony in my CD player. Emiko sat in the front seat, and the guys were in the back. It started to rain, not a drizzle but a downpour.

"Damn, we're hitting every yellow light," I said, slowing down.

"Once you get one, you get them all," Finn said in the back seat.

"You have to pass one, break the rule once, and you're free." I laughed. "It's the only way to break away from conformity."

"Sounds like you might be her first yellow light, man." Finn chuckled in the back seat.

I smiled at Marc in the rearview mirror.

The next light on the main road turned yellow. I put my foot on the gas to "break free."

"Maleeka, stop!" Emiko called out before the loud smash put a ringing in my ear. The car filled up with a dusty haze, and the airbags were in my lap. Everything froze and got silent for a moment until I realized what had happened.

"Maleeka! Babe!" Marc yelled out. He was already outside and pulled the handle to open my door. The front hood was pressed in toward the dashboard, which made it difficult to open the door. He screamed through the busted window, "You're bleeding!" He pulled on the door in a panic, and I pushed as he pulled.

"Babe." He grabbed me. "Are you okay?"

"Fuck! I am so sorry, oh my God, I am so sorry," I said, looking up at him.

"Are you okay?" he said again, wiping my eye with his sweatshirt. There was blood all over the cuff.

"Yes, yeah, I am fine." I pressed against my left eye to try to make it stop.

Emiko was coughing.

"Emiko," I yelled, "are you hurt?"

"I'm okay," she said as Finn pulled her out of the car.

The damage looked even worse outside of the car. The windows were shattered, the hood distorted and mangled. I couldn't believe we were all alive and on our feet. I looked over at the car I hit through the heavy raindrops. I could barely see the man's upper body hunched over his steering wheel.

"Oh my God!" I put my hands to my mouth. "I killed him!"

"I'm going to go check on him, are you sure you're okay?" Marc said, pulling my wet hair back.

"Yeah, I'm fine." I covered my face with my hands.

"You sure?" He took my hands down. "Look at me, babe, are you sure you're okay?"

"Yes, I swear."

He and Finn ran over to check on the guy, who had a few witnesses around the car. Nobody touched him, but someone called an ambulance.

"He's okay." Marc walked back to me.

"Are you sure?"

"Yeah, he's going to be okay. He wants to get checked out."

"Checked out?" I looked at him and over at Finn. I heard the sirens howl. I backed away from Marc with my hands on my forehead. "Oh my God, you have to leave!"

"What? I can't leave."

My whole body rattled as I walked away. I didn't know what to do, or where to run. I was a mess, wet, frazzled, and bleeding. I shook uncontrollably, not from the cold but from my fear.

"Maleeka, I'm not leaving you." Marc grabbed me to stop me from pacing.

I knew he was being honorable by insisting on staying with me in such a situation. But I didn't need anything from him; all I needed was for him to leave.

"No, no, no, please, you don't understand. You have to leave. They're on the way. You can't be here. Finn, please, take him and leave."

"We can't leave, Maleeka. The police are pulling up," Finn said.

"I don't care about the police, I'll tell them you were walking by." I looked back at Marc. "You don't understand, you have to leave. They can't know you were with me. My parents can't—"

"Are you crazy?!" Marc snapped at me. "We just totaled the car, we could have died! I am sure they don't give a fuck if I'm here! That's the last of anyone's worries right now." He turned to walk away and pulled his pack of cigarettes from his pocket.

I couldn't see straight. All I could think about was the look on my dad's face if he saw Marc. The rage, the panic, the consequences. My life would never be the same. I walked up to Marc so only he could hear me. I grabbed his hands before he lit up, and I pleaded.

"Please, I know this doesn't make any sense to you, but please listen to me and leave." He tried to get a word in, but I wouldn't let him. I squeezed his hands harder to get my point across. "I can't have you here. If they see you here, I'll never see you again."

He pushed my hands off his and put his cigarette up to his lips to light it.

"Finn, let's go, man." He sucked in until the cigarette lit and didn't take his eyes off me.

"You sure?" Finn asked. "Are you going to be okay, Maleeka?"

"She's fine," Marc answered for me, still staring. "She's got this all under control. Let's go."

He pulled up the hood on his sweatshirt and walked away before the cops saw them. He didn't even say goodbye.

By the time my parents got there, the guy I hit was taken away by ambulance. The cops confirmed he was okay, but he wanted to get checked out for his bumps and bruises. Mom got out of the car and went straight to the officer, but Dad ran straight to me.

"You okay, *habibti*?"

"Yeah. I am so sorry, Dad."

"Don't be sorry. They call them accidents for a reason. I am glad you're okay." He kissed my forehead while Mom glared at me. She was pissed Emiko was with me.

"You know she just got her license. She wasn't supposed to have anyone in the car with her," she told the officer.

"It's okay, we won't cite her for that. We'll let that one go as a warning." He looked over at me. "Next time, it will be a ticket, okay?"

I nodded and kept close to my dad, appreciating his grasp. I couldn't wait to go home, get warm, and hide in my bed.

Emiko's parents picked her up, and I got in my mom's car. The ride home was silent. Dad had more of a temper, but when Mom was mad, it was hell. Her eyes were terrifying. When we were young, we would say she had the devil in her when she was mad, because her eyes would get red. We walked inside the house, and she laid into me.

"I want to know what the hell you were doing on that side of town!" she yelled, throwing her purse on the kitchen counter. "And with Emiko in the car!"

Mom was pissed at me for breaking a rule with Emiko in the car, what would she or Dad do if she knew Marc and Finn were with me and we were on our way to buy an ounce of weed?

"We were driving around listening to music."

"Go to bed," she told me. "I can't even look at you right now."

I walked upstairs and saw Rasheed in the office on the computer. It wasn't out of the ordinary to walk by Rasheed and not say anything to him. I kept walking.

"Why were you on Folding Street?" he asked with his back toward me. I stopped and looked at him. He couldn't even ask if I was okay.

"Why does that matter?"

He stood up off the chair fast enough for it to roll back and slam into the wall. "Because it fucking matters." I guess he found out who recently moved to that side of town.

I stood still. I didn't want him to think he could intimidate me. "We went for a drive."

"Bullshit." He walked past me.

Still didn't even ask if I was okay.

Dear Journal, Feb. 25th, 2002
   I hate that I have to hide him
and make him feel like he isn't good
enough. Good enough... God he is so good.
He cares about people.
I crashed a brand new car, almost killed
my friends and a helpless man, and all
I cared about was protecting myself.
→ He is a better person than me. ←
I'm a selfish, careless liar. It's crazy how
good I am at lying. It scares me how
easy it is for me to lie.
Dad thinks his rules are to protect me,
but they're only turning me into someone
I don't want to be
      A lying, selfish bitch.

Every lie that I give — I get better
my eyes, they don't flinch — I get better
Tell them what they want to hear
  I'm no better
Than what they think I am

But you, my God you, you are better
than anything I can pretend to be

"Hey." I walked up to his patio the next day after school. He sat on the edge of the love seat they had outside, with his elbows on his knees, smoking a cigarette alone.

"How'd you get here?" He looked up at me.

"Sam dropped me off." I stopped before I got too close. It didn't look like he was happy to see me. He didn't even get up to greet me.

"Is the car totaled?"

"Yeah."

He nodded his head. "Bummer."

"It's okay, I didn't really like the silver anyway." I smiled at him.

He didn't smile. Bad time to make a joke about my privilege.

"I'm sorry I freaked out, Marc," I told him. He kept his head down. "I'm sorry I asked you to leave."

"You cared more about me leaving than you did about the man that looked dead," he said, looking at the floor. He wouldn't look at me. I knew he was disappointed in my character. All he worried about that night was everyone else, especially me.

"I was scared."

"We were all scared, Maleeka, that crash was fucked up, seeing you stuck in between those airbags scared me more than anything." I realized then I didn't even ask him if he was okay that night.

"I'm sorry, all I could think about was that I would never see you again!" I told him, hoping it would scare him too.

He lifted his head up fast. "I can't understand this, I can't imagine they'd care *that* much if I was there."

It got quiet. Marc knew my dad was strict, I told him he'd lost it at times, I told him I wasn't allowed to have a boyfriend, but I left out details. I wasn't sure if it was to protect myself or to protect my dad. I sat next to him on the edge of the love seat and looked up to the sky.

"When I was in eighth grade, I went to the movies with Lauren," I said without looking at him. "Shelly took us to meet up with the guys."

He looked over at me, but I didn't take my eyes off the sky.

"Rasheed found out and told my dad. He lost his mind. He didn't want me hanging out with Lauren, let alone a bunch of guys."

"That's ridiculous." Marc shook his head.

"I told him that." My voice cracked. I looked down at my lap and bit my lip while I took a deep breath in. I was scared to tell him the rest, but I needed him to understand me and why I was scared of my dad. I never told Marc about the night he threw a chair at me or about the time he threw the TV on the floor while fighting with my mom. And I never told anyone about this night. "I told him it wasn't fair. I said all girls have boyfriends. I told him I wanted one."

"What'd he do?"

I leaned back against the sofa and cried into my hands cupped over my face. I didn't want to paint my dad to be a monster. But I needed Marc to understand.

"He pulled his arm back."

Marc turned around to face me. It was the first time Marc had seen me cry. "What the fuck, did he hit you?"

I nodded my head and let my hands fall down to my lap as I tried to catch my breath. "He told me he wasn't raising a slut."

He clenched his teeth and put his fist up to his lips.

I pulled his hand down. "Please don't hate him, my dad's a good man, Marc. He loves me, but I'm terrified of him. I didn't tell you this so you would hate him. I just want you to be able to see why I lie and hide to protect myself."

He shook his head softly. His eyes looked sad while he tried to figure out what to say or what to think. I couldn't imagine he'd understand why I was still calling my dad a good man. But I could tell he tried to. He pulled me into him and said, "I hate that you have to live life in fear."

Dear Journal, Feb. 26th, 2002
  I do live my life in FEAR
I'm always on edge around them, plotting
ways to live a normal life that they
won't find out about.

Raneem told me I was brave, but I'm
always scared and always holding back.
Scared to get too close, scared to love,
scared to live.

I don't want to be scared. I want to live
and love hard, like Marc does.

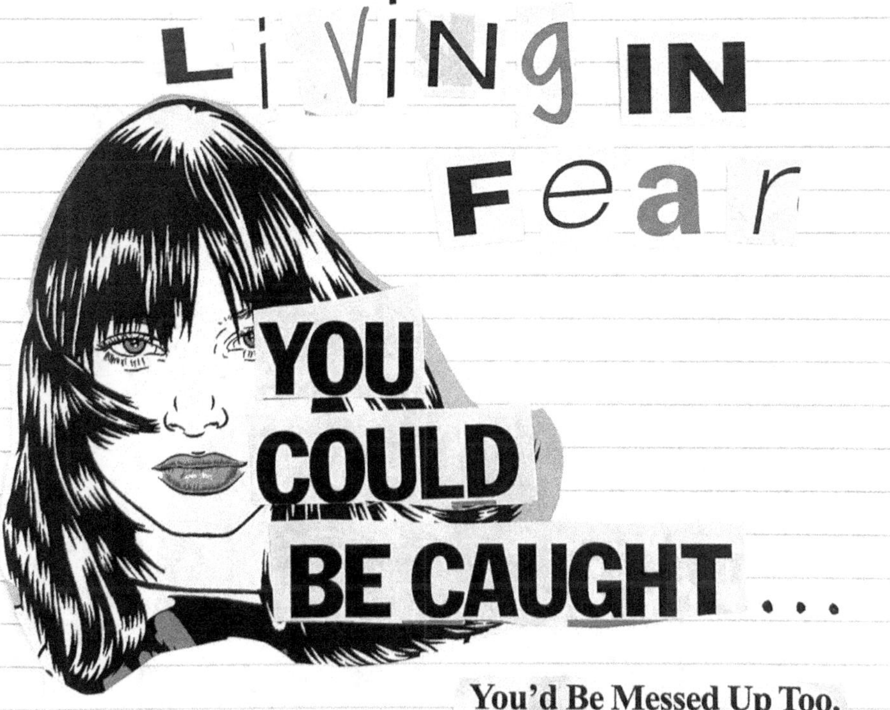

a Masterpiece

April 13th 2002

Dear Journal,

I love sitting next to him as we both write in our notebooks. Me writing about him, and he's writing about me. I know he is because he keeps looking up, smiles at me, bites his bottom lip and goes back at it.

I love that he writes about me, it's proof that I exist. It's like a part of me will live forever on his pages.

And marc can turn me into a

Masterpiece

with his art.

Press me against your paper
Capture me with words
Force me to last longer
Use your metaphors
Unsure of what you're writing
I know it's about me
I hear your pen engraving
the intensity
Those pages know my details
You've let them feel my heart
You've turned me into a masterpiece
with your art

It was prom night. If Marc were still in school, he'd be a senior and able to go. But he wasn't. Instead, he was in his dark, messy apartment, stoned with his girl. I sat on the far right side of the couch with my feet on the coffee table, writing in my journal while he wrote in his notebook on the other side. I put my pen down and looked over at him.

"What are you writing over there?"

I figured he was writing something brilliant as always. I could hear his pencil moving fast, scratching the notepad on the other side of the sofa with his feet tucked under my thighs facing me.

"I'm drawing," he told me, tilting his head and biting his bottom lip.

"I thought that was your poetry book."

"It is, but this is another form of art."

"Let me see it." I leaned in over his notepad. "Oh my God, Marc! Is she naked?!" I looked a little closer. "Is that me?" He had sketched every detail of me—the dips of my eyelids, the height of my cheekbones, and the cleft in my chin you could only notice at a certain angle.

"Yeah, can't you tell?"

"That does not look like my body. You have to add a few rolls of fat for it to be me."

"Maleeka, stop. This picture doesn't do you justice."

I shook my head and grabbed the notebook. "You had to add my birthmark?"

I have a birthmark under my right ear, at my jawline, a few shades darker than my olive complexion. My siblings and cousins used to say it looked like I had shit on my face. It wasn't anything I was proud of.

"Of course I do, it's right next to my favorite place to kiss you." He leaned in to kiss my neck as I flipped through the pages. "Come on, babe, you don't want to see what else is in there." He grabbed his book back.

"Why not? Let me read them. If nothing else, let me read the ones about me. I have a right to those. Your art wouldn't be without me."

"Someday," he told me.

"Okay, but promise me if you ever publish your writing, you'll change my name, so my dad won't know all my secrets."

"I would never change your name." He put the brown notebook in his lap and smiled at me. "It's part of who you are. Unique, gorgeous, and alluring."

I looked down, shaking my head. "You have to. Shit, my dad would kill me if he knew anything about us."

"What about your journals? What would he do if he read those?"

"How do you know I write about you in my journals?" I teased him.

"Well, if you do write about me, I have a right to know what you're writing. It wouldn't be without me."

"Someday." I smiled at him. "Maybe I'll publish my journals."

"You have to share your art, Maleeka," he told me as he threw his poetry book on the coffee table.

"I wish, but I could never share what's in here." I laughed and grabbed his notebook. "Come on, read me something. It doesn't have to be about me." I handed him the book and got comfortable on the couch.

He read me lyrics he wrote while in his band. I listened, admiring his talent.

"I want you to get back together with Absence. I want to see you in that light again. How cool to go see you at your shows."

"Would you be one of my groupies?" He laughed.

"I would *not* be a groupie," I objected quickly.

"Maybe I could get you onstage with me, and you could sing."

"Sing what, punk rock? I wouldn't sound good screaming."

"You can do a soft hook, some kind of intro."

"Yeah, right. I'd be too scared. I would stand in the back and smile at you to be your inspiration."

"You are an inspiration," he said, "but it's not going to happen. Not now."

"Why not?"

"We're not in it like we used to be. Too many distractions."

"What, like me?"

"Nah, not you. Just other distractions."

Before the conversation could be finished, Rob and Carson slid the door open. They were going to prom that night with Amelia and Karen, and they stopped by Marc's to get stoned before picking up their girlfriends.

"You like my handkerchief, Marc?" Carson laughed as he sat between Marc and me. He pulled it out a little to show it off. Rob sat on the futon, laughing while Marc loaded the bong.

"You guys look good," I told them as I got up off the couch. "And I'm sure the girls are going to look beautiful. Amelia and Karen are gorgeous."

"You should be going with us, Marc," Carson said, nudging him on the couch and looking up at me. "You should be taking Maleeka to the prom."

Marc smiled before pressing his lips on the bong.

"Yeah right," I said. "Even if Marc were in school, he would never go."

"Why do you say that?" Marc asked me, blowing out his smoke to the middle of the room.

"It isn't your thing." I shrugged my shoulders.

"Well, it's obvious this *is* Carson's thing, but you think Rob cares about prom?" He laughed. "If you wanted to go, I would take you."

I laughed, taking my turn to hit the bong.

"Why are you laughing?" he asked with a smile on his face.

"'Cause, we are different. I can't wait to go to prom next year. I love that stuff."

Marc shook his head a little with his smile still pressed on his face.

The guys got up to leave. Marc and I walked them out. After the accident blew over at home, Dad got me another car to replace the one I totaled. Mom wasn't happy about it, she called me spoiled, but I promised I would be careful and I swore to her I wouldn't have anyone with me in the car until the six-month rule ran out. I kept one promise; I was very cautious while driving, but I broke the six-month rule often. We were going to go for a drive that night to get out of the apartment for a bit. Since I wouldn't go anywhere in public with him, we took drives often.

Marc gave the guys a high-five handshake, and I called out, "Have fun, you guys! Take lots of pictures!"

"Good night, Maleeka!" they both said.

"You ready?" I asked as I got in the driver's seat and put my key in the ignition.

"I'm going to finish this cigarette." He stood at my door, leaving it open and looking at me as I pulled out my phone to check for any missed calls. "What do you love about it?" he asked me.

"What?" I looked up to him.

"The prom, what do you love about it?"

"I don't know, it's fun to get dressed up and take pictures and dance."

He put his cigarette out on the ground and reached for me. "Come here for a second." He grabbed my hand.

"Why, what are you doing?"

"I would go anywhere with you," he said as he pulled me close and kissed me on the cheek. "Dance with me," he said near my ear.

"What? No, we're outside."

He didn't care; he reached in the car and raised the volume on the radio that played the only song I knew of S Club 7, "Never Had a Dream Come True."

"I want to see if you're any good at dancing."

I put both my arms around his neck; that's how I knew how to dance. I had slow-dance swayed with guys before, with enough awkward space between us to put another person. But Marc knew how to really dance; his mom taught him when he was twelve years old before his first middle school dance. He took my right hand off from around his neck, looked down at it, and wrapped his fingers around my palm.

He put his other arm around my waist and held the small of my back tight so I was pressed up against him. I held on to his bicep and leaned my head against his. I could smell the cigarette left over in his hair, with a hint of Cool Water shampoo. His sideburns brushed against my cheek, and his breath ran down my neck.

"Maybe this can be our song," I told him.

"You're joking, right?" He leaned back to look at me.

"No, it's perfect."

"Come on, babe, there are so many better songs out there." He laughed. "I will give us a song. Fuck, I'll give us a whole soundtrack."

I laughed with him but loved every second of that song. He *was* the first dream I had come true.

"I love you, you know that?" he said, brushing my bangs off my forehead.

"Yes, I know that. More than anything else, I know one hundred percent you love me." I smiled at him.

"Let's go, I want to take you somewhere special."

Fucked Up

"Is this it?" I smiled as I got out of the car. "You think we'll see a train pass?"

"It depends how long we stay." He shut the car door and grabbed my hand to take me down the path.

It was a secluded spot buried between tall Douglas fir trees. There was an old, abandoned train station, barely held up by rotting beams and broken wooden steps that sat on a slab of concrete. Nobody went there, trains didn't stop there anymore, but it was Marc's spot. He would walk to the tracks to help clear his thoughts and write. I knew how much he loved that landing.

"Wow." I walked past him, looking at the run-down station lit up by the bright moon between the trees. "It's kind of cool looking."

"It's not the prettiest place, but it's got character."

"I love it." I turned around to look at him and made my way over to the concrete floor to sit down. "So this is where you write?" I smiled at him.

He sat next to me and leaned back against the dirty beam, looking at the moon. "I sit right here and reflect with the moon."

"Don't you ever get scared being here alone?"

He grabbed my hand and smiled at me. "Nothing can get me out here."

It did feel safe out there, alone and peaceful. Like we were the only people in the world existing without any expectation or pressure. Without fear.

"I admire you, Marc. You're the bravest person I know." I leaned in to kiss him. "I love you," I whispered in his mouth with my eyes closed.

That set him off. I didn't say love often, the word *love* scared me, but that night I didn't want to live in fear.

He grabbed my neck and had me lie on the dirty concrete floor. He unbuttoned my pants to do the usual.

"I want you inside of me," I told him. I had said that to him before, but only to turn him on. That night I meant it. It was the perfect place; hidden, moody, romantic, and most of all safe. I knew it had to happen there, in his spot. I unbuttoned his pants and pulled out his dick, hard between my legs.

"Babe, you can't keep saying that shit to me." He pulled back, looking down at me.

I took off my shirt to entice him and grabbed his face, kissing his neck. "Don't stop, Marc." My chest pounded on his, and I could feel his heart rate increase. But I wasn't scared like before in Carson's truck. I felt empowered and sure of it. Nothing scared me out there.

"It's okay if you don't have a condom. You can pull out," I said, sounding like an expert on teenage sex.

I grabbed his dick to put it in. In seconds he was inside me, but instead of going all the way, he pulled himself out and fell to my side with his hands on his head.

"I can't, Maleeka," he panted in agony. "I can't fuck you like that. I'm too fucked up."

"It's okay, I smoked too," I said, getting on top of him, kissing him again.

"No, Maleeka, you don't understand, I'm too fucked up right now." He pushed me off him. How fucking embarrassing.

I looked at the ground while doing a replay of the evening to figure out how he'd be so fucked up. Yeah, we all smoked, nobody was drinking . . . but then I remembered he'd stepped in the other room with Rob.

I grabbed my shirt and pulled up my pants. "Babe," he said, and I didn't answer back. "Babe?" he said again as he tried to keep my pants undone. "Let me go down on you."

"You're too fucked up." I shook my head, looking the other way.

"I don't want to do it like this," he told me.

I stood up and wrapped my arms around my chest. "Let's go. I'm sorry I brought it up. This was a bad idea."

Back at the apartment he spent the rest of the night telling me how much he adored me. He brought up the night in Carson's truck and how horrible he felt after the fact. I insisted this time was different. He said he wanted to fuck me, but not like that. Not when he was fucked up and sticking it in with hesitation. I couldn't stop wondering how and why he was so fucked up, but I was scared to ask. It was easier to just let him go down on me and pretend it never happened.

I woke up early in Marc's bed, fully dressed in my clothes from the night before and bundled up under the covers. His fan beside the bed ran on high. It was freezing. I hated that fan, but Marc couldn't sleep without it. I got up to freshen up before meeting the girls for breakfast.

"Come here." He opened his eyes and reached for my hand. "Are we good?" he asked as I knelt to his side.

"Yeah, we're good. Just promise me you won't tell anyone you rejected me."

"Babe, I didn't—"

"I'm joking," I said before he went off again about why.

"You're so beautiful," he told me as I sat on the floor next to him and brushed foundation over my eyelids in front of a small compact mirror. He didn't have a mirror in his room. "You don't need that shit."

"Yeah, but feel this." I got closer to him. "Close your eyes." I took the soft foundation brush and wiped his eyelids with it. "Doesn't it feel amazing?"

"Yeah, I guess," he told me.

"Come on, relax. Close your eyes and really feel it."

"You're crazy," he told me while lying still to let me do as I wished.

"You like it." I laughed.

He rolled over to his side and put his hand on my face. "Stay here with me."

"I can't, Marc. I promised them. I'll try to come back." I grabbed my purse off the floor.

"I love you, Maleeka Munir!" he yelled as I ran out.

We met at our favorite breakfast diner. It was our spot when we were younger and dependent on Lauren's mom. She'd take us for pancakes and hash browns and ask us about our crushes. I remember writing out the initials of the guys we liked with ketchup over the hash browns. We shared lots of adolescent secrets in that diner. I sat at the booth while the girls gave me all the details from the night before. I didn't give them any details of mine. I didn't want them to know I didn't go to the party with them to get rejected.

"He called her every hour," Emiko told me after Lauren got off the table to take Zach's call.

"He's crazy," I told them as I sipped on my hot coffee.

"At least he let her go without him," she said.

"He *let* her go? What a good guy." I rolled my eyes over the rim of my cup.

"He's coming," Lauren said as she came back to the table. "Remember, we stayed the night at your house, Sam."

He walked in with his hair in perfect place, like his jacket, watch, and fake-ass smile.

"Hi, girls," he said with his snarky voice before kissing Lauren good morning.

We all nodded and said hello as he played nice and asked about their night. They kept it vague so he wouldn't know details. Sure, Lauren did as she was told and didn't drink or smoke, but she did sleep at another guy's house. Even though he was her harmless friend, Brandon was still a guy.

"I'm glad you had fun, Ren, but I hate when you go to parties without me."

I rolled my eyes right out of my head. I couldn't help it. "Oh my God," I said louder than I should have.

Zach pounded his fist on the table. "I'm talking to my girlfriend," he told me. "Stay out of it."

"Zach!" Lauren said, jolted by the thud on the table.

"This is exactly the shit I'm talking about," he told Lauren.

"Let's leave." Lauren grabbed her purse.

"Even better." He smiled at me.

Lauren got up in a hurry as Zach followed behind her without either of them saying bye.

"He's fucked up," I said, shaking from the inside out. "Guys, he's so fucked up."

"Leek," Emiko said calmly, trying to ease the situation out.

"No, don't brush it off, Em. Didn't you see him smiling at me like a fucking creep? He's fucking crazy." I couldn't stop shaking my head. "I hate him."

"Well, it's obvious the feelings are mutual," Samantha said, taking another bite of hash browns.

I'M WATCHING YOU

"What do you want to do this weekend? Let me take you out on a real date," Marc told me while I lay in the dark with the phone up to my ear. Marc pushed us to go out in public often, but I always found a way out of it. I was much more comfortable in the haven of his place.

"We don't need to go anywhere, that's what your apartment is for."

"Come on, babe, don't you get tired of sitting around the apartment all night? Let me take you to dinner."

"Let's order food, and we can watch *The Sopranos*. I still haven't seen it." I knew he'd be down for that. Marc loved *The Sopranos* and always tried to get me to watch it with him. Rasheed also loved that show. I would never tell Rasheed this, but I let Marc borrow the first two seasons Mom bought him for Christmas on DVD.

"Okay, fine, but promise me we'll do dinner soon."

I sat up in bed in a panic and didn't say anything.

"Maleeka?" he asked.

"I got to go, Marc, I think the house phone is ringing."

"This late?" he asked.

"Yeah, it's definitely ringing. I'll call you back." I threw my phone and ran to the office, praying it wasn't for me. Nobody called the house for me anymore. When I picked up the phone, I heard Rasheed had picked up as well. Thank God Dad was out of town. I took the phone back to my room and listened in.

"Hello?" Rasheed said, half-asleep.

Nobody answered. I shut my bedroom door and sat on my bed.

"Who is this?" There was only heavy breathing. "Hello?" Rasheed said again.

"Maleeka's a whore," the voice whispered.

My shoulders and my stomach dropped.

"Who the fuck is this?" Rasheed's voice became aggressive like he was ready to fight, but fight who?

"Your little sister's a slut," the voice said, and hung up. I knew whose voice that was. Zach knew what happened to me last time he called the house late; he must have wanted it to happen again.

I heard Rasheed's footsteps approaching. I threw the phone under my bed and covered myself under the blankets. He stormed into my room and turned on the lights. "Are you sleeping?"

"What's going on?" I rubbed my eyes, pretending I just woke up.

"Someone just called the house, saying fucked-up things about you!" He paced back and forth. "Is anyone giving you a hard time at school?"

"No, not at all," I assured him. "What did they say?" I had to act like I had no idea.

He shook his head, clenching his teeth. "They called you a slut."

I put my head down. I felt worse hearing Rasheed tell me what they said than actually hearing them say it.

"I bet it's that fucker."

"What fucker?" I looked up at him.

"Marc!" He stopped and yelled at me, "Who else?"

"No way, Rasheed, Marc wouldn't do that." I sat up in bed in defense.

"How do you know what Marc would or wouldn't do?"

I couldn't tell him Marc was on the phone with me when the call came in or that Marc loved me and would never call me a slut.

"I don't know," I backtracked. "I'm just saying, why would he be calling now? It's been so long, he doesn't give a shit about me. I'm not on his radar."

"You're going to kill Dad. Imagine if he had been home and answered. You think he wants to hear someone call his daughter a slut?"

"What about me, why does this have to be about Dad? They're calling *me* a slut."

"Obviously you're doing something to make them say that about you."

That hurt.

"They're too easy on you, Maleeka. You need to grow up and consider what you're doing to your parents."

"I'm not doing anything!"

"I'm watching you, Maleeka, I swear to God. You aren't invisible." He stormed out and left me feeling overwhelmed about all the lies I fed him and my parents every day.

Keeping both worlds separate was hard; being a compulsive liar was hard. No matter how much I wanted to keep Marc a secret, I knew I couldn't control every situation. There would always be someone or something that would get me caught. Anticipating it and also facing it wore on me. It was constant work. I could never relax and bring both worlds together.

Dear Journal,

April 30th 2002

I'M NOT ON HIS RADAR...

I kiss him every day
I lay with him in bed
I smoke weed with him
Laugh with him
and tried to have sex with him

But no Rasheed, he doesn't give a shit about me...

I'm going to hell someday.

Seventy-five degrees in Oregon in late spring was like a holiday. Everyone stopped what they were doing to enjoy the sun, even if it meant calling off work. It was warm enough for us river rats to head to the Misty River to lie out and do stunts in the ice-cold water. I picked up Emiko and Jake to meet Lauren and Samantha, who were already there with their boyfriends.

"What's Marc up to today?" Jake asked me as he took charge of the music in the front seat of my car.

"He's hanging out with Carson."

"Call him, have them meet us there," he said.

"I'll call him later," I said. I didn't want to admit to Jake that I was scared to bring Marc to a public place not knowing who all would be there, especially after Rasheed insisted he was watching me.

We walked down the hill leading to the shore full of people. As we got closer we found our friends spread on the sand with coolers, camping chairs, and towels laid out. I could see Lauren on Zach's lap, talking to someone next to them. I couldn't see who it was, but I could see smoke blown around them.

"Is that Marc?" Emiko turned to ask me.

I froze.

"Guess you don't have to call him." Jake walked past me.

I felt like an asshole. Marc had asked me to hang out that day, but I told him I'd be busy with the girls. I didn't mention the river, or that their boyfriends would be there. I'd played it off as a girls-only day. I could have invited him.

Marc put his cigarette out and walked over. "Why didn't you tell me you were coming here?" he asked as he put his arm around me and gave me a kiss on the cheek. He aimed for my mouth, but I blocked it. My conduct was on shield. I hadn't had to hold back for a while, but Waleed's football team was about ten yards away from us.

"You okay?" he asked me as I slithered out of his grasp.

"Yeah, I'm fine," I said. "Sorry, I didn't realize all the guys were coming." I walked off to say hi to everyone and left him with Jake and Emiko.

"What's up, Maleeka?" Zach said to me. I said hi back—I knew it needed to be done to avoid any more friction or late-night calls—and gave the girls a hug. I didn't tell the girls about Zach's prank call; I knew Lauren wouldn't believe me, and I didn't want to strain our relationship.

I sat next to Samantha, who wore a bright-pink string bikini. Lauren wore the same one but in yellow. I wished I were more like them, comfortable, confident, and at ease in their skimpy swimsuits on their boyfriends' laps. Even Emiko; she got undressed in hers right when we got there, and Jake had her under his arm, shirtless. I on the other hand stayed in my linen shorts and tank top and ignored my boyfriend.

"Maleeka, this song's for you!" Brandon yelled over to me as he played Eminem on the portable CD player.

"Thanks, Brandon." I smiled and raised my beer to cheers him in the air. Samantha handed me a joint that was being passed around. I put my head down and took a hit, and as I looked up to exhale, I caught eyes with Marc. He stared at me as he sucked in his cigarette. I looked back down and brushed my foot through the sand.

"You didn't bring your swimsuit?" He eventually approached me and sat on a rock behind us.

I looked back at him. "Nobody wants to see that."

"Oh, come on, Maleeka. I've seen every inch of your body, and trust me, anyone here would want to see it too."

"Stop talking like that, Marc!" I got up, and he did too.

"It's the truth."

"Okay, stop."

"Tell me what's going on, what's wrong with you?"

"Nothing," I insisted without looking in his eyes.

"How am I supposed to believe that?"

"Believe it! What do you want from me?"

"I want you to act normal. Even now, you're backing away from me." I hadn't even realized I was taking small steps away from him.

"You're making a scene." I turned my head the other way.

"I'm not making a scene, Maleeka, I am trying to have a conversation with my girlfriend." He didn't yell, but I freaked out.

I waved my hands in the air. "Shh, stop, Marc." I was pissed off at him for saying the word *girlfriend* in public.

"Are you kidding me?" He glared at me.

"Why are you doing this?"

"Doing what? We can't even talk? You've been dodging me this whole time."

I shook my head. I couldn't admit to his callout. "Lauren, can you take Emiko and Jake home?" I said over Marc's shoulder.

"You're leaving?" he asked me.

"Yes, I'm leaving. You can't act like this in front of people." I grabbed my purse and walked away.

"Act like what?" he said louder. "We're just talking!"

He stopped me in my tracks. If they didn't hear *girlfriend*, I'm sure everyone heard that. I got closer to him and said as calmly as I could, "I care, Marc. You know I care, so lower your fucking voice."

I stormed off. How many times did I have to tell Marc I couldn't be seen in public with him? As much as he told me he understood my situation and accepted it, he acted like he had no idea why I dodged him, and even worse he made me feel bad for it.

As I walked to my car, my phone rang. It was Rasheed. I panicked, assuming he found out I was there with Marc.

"Where the hell are you?" he asked frantically. "I've called you like five times."

"I didn't have my phone, what's wrong?" Rasheed never called me, especially five times.

"Jiddo is dying."

Everything stopped. There was a ringing in my ear. I didn't know if

I heard him right. My jiddo was diabetic and spent time in the hospital on and off. Dad told me all week to go visit him, but I assumed he'd be out soon enough.

"Maleeka!" he yelled. "Did you hear what I said? Dad wants you here, now."

"I'm coming."

his HANDS

The elevator stopped at the third floor, and when the door slid open, I could see the entire family in the waiting room. There wasn't a place to sit and hardly a place to stand. They all looked up as I walked out, but nobody said a word. I had never seen my dad's family be so quiet together. I timidly stood behind Waleed and Asma without speaking. They nodded to me.

"Maleeka," my uncle called out to me.

I didn't move.

"Maleeka, go," Asma whispered to me. "It's your turn." Everyone took turns to tell him goodbye. I watched them as they walked in quietly, hoping for a miracle, and came out in hysterics after seeing the reality. I was scared to face it. I had never been close to death.

"Come closer, *habibti*," Dad told me when he saw me approach the room. "Hold his hand." He grabbed my dirty hands that just got done drinking beer and smoking pot on the beach and placed them in my grandfather's for the last time. I wrapped my fingers beneath his palm.

"*Baba*," Dad said in his father's ear. "It's Maleeka. Maleeka came to see you," he told him in Arabic.

Jiddo wasn't responding. He lay still with his hand in mine, unresponsive.

"Talk to him, Maleeka." Dad nodded to me.

Talk to him? I wondered what I was supposed to say? I'm sorry I didn't come sooner? I'm sorry I didn't spend your last days with you? Goodbye? Was I supposed to let him know I knew he was dying?

"I-I," I stuttered. "I love you, Jiddo," I said to him in English. Jiddo always told me to speak Arabic to him, but "I love you" was understood by all. Still, I wondered if he could hear me or if he thought, *Speak in Arabic,* as I said those words to him.

His breathing changed a bit as he tugged on my shivering hand. He knew I was there. He always gave me a hard time for not coming around often enough, but when he'd see me, he always smiled, relieved I was with the family. His tug reminded me of his smile and made me realize his smile wouldn't be there anymore. I kept my head down and closed my eyes; my tears fell onto his hands. I wiped them off his knuckles, staring at his dark, solid hands, hoping I'd never forget them.

I WAS CAPABLE

My jiddo died that Saturday night. Dad didn't come home until 2:00 a.m., and the next morning we all got up to go to my sitto's house. Family from all over the country had already flown in, and the community trickled in to give their condolences. My grandparents' house was big, but not big enough to fit everyone. Dad and his siblings sat next to their mother as she grieved. The in-laws stayed close to show their support. The older women cousins served coffee to each guest that sat in silence, and the guy cousins stood outside silently smoking cigarettes, welcoming all who came. Each new group that walked in to pay their respects would bring another wave of emotions, reminding them of the good old days they shared with my grandfather.

Everyone wore black. I had never seen so many shades of black, so many flower arrangements, or so many tissue boxes. And I had never seen my family cry. Men I was always terrified of were bawling like baby boys, with their hands cupped over their faces, their gold rings brilliant against their dark skin. My uncle Salim cried at the fireplace while my dad held him like a child. The women I normally found petty and judgmental were somber and hardly spoke unless they were in the kitchen, and they only discussed who was waiting for a cup of coffee. I watched my bitchy older cousin Antoinette dab her high cheekbones delicately with a tissue, and I forgot all the stupid, offensive shit she said. My dad told me once that so long as you feel sorry for someone, you won't be capable of hating them. I felt sorry for all of them.

"Hi, Merched," Raneem said quietly, approaching our cousin outside.

Merched was at least twenty years older than I was; he scared the shit out of me when I was a kid. He didn't speak much English, and when we'd play too loud in the other room and wake him up from a nap, he'd lose his shit and freak out, screaming in Arabic. He'd often kick a toy before he left the room. The men in my family all had short fuses and mean tempers. But that day, he was soft and sweet. He put his cigarette out and grabbed Raneem under his dark, hairy arm. Seeing each other made them both cry, which made me cry too. I followed them inside.

"Hi, Mom," Raneem said to Mom, and gave her a side hug before putting her purse on the floor. She looked up as Dad approached her. "I'm sorry I didn't make it sooner, Dad." He broke down and grabbed her, crying in her arms.

The whole room wept seeing them cry together.

"Raneem!" Sitto yelled. "Raneem, he's gone!" she screamed in Arabic.

Raneem sat by our grandmother's side and rubbed her back, repeatedly telling her how sorry she was. She knew how to put her nerves aside and be there for everyone in such a tragic time. She didn't hold back from holding them or pulling their hair off their faces or wiping their cheeks with a tissue. I couldn't do that. I stood back and cried alone. I was scared, and I didn't know how to connect with them. I think others assumed I didn't care, but it wasn't the case.

Dad made his way back to his chair, wiping his tears. "Maleeka," he called me over to sit by him on the couch. I sat silent next to him, staring at the floor. His heavy breath and waves of tears made me feel for him. "I love you, Maleeka," he sobbed as he put his arm around me and pulled me into him, kissing the top of my head. It was the same place where Marc would kiss me after we were done fooling around and I'd fall asleep on his chest. I loved those kisses, which weren't given to arouse me. I loved feeling him press his lips against the top of my head like he would do anything to protect me, like a father would, like my dad would. *Oh my God, what was I doing to my dad?* I thought to myself. He just wanted to protect me. Maybe Rasheed was right. It was time for me to grow up.

"Go make another pot of coffee," Dad told me, wiping his face with a tissue.

"Four scoops?" I asked him quietly.

He nodded with a little grin. Dad had shown me how to make Arabic coffee when I was eight. I would pull the kitchen stool up to the stove as he stayed by my side, watching and counting four scoops out loud with me. It had been a while since I last made it.

"Oh, Maleeka, you don't have to do that," Antoinette told me, getting up to beat me to the kitchen. "I'll do it."

I backed away.

"Let her do it, Antoinette," Dad said.

I think he wanted everyone to know I was capable of contributing, that I wasn't a screw-up stressing him out. Passing the tray to each guest gave me purpose like I belonged there.

Rest in Peace Jiddo ♥   may 14th 2002

I know he lived a full life and he accomplished so much, but 75 seems too young to die. He could have done so much more with another ten years.

I have never cried this much. Being around death and all the emotions that come with it is so devastating.
I can't stop crying.
I always get emotional before my period comes so thats contributing to it I'm sure, but it's non stop.

It's not only about losing Jiddo, I can't stop thinking about how much I am letting Dad down. Am I a terrible person? God if he only knew what I do, it would break his heart.

"Have you talked to Marc?" Lauren asked me after school on Monday. She came over to make sure I was okay after my jiddo died, and after my fight with Marc. I was about to head over to my sitto's house.

"He left me a message last night. Jake told him about my grandpa."

"Did you call him back?"

"Not yet, I don't know what to say to him. It's easier when it's just the two of us. I hate being in public with him," I said as I dug in my closet drawers.

"Why are you changing? You look cute."

"I can't go over like this."

"Why not? It's a sweater, you're hardly showing any skin." Lauren smiled. She was used to me changing my clothes around my family to cover up.

"A bright-red sweater. You don't understand, everyone there is dressed in black from head to toe. I can't wear this." I searched through my closet for anything black to wear.

"You're not wearing that, are you?" Raneem said, standing in my open bedroom door, dressed in loose-fitting black slacks, a tight black T-shirt, and black Converse shoes.

"See." I looked over at Lauren.

"Hi, Lauren." Raneem smiled.

"Hey, Raneem," Lauren said, getting right back to her questions on the rules of mourning in our world. "I know you have to wear black to a funeral, but now?"

"Some wear black all year after someone passes," Raneem told her.

"All year!"

"Yeah, and you don't go to any parties or social events 'cause that would be extremely disrespectful, and everyone will talk shit about you."

Lauren looked over at me with wide eyes.

"She's right," I said. "We have rules for everything around here."

"What happens if you don't wear black?" she asked.

"They'll talk shit about you," I said, matter of fact.

"God, that's intense," Lauren said.

"Yeah. Are you ready soon?" Raneem asked me.

"Yeah, I just need to find something to wear," I told Raneem as she walked out the door. "I'll meet you there."

"Sounds good. I'll see you soon, Lauren," Raneem said. "And wipe your face off, makeup whore!" She laughed.

"I know!" I yelled out. Going over with a face full of makeup would appear insensitive.

"She looks good," Lauren told me.

"Yeah, it's good to have her back," I told her as I put on a black blouse.

"Jeez, how do you keep up with all these ways of living?" she asked.

"It's embedded." I shrugged my shoulders. "But honestly, it's easier. You don't have to think about how to act or what to do; you do what you're supposed to. And for something as complicated and hard as death, it's easier to have a rule book."

I sat in the full house at the kitchen table with Antoinette and Dunia, going through the endless cards attached to the arrangements delivered to the home. We kept track of every family that sent flowers so we could remember to send them a thank-you note after the funeral. I stacked the notes passed to me neatly in a shoebox and even put them in alphabetical order.

"Whose phone is that?" Dunia said, looking around the kitchen. I jumped up to grab my purse. "Turn your ringer off," she scolded me.

"Sorry." I looked at the phone and saw Marc's name. I went to the staircase to take the call from my secret boyfriend.

"Hi," I said. I didn't know what else to say except hi.

"You okay?" Marc asked me.

"Yeah, I'm okay. It's just sad, you know."

"I know, babe, I'm sorry. Why don't you come by tonight, try to take your mind off things."

"I can't leave them. Everyone's here. I can't be the only one that's not."

Nobody left the house. They were there from morning to night, exhausted by tears and fueled with coffee.

"Well, what about tomorrow?" he asked me.

"I can't, Mar—" I stopped myself from saying his name as my aunt walked up the stairs. I whispered, "At least until after the funeral. I have to be here."

"When's the funeral?"

"Thursday morning."

"I want to be there for you."

"You can't be there," I insisted, shocked he would say that.

"Not there at the funeral. Just in general. You're my girlfriend. I want to be there for you."

"Oh, you scared me," I said.

"Maleeka, at the river—"

"Marc, you know I can't—"

"I know, I know. I guess I want to know how long we have to keep this a secret?"

I hated his timing. "Why are you asking me this? There's no way, not now, not—"

"Ever?" he interrupted me again.

"I don't know." I looked up and saw Asma walking toward me. "I have to go, I'll call you later."

"You have to go?"

She got closer.

"I'm at my grandparents' right now. I have to go."

"Okay, okay. I love you, babe," he told me.

I knew he wanted to make me feel better by telling me he loved me, but hearing those words in that house didn't do so. I stood up and turned my back to Asma.

"Maleeka, I said I love you," he told me again.

"I know. I'm sorry. I'll talk to you later," I said, and I hung up without saying goodbye. Which is technically hanging up on someone, right?

"Don't hold back because of me," Asma said as I turned around to face her. "What's his name?"

I smiled at her as we both sat on the stairs. "His name is Marc."

I told her all about Marc, all the good about him. How smart he was and how kind and how much he adored me. She thought the cupcakes in the mailbox were sweet and the dance outside of my car was like a movie. But she had hesitations.

"Make sure you're careful, Leek. Your dad would go crazy if he found out. God, I mean, everyone would freak out. I don't even know what they would do to you or what they'd do to him."

"Oh, trust me, I think about that all the time, but he loves me so much."

"More than your family?" she asked. If it were anyone else asking me that question, I would have jumped to defense. But Asma wasn't lecturing me, she was asking me.

"It's different. He loves me because he wants to love me, not because he has to. He knows and he loves everything about me. Nobody here knows anything about me. They love me because you're supposed to love your family."

She didn't say anything.

"I'd like more connection than just obligation because we have the same last name to feel love," I told her.

"Well, I love you, and I think I know you pretty well." She leaned her head on my shoulder.

"You're different, Asma." I put my cheek on the top of her head.

STRONG
in that stampede

The Orthodox Church was filled over capacity, flooding people outside. I walked in behind Raneem and sat in the pews at the front, reserved for family. Mom and Dad were in the front row with the other siblings and spouses. I could see my mom's hand resting on my dad's thigh. I was grateful for her peaceful gesture. My dad always told me two occasions brought people together when they stood adrift: weddings and funerals. Both events were opportunities for people to come together and forget about their disconnect and pride, to be there for one another.

Rasheed, as well as the other male cousins, stood as my grandfather's legacies at the altar in their crisp black suits. His casket was open, so I was able to stare at him the entire time. He didn't look the same. He was puffy, and his skin tone was off. I didn't take my eyes off the coffin throughout the service, done mostly in Arabic, with biblical chants and incense tossed in the air. After the priest gave his final prayer, everyone made their way up from the back of the church to the front to tell his body goodbye. Some kissed their hands and placed them on his forehead. Some placed their hands on their own foreheads, then chest, then one shoulder to the other, making a cross, and walked away. And some lost it in hysterics, held up by the young men who were strong enough to escort them out gently.

"I can't do it," I told Raneem as my dad's cousin collapsed on the casket, crying. My grandfather basically raised her, and she didn't get the chance to tell him goodbye. It was hard to watch.

"We can go together," Raneem told me.

"Can I go with you guys?" Asma approached us as we stood up for our pew to file out.

"Of course, Asma, you're our little sister." Raneem grabbed her hand, and I followed behind them.

Raneem put her head next to Jiddo's and kissed him, stroking his hair. Asma grabbed his forearm, and I heard her whisper to him, "I love you, Jiddo," before she placed a note in his pocket to go with him.

I stood back while my heart raced. I couldn't get closer but knew I had to. People were waiting for their turns. I touched the lapel on his suit with my shivering fingers and ran my hand to his lifeless grasp. I knew my grandfather loved me. He showed me love every time I saw him, guilt trip or not. I could hear him call out, *"Ya hala, ya hala, ya hala,"* in my head, like he was saying it right there. I caught a quick breath before I lost it. And before I could hit the floor like my dad's cousin, Rasheed put his arm around me.

"It's okay, Maleeka. He knew you loved him," he told me. Rasheed hadn't had his arms on me since we were kids and he had me in a headlock. He almost felt human, like he was capable of loving me.

The family arrived last to the burial site, and the entire community stood waiting for us. We all got out of our cars without a word, and I lined up behind my cousins. My dad's oldest brother was at the front of the line, holding his mom while she cried. We were like a wolf pack following our leader in synchronized steps. Without practice, we walked at the same pace, had the same somber mannerisms, the same quiet tears, and what seemed like the same broken hearts. As devastated as I was, I felt strong in that stampede.

The funeral was an all-day affair, and by the time of the mercy meal back at the church hall, I was exhausted. Food is a big deal in our culture. It serves to welcome and show appreciation to our guests. I sat with my younger cousins with a plate of food in front of me, but I didn't touch a thing. I hated that we were all there without him. The priest got up to pray before everyone ate, and afterward Rasheed got out of his seat.

"What's he doing?" I asked Raneem.

"Dad asked him to give a speech."

Rasheed stood at the podium in his black suit, his matching tie, and his new watch left for him by our grandfather. In his eulogy, he told the story of how our grandfather left the old country and moved the entire family to the States for better opportunities. He spoke of his values, his sacrifice, and ended with the legacy he left behind.

"Family was the most important thing to my grandfather—sticking together, strong, as one family no matter how big we get. He built this empire, and I plan to keep his legacy going, keeping the Munir family as one, because no matter what's out there in this world, family comes first. We are who we are because of him and our grandmother, and we owe it to them to keep the family name reputable and our unit strong."

It was as if he was talking directly to me.

GUILT

After the funeral was over, things returned to normal. Well, kind of. Raneem went back to Boston to clear out her dorm room and spend a couple of weeks there for the summer. My sitto was home as a widow, devastated. Dad and his brothers had set shifts to go check on her so she wouldn't have to be alone. Mom was sweet to Dad; they were soft-spoken and kind to each other. And I couldn't get Rasheed's speech out of my head. His words, which I'd heard before so many times—"we owe it to them"—resonated for the first time. I knew I wasn't keeping the family name reputable.

"Do you have this song on repeat?" Lauren asked, lying on my bed while Ben Folds sang "Brick."

"Yeah, I love it."

"Isn't it about abortion?"

"Yeah," I told her as I sat at my vanity with my back toward her and my chest caved in. "It's also about lying."

"It's so sad," she said, staring at me. "Are you sure you're okay, Leek?"

"Yeah, Lauren, I'm fine." I looked at my reflection. It was getting hard to look at myself, knowing how much I let my family down behind their backs. I grabbed my compact and wiped my face with the same brush I used on Marc's eyelids. It felt good. "I'm going to miss him," I told her.

I walked up to the back patio. Marc got up and put his cigarette out to give me a hug. It was a long hug with no words and a kiss in the same spot on my head where my dad had kissed me. I had waited a couple of days before going there after the funeral, sitting with confusion, fear, and sadness.

"Hi," I said as I backed away.

"You good?"

I nodded.

"I'm glad you're back. I thought I was going to lose you to your family." He laughed as if he were joking, but it was more like "I meant it, but I can tell you're not happy with what I am saying—let me turn it into a joke."

"Why are you saying that?"

"I'm sorry, I'm joking. Let's enjoy the night. I've missed you." He put his arm around me and walked me into the living room, where Finn and Rob were hanging out.

"I'm sorry to hear about your grandfather, Maleeka," Finn told me, handing me a pipe.

"Thanks, Finn," I told him, and took a couple of hits.

Normally I loved where my mind traveled while stoned, but I didn't like the direction it headed that night. I kept staring at everything in the room, wondering if I belonged there with Marc lying on my lap and a cloud of smoke blown in my face. There was a giant bag of Doritos spilled out on the table next to shake from a joint that they rolled. I saw a pink bath towel on the floor that I assumed was used to clean up or cover up a mess, and the carpet needed a good scrub. The dishes were piled in the sink, and it smelled like old food, dirty guys, and stale weed. It was just as Lydia described Henry Chinaski's place in the novel *Women*, even down to the shit ring in the toilet.

Marc sat there like a king, with his girl by his side, his drugs on the table, and his friends all around. "You okay?" he asked me.

"I'm okay," I told him, biting my thumbnail.

"Maleeka, I think your phone is ringing," Rob said, pointing to my purse.

"Oh shit," I said as I jumped up to grab it. "Fuck," I said, looking at the screen.

"What's wrong?" Marc asked.

"It's my mom, don't say anything."

"Where are you, Maleeka?" she said before I said hello.

"I'm with the girls."

"Why did I just see Lauren and Samantha at the store?"

"They were grabbing snacks, I stayed at Lauren's." I was quick with my lies.

"Are you sure, Maleeka?"

"Yes, Mom, do you want me to come home?"

"I just want to make sure you're not lying to me."

"I swear I'm not lying."

Finn looked over at Marc with an uncomfortable smile. "She's good," I heard him tell Marc.

Marc shook his head. "Fucked up, right?"

"I promise, Mom, I'm at Lauren's. I'll be home in the morning."

"Is everything okay?" Marc asked as I hung up the phone.

"Yeah, everything's fine," I assured him as I put my feet up on the coffee table. There was a bong on the table with a couple of baggies of weed next to it. Stacks of books, a couple of skate magazines. Everything I had seen before, except I noticed an orange pill bottle with a white lid.

"What's that?" I asked him.

"Vicodin, Finn hurt his back last week. You want one?" he asked me.

"I'm not in pain."

"You don't have to be in pain to take it," he said, and Rob dipped his head to his chest and chuckled in his armpit.

"I'm good."

"Well, if you want it, it's yours," he said.

It was just a pill. A prescription given to Finn by his doctor. Nothing I thought I needed to worry about or be scared of. Pills weren't part of the war on drugs at the time. So I didn't think anything of it. Not like I had the capacity in my mind to do so anyway.

"I'm going to go lay down for a bit."

I threw my purse on the floor and looked around his filthy, dim room. How did he live like this? I fixed the bed by pulling the one quilt he had on it tight around the edges and lay on top without getting under the covers.

What would my dad think if he saw me there? He would be disgusted and disappointed. I knew there was more to all of them than the filth. I sat in it too, and I had a kind heart and head full of dreams. I wasn't any different from any of them, but I knew the family thought I was.

Well into my thoughts, his door opened, and he sat on the bed and put his hand on my waist.

"Are you okay, babe?"

"Yeah, I'm fine," I said with my arm over my eyes, avoiding contact with him.

"I know what will make you feel better." He smiled and pulled my pants down, kissing my midriff.

I let him go down on me. But it didn't work, the darkness didn't go away.

Dear Journal,
May 27th 2002

I can't sleep, tucked under the sheets
My eyes are wide open, staring at the street
Your eyes softly closed
    as you breathe through your nose
And the fan behind you goes wild

What if they knew all that we've done
You've just gotten off, my pants still undone
I try to ignore
know they'd call me a whore
While the fan behind you goes wild

What would they think if they saw
        you with me
Your arm around my waist
Your breath against my cheek
Your hands down my pants, stuck in
        your trance
Still behind you, the fan goes wild

That Wasn't COOL

A couple of weekends later, we were officially on summer break. I decided cleaning Marc's messy apartment would help me feel better about the environment I was in. What does that Smashing Pumpkins song say about cleanliness being Godliness? Marc didn't have a vacuum at his house. So I went to the garage. My mom was having a garage sale and had a fully functioning vacuum up for sale she didn't need after her recent upgrade.

A man stood at her table, buying an old radio. He wore a brown button-up shirt with khakis and a pen in his shirt pocket that he pulled out to write a check. When he smiled, his blue eyes creased like Marc's.

"This is my son," the man said, pulling out a picture from his wallet like all dads do when they show off their family. Mom politely nodded along with him. "He is dating your daughter."

That's why his eyes were like Marc's. I had never seen his dad before. I couldn't believe he was in my garage busting my cover. My insides hollowed out. I could hear my heart rate pumping through my chest.

"Maleeka, you know this boy?" my mom asked me, pointing at the picture.

"Hello, Maleeka, it's nice to meet you finally," his dad said to me.

I wanted to disappear, but I had to acknowledge him. I gave him a half-ass smile as I swallowed my nerves and looked back at my mom. "Yeah, he's my friend, Mom."

"Friend, or boyfriend?" Mom asked.

I looked at his dad. Ken was his name. I knew his name, I knew what he did for a living, I knew where he took his family on vacation, and the "dope" omelets he'd make on Sunday mornings. But I couldn't let on to any of that.

"He's just my friend, Mom," I lied, and took a few steps back, knocking into the table behind me. A basket with silk flowers fell to the floor, and I dropped down to pick them up. I could feel my fingertips trembling.

"Let me help you." Ken grabbed a couple of stems and handed them to me. I pressed my lips together and grabbed them without looking him in the eye. I couldn't look at him after lying to his face.

Everything closed in, and I didn't know what to say to make it all go away. I had to get out of there. Luckily Mom was approached by another customer to give me the chance to get out. "I'll be back," I said as I ran out of the garage without saying bye to Ken, hauling the vacuum with me. I told Mom I was giving it to Lauren's mom.

His apartment sparkled by the time I got done with it. I was taught how to clean by the best of them. Aside from being a good cook, being a meticulous cleaner was also a selling point for an Arab girl. Marc did the dishes while I wiped the countertops, the coffee machine, and the crusty spaghetti sauce off the stove. I even did the creases in the cabinet faces.

"Damn, you're going after it," he said, watching me tackle the bottom cabinets.

"Hey, at least I'm not doing the walls." I laughed. I used to watch my sitto clean the baseboards and walls every Saturday like clockwork.

I finished vacuuming while he stepped out to have a cigarette. I vacuumed in perfect strides to put stripes in the carpet and walked out the sliding door to do it up to my last step. I wanted that place pristine.

"You done?" He smiled at me.

"Yeah, this patio is next."

Marc's phone rang.

"It's my mom," he said, about to answer.

"Marc, wait. Don't answer yet." I put my hand on the phone.

I told him what had happened at the garage sale.

"Please explain to your parents why I lied," I told him. "I'm embarrassed, I acted like an idiot. I didn't know what to say."

"Don't worry about it. I'm sure my dad didn't think anything of it," he said.

He called his mom, who knew about the awkward encounter. I could hear through the phone; she obviously thought something of it.

"That wasn't cool, Marc," Suzy said.

"She had no choice, Mom, she isn't allowed to date."

"Well, why does she?" she asked him. "I don't know if it's such a good idea for you to be tied up with her."

My eyes widened, and I took a deep breath. He got up to go talk to her privately.

"I know it doesn't make sense to you, Mom. But you know I love her," I heard him say before getting too far away. I envied the fact that he could be open with his parents.

I sat alone, tearing my already torn jeans, nervous and embarrassed I had put him in this situation. I didn't want his family to hate me for lying to my parents, but I also didn't want them to hate my parents, who they didn't even know, for not letting me date their son.

He hung up and came back to sit next to me.

"Don't worry about it," he said to me as he put his arm around me.

"She seemed so annoyed."

"It's fine, babe. She'll understand."

"Please tell her I'm not a bitch."

"She would never think you were a bitch. My mom will always love you because I love you."

"Ugh, I feel awful." I buried my head into his shoulder.

"Are you going to get in trouble?" he asked me.

"No, it will be fine. I'll think of a lie to get her to forget about it."

"What kind of lie would make her forget? I mean, he flat-out told her you were dating his son."

"I'll think of something."

He shook his head. I hated when he shook his head like he was disappointed in me. I knew he hated that I was a pathological liar. "Promise you'll never lie to me."

I couldn't agree to that, but I did anyway. My stomach turned, knowing I was a piece of shit betraying everyone that loved me. I couldn't stop, and it was getting harder to control.

I got home late that night. Dad was out of town, and I wanted to avoid seeing my mom. I hoped if enough time passed, she'd eventually forget about it or not bring it up. I walked into the house with my shoes in my hand so I wouldn't make noise on the hardwood floor. I turned the corner to find Rasheed on the couch.

"Hey."

He didn't say anything to me.

"I'm going to bed. Good night," I told him.

"Why are you just getting home?" he said, looking straight at the TV.

"I lost track of time. I was with the girls, watching a movie, and I fell asleep."

"You know I don't believe a God damn word that comes out of your mouth, right?" He glared at me.

"What do you mean?"

"You're full of shit. You're lying to everyone in this family, and it better stop."

"I have no idea what you're talking about." I shook my head and turned to walk away.

"Don't insult me, Maleeka." He turned off the television and sat up at the edge of the couch. "I'm not a fucking idiot. You can play Mom and Dad all you want, you make them look like fucking idiots. But not me. I don't believe shit about you, I don't trust you, and I can't even look at you."

"I'm not playing anybody, I was just . . ."

Rasheed got up off the couch. He couldn't listen to another ridiculous lie. He got close to me. I could tell his insides were shaking, but he kept his composure on the outside, still and stern.

"Listen, you don't know any better, so I will make this easy for you to understand. I swear to fucking God if you're still dating him tomorrow at this time, Dad will find out and I will make sure you never see him again."

"I don't know better?" I glared at him.

"Maleeka." He took a deep breath. His face was red and his eyes bulging. "You'll never fucking see him again," he said, putting his finger close to my face. I didn't know if he'd rather beat the shit out of me or Marc at that moment. There was nothing I could say. I knew it wasn't an empty threat. When it came down to it, the men in my family scared me. If he told Dad, or any of my older cousins, I *did* fear what they would do. Not only to me, but to Marc. I kept my eyes on the ground, waiting for him to back off and storm to bed.

I knew there was no way Rasheed would let this go unless I broke up with him. I sat up on my roof and loaded a bowl from a bag Marc had given me. *The girls are going to be bummed about losing free weed,* I thought to myself while I blew my smoke out and rested my head on the siding outside my bedroom window. The sky was full of stars that night. I got lost in them for a minute.

I wanted to protect Marc, I wanted to protect my family, and, in a way, I wanted to protect myself. I knew Marc wanted me to be strong enough to stand up for what I wanted, but I couldn't go against them. Especially after mourning my grandfather's death. It was easier to not give a fuck when I hated them. But it was different now.

Dear Journal,					June 15th 2002
	I have to let him go.
But I know he wont let me go if it's
because of them. He'd fight for me.
I have to convince him that I don't want
to be his girlfriend anymore.
I have to convince myself that I don't
want to be his girlfriend anymore...

I'm not allowed to know you
		or lay down by your side
I'm not allowed to have you
		they've caught on to my lies
I'll swear to you and to the world
		that friends is all it is
I'll force my lie upon you
		they'll never get past this

What I Want

"What's up, Maleeka?" Finn said as he opened the door to the apartment for me.

"Hi, Finn," I said, holding on to my neck with my head down. I couldn't look at him.

"Marc, Maleeka's here!" he yelled out. Marc was outside on the patio, having a cigarette. He walked in and smiled when he saw me.

"I didn't see you pull up," he told me as he got close to give me a hug.

I had parked on the other side of the building so I could hide in the side parking lot while rehearsing my speech and pumping myself up for what I was about to do.

"Can I talk to you for a minute?" I asked him quietly, immersed in his arms.

"Yeah, let's go to my room," he said. "Finn, hold off on that bowl. We'll be out in a minute."

Finn looked concerned. I knew he could tell something was up by my request and lack of eye contact.

"What's going on, babe?" Marc said as I shut the door. I took a deep breath.

"Hi," I said, standing at the door, trying to smile at him, nervous to say anything else.

I couldn't take my eyes off him; he wore jeans with a white T-shirt and an unbuttoned flannel shirt; there was that effortless white

T-shirt again, making his eyes shine bright. I remembered the show, the first time I saw him, when I decided I wanted him. I chose him and got him and loved him. Maybe I wasn't ready to start on my script. My mind ran wild, telling me, *Maybe I don't want to break up with him, maybe I can make this work. I'll keep hiding it, or fuck it, I don't care if they do find out. I don't need them, I don't need their love like I do his.*

He walked up to me. I too wore a white top; I had a necklace that hung so low it fell in my cleavage. He took it out and placed it on the outside of the neckline.

"You okay?" he asked me with his hand on my neck, standing close and staring into my eyes. I looked down so he wouldn't see the confusion inside of them and reached my hands up like I normally would when he had me up against the wall. But before I grabbed him, I pulled them back in and cracked my knuckles.

"What's going on?" He moved my hair off my face and pulled my chin up. I couldn't look at him, so I closed my eyes and kissed him intensely. I kissed him out of anger and confusion and lust. I kissed him because I loved kissing him and knew this would be the last time I could.

It gave me an outlet to express myself without words. I pushed him back to his bed aggressively and got on top of him, still kissing him; his hands were all over me, in my hair, on my neck and my waist. I shoved him onto his pillow and took my shirt off. He pulled me into him. "I fucking love you," he said in my ear, snapping me back to reality. He did love me, and I couldn't be with him.

I collapsed on his chest and rolled over to the side of him. "I can't do this, Marc," I said, and grabbed my shirt to put it over my head.

"Do what?" He sat up. "What's going on?" His eyes broke my heart. I got up off the bed. I couldn't sit next to him and his eyes.

"I think we need to be friends. I think it's better if we're . . ." I paused. He gave me the time to finish my thought. "I can't be with you anymore."

"You can't be with me? Or you don't want to be with me?"

"Is there a difference?" I kept my head down.

"Fuck yeah, there's a difference. I knew this would happen."

"What's that supposed to mean?" I shot my head up at him.

"You've been acting weird ever since your grandpa died. Ever since you spent all that time with your family."

"This has nothing to do with them."

He shook his head. "I don't believe you."

I couldn't breathe; there were cotton balls in my throat. "Believe me," my voice muffled out.

He stood up to be eye level with me. "I know you don't want to tell them about me, but, babe, you don't have to. They don't have to know anything." He tried to grab my trembling hand, but I backed away before he could feel it shaking.

"This isn't about them, Marc. It's about me and what I know is best for me. We're better as friends."

He shook his head. "I'm sorry, I don't believe you."

I hated that he doubted me but also hated it because he was right.

"I know you want this." He reached for my hand again. This time I didn't move. "Maleeka, what we have is big." He kissed me. "*This* is what you want," he said as he backed away and looked at me.

"Please don't tell me what I want," I said quietly.

"What?"

I swallowed big enough to clear the cotton from my throat. "I know what I want; you don't have to tell me. Nobody does! I don't want to be with you anymore, this is too much, all of it is too much!"

He took a couple of steps back and put his arms out. "You were just on top of me, and now you've decided you don't want to be with me. How the fuck does that make any sense?"

"I don't know. God, I don't know." I ran my hands through my hair as I walked toward the door.

"Where are you going?" His tone softened up again. "Please don't leave, Maleeka," he pleaded, "please stay."

"I can't stay, Marc. I'm leaving," I said, staring at the door handle. "We're done, okay?"

"How can you say that so easily?"

I looked back at him. "You have no idea what's easy for me." I turned the door handle. "I don't want to be with you anymore. That's all you need to know. The rest is my problem, not yours."

I walked past Finn's room and out the door timidly. When I got outside, I turned back to see him through the window, still in his room, standing at his dresser, looking at the Valentine's box I made him months before. It was a decorated shoebox with my favorite things about us. Letters and song lyrics and excerpts from instant messages I had printed. I even glued magazine cutouts and sweetheart candies all over the top, saying things like "I'm Yours," "True Love," and of course "I Got You Babe." He looked at me with broken eyes and threw the adolescent love box I made him at the floor.

Dear Journal,   June 16th 2002
    I broke his heart. I'll never forgive
myself for breaking his heart.
God, if ~~you~~ you could've seen his eyes ...
He loves me so much.

Who loves me most? Them or you?
It's not fair that I have to choose

They don't know me like you know me
They don't see me like you do
With them it's superficial
It's all so deep with you

I can't sit and watch you beg me to be free
I can't blame it on my family
      it has to be on me

You use your words and reason
You use our passion too
It pulls me in your direction
but I'll never follow through

I'm not strong enough

<h1>CHECK ON YOUR Sister</h1>

That next day, the girls were calling nonstop. But I couldn't answer. I sat in my room alone while everyone went about their business. My dad in the garden, my mom in the kitchen, and Rasheed at the computer outside my room with Waleed. I'm sure he knew I did what I was told since I hibernated in my room with the S Club 7 song on repeat.

I joked the song was ours while we danced outside my car, but as I listened to the words, maybe it really was our song. Cheesy or not. He *was* the first dream I had come true, and now I had to leave that behind only to regret it. It was only a day after the breakup, and the regret ate away at me. It wasn't only my boyfriend I let go; it was my best friend.

"Is Maleeka okay?" I heard Waleed ask Rasheed through my bedroom door. He could hear my music.

"Did you know she was dating that motherfucker?" Rasheed said.

"She mentioned she was hung up on him, but she swore to me they weren't dating."

"Why the fuck wouldn't you tell me that?"

"Because, man, she didn't say they were dating, she just told me he was a good guy."

"And you took her seriously? She's such a drama queen, and obviously you are too." I heard him get off the squeaky computer chair.

"Dude, she confided in me. I told her I wouldn't say anything, and she told me she wouldn't date him. I'm going to be there for her. You can't be a dick and have her respond to that."

"I was a dick the other night, and she obviously responded."

"Did she break up with him?"

"She had no other choice."

"Well, what the hell, man, are you going to check on her?"

"No, Waleed. She did what she needed to do; she'll get over it."

I cringed.

"I'm going to go grab a burger, you want to come?" he asked.

"No, man, I don't want a burger," he snapped. "I'm going to go check on your sister."

Waleed knocked. "Leek? It's me, can I come in?"

"Yeah, come in," I told him, sitting on the floor with my journal next to me.

"You okay?" he asked me with his big bear eyes.

"I'm fine."

"Let's go on a drive."

"I want to be alone."

"Come on, Leek," he said as he turned to walk out of the room. "And when you get home later, clean up your room. It's disgusting in here."

It felt good to get out of the house, to get some air and listen to music other than that S Club 7 song. Waleed played the new Eminem album his parents bought him. They had no idea what parental-advisory tags meant. The fifth song on the CD played.

"Remember when we had to do square dancing in sixth grade?" He laughed as the chorus of "Square Dance" started.

I nodded and put my feet up on the dashboard.

"You had such a crush on Kalvin Stump, I could tell."

"Who didn't?"

"I was pissed at him for not being your partner."

"He wanted Lauren."

"Still, I was pissed off because I knew it hurt you."

That's why I loved Waleed; he wasn't pissed at me for liking a boy; he was pissed 'cause I was hurt.

"Rasheed told me what happened," he said as he slowed down at the stoplight.

"Well, whatever, he got what he wanted. You all did."

"Are you okay?" he asked me. Waleed was more of a brother to me than Rasheed was, the kind of a brother I wanted.

"I'm fine." I pulled my purse up from under my feet, and I grabbed my pipe. "Do you mind if I smoke?"

"That's fine, but duck down," he told me. "Maleeka, I know you love him," he said calmly while I leaned beneath the dash and lit the bowl. "But you have to believe me, you can do better than him."

I blew my smoke out the window and shook my head. "Waleed, I know in our family's world he might seem like a bad guy, but all kids have fun, especially in high school. Everyone smokes, everyone drinks, it doesn't mean they're bad people. Am I a bad person?" I leaned down to light the other side of my bowl.

"You're not a bad person," he said to me as he rolled down the back-seat windows. And I knew he believed it, even though I got stoned right in front of him.

"Neither is he. He's kind and smart, and I swear to God, Waleed, he loves me."

"Maleeka, when a guy loves a girl, you can see a change in his life. They'll try bettering themselves. Is he bettering himself?"

"He doesn't need to better himself! He's fine," I snapped at him.

"I'm not trying to fight with you, I'm not like Sheed," he told me. "I'm here for you, Leek. We're family."

I closed my eyes and nodded. Waleed was always going to be there for me. I put my pipe back in my purse and grabbed a folded note I wrote that afternoon. I couldn't leave things the way I did the day before.

"Waleed, can you take me there?" I asked him, staring at the note.

"Where? To Marc's?"

"I wrote him a letter. I need to take it to him."

"Tell me how to get there," he said, nodding his head, looking straight ahead and paying close attention to the road.

Luca Brasi

"I'll stand back here," Waleed told me at the walkway to Marc's front door.

"Come stand next to me, you look like a creep back there."

He walked up to me with his hands in his pockets. Waleed had never met Marc and only knew what he had heard about him. All the bad things, of course. I knocked on the door and kept my head down.

Finn opened the door. "Maleeka, hey."

"Hi, Finn, is Marc here?"

"Yeah, come inside," he said, sure I'd follow. But I couldn't take Waleed in there. Seeing Marc's apartment would validate everything he had heard of him.

"I'm going to stay out here, Finn. Will you grab him for me?"

"Yeah, for sure. I'll be right back." He turned around, and turned back, realizing he'd completely dismissed Waleed. "I'm sorry, man, I'm Finn." He put out his hand to shake.

"Oh, I'm sorry, I didn't even think to introduce you. Finn, this is—"

"Waleed," Waleed interrupted me, shaking Finn's hand.

"You Maleeka's brother?"

"Basically," he told him. "She's my little cousin." I was only three weeks younger than Waleed, but he always called me his little cousin.

"Sweet." Finn smiled at us. "I'll go grab Marc."

"Marc," he hollered. "Maleeka's here with backup." He laughed. "Careful, man, he's big."

Waleed looked at me and shook his head.

Marc didn't look good. He had dark circles under his eyes that I could barely see beneath his baseball hat. "Hi," he told me without looking at Waleed.

"Hi," I said to him. I looked over at Waleed.

"I'll go wait in the car, Leek," Waleed said. I don't think he wanted to shake Marc's hand and double-cross Rasheed.

"Okay, thanks." I looked back at Marc.

"Is he here to intimidate me?" he asked after Waleed got in the car.

"No." I shook my head. "It's not like that. We were on a drive, and I asked him to—"

"What are you doing here?" He looked at the ground for a second, collecting himself before he looked up at me. "Obviously, you're not staying since you brought Luca Brasi with you." He smirked a little.

"Don't be mean." I tried to hold back my smile.

"Come on, you know I'm joking," he said as he reached for my hand. I backed away a few inches and handed him his letter.

"I came here to give you this."

"What is this?"

"Please read it. And consider it."

He stared at the note. He looked broken, and I wanted to fix him. I wanted to make him feel good, the way I did the night I asked him to be my boyfriend. I knew I had to leave.

"I better go." I turned to walk away.

"Maleeka, wait."

"Yeah?" I turned back.

"Thank you for coming." He held up the note.

"I'll talk to you soon, Marc."

"All right, ba—" He stopped himself from saying *babe* and shook his head. "All right, Maleeka."

My stomach dropped. I hated that he called me Maleeka, but I wasn't his babe anymore.

Dear Marc,

I can't believe I am sitting here writing you this letter under these circumstances. I know I said I don't want to be with you anymore, but that's not what it means entirely. I don't want to be your girlfriend, but I don't want to lose you either.

I'm not doing this so that we never speak or see each other again, I'm doing it so that we can. If that makes any sense... So many couples end on a bad note, and I don't want us to ever be like that. If we end it now and stay friends, we will never lose each other. You always said I love my friends more than anything, and just like I love them, I love you too, Marc. You ARE my best friend. You are my favorite person on this earth.

Please, if you can, stay my friend. I can't lose you completely. I need you. And Marc, I think you need me too.

Please consider a friendship with me, please try.

I will always love you more than you can imagine... as a friend.

Love always, your biggest fan,

Maleeka ♥

ACKNOWLEDGMENTS

There is a handful of people that have contributed to these pages being published.

You know who you are, and I thank you with all my heart for your support and encouragement through my highs and lows while pouring my soul into this over the years.

And thank you to those that have inspired me, those living and those lost.

You will never be forgotten.

ABOUT THE AUTHOR

Rowen Lee lives two lives. One life doing what her family and her social media accounts see, a world that feels a little phony as she plays by the rules of what feels acceptable. A nine-to-five corporate job with health insurance and a 401(k) and a babysitter to help her manage the responsibilities of being a working mother. The second life is where she feels like her most authentic self by nurturing her passion. After she tucks her son into bed at night, she devotes the time she should be sleeping into her writing. She finds peace in her smoky garage with her laptop, music playlist, and cup of coffee, while her dog stares at her, wondering what the hell she is doing up so late.

Her writing has been described as lyrical, insightful, direct, and proud. She has dug up the muck of teenage youth and made it accessible and relatable to adults and teens alike. Being a keen observer with a loving heart, Rowen Lee combines undiluted honesty with a delivery that makes you feel safe.

www.ingramcontent.com/pod-product-compliance
Lightning Source LLC
Chambersburg PA
CBHW070451300726
48975CB00007B/2126